ASTRID DARBY & THE LAUGHING COFFIN
THE SECOND ASTRID DARBY ADVENTURE

ELEANOR PROPHET

An imprint of Diogenes Club Press

Worldly, Whimsical, and Weird Books

www.diogenesclubpress.com

Dallas, TX

DC Dreams, an imprint of Diogenes Club Press
8619 Reva St. Dallas, TX 74227
www.diogenesclubpress.com

The characters and events in this book are fictional. Any similarity to real persons, living or dead, is coincidental and not intended by the author.

ISBN: 9781622010066

Library of Congress Control Number: 2017955889

CHAPTER ONE

A kaleidoscope of colours filled the brilliant blue afternoon sky as dozens of bulbous balloons lifted into the air with the softest hiss of hot air. The watching crowd erupted in a smattering of delighted applause, turning to their neighbours to commend the flawless ascent. The highly anticipated maiden launch of the revered Mr Thaddeus Rush's Gertrude, a ship most highly venerated as a revolutionary mechanical achievement of steam and air, was scheduled for five minutes hence.

"Though my young cousin seems to have overcome his particular aversion to the flying beasts, I find my heart still justly flutters when I watch them lift off," I admitted, turning my head to address Mrs Elisabeth Hawkins nee Weston at my flank.

The Lady Elisabeth smiled in a most conciliatory way. "I thought you might not relish the launch as much as your young cousin, who favours science and innovation above all things tender, but do try to enjoy yourself, Astrid. Mr Rush was most insistent that you accompany Sir Benedict and I, so deep is his admiration for you since your work for his esteemed corporation several months past."

She was all beauty and good humour, in her customary mode, and I found myself quite unable to resist the merriment upon her smiling countenance. "I assure you, Lady, I will be most delighted to see the good Mr Rush ascend safely into the heavens. I am unable, however, to rid my mind of the sad memory of my dear Nathaniel who, as you know, had most unfortunate luck in such a similar craft."

"Ah. Astrid, I regret your loss deeply."

"Thank you, Lady. I am most pleased, nevertheless, to see young Xander enjoying himself so thoroughly. I would have expected a lithe lad of his youth and good looks to value rather more unsavoury pastimes, but he remains as steadfastly dedicated to the science of invention as my late husband."

"He is truly an extraordinary youth. But where is young Knightly? I have not laid eyes upon him since the tea."

I laughed, lifting my lace-gloved hand to point towards the garish Gertrude, whose sheer size and stunning colour threatened to eclipse all but the most brilliant and distinctive dirigible. There, tethered to the podium, Gertrude drifted serenely over the plush, green courtyard, casting a swollen shadow across the gathering. Mr Thaddeus Rush, dressed in his most adventurous brown leather suit and flowing white scarf, his gleaming black hair flattened beneath a worn aviator hat and shining brass goggles, leaned over the side of his ship's gondola. He was speaking animatedly to the young, black-haired youth at the foot of the podium, his dark eyes alight with the thrill of his exhibition.

Lady Elizabeth laughed. "But of course. Trust the lad to be in the thick of things. And I am sure Mr Rush highly values such a keen and intelligent youth to whom he might flaunt his cleverness and good fortune all the day."

I snorted, covering my mouth delicately with my hand. "Now, Lady Elisabeth, that's very ungracious of you."

"Forgive me, Astrid. I do find him tiresome, though. When he comes around to call upon Sir Benedict, I admit I am most eager to find anything else to be doing, rather than listen to his endless espousing of his latest business deal or innovation. I am convinced the majority of his cleverest innovations have, in fact, been the work of eager young men such as your cousin. I should warn him away from the old fraud, indeed."

I smirked. "Xander is not one to be so easily duped by a scheming charlatan. He is clever, my young cousin, and he is perfectly adept at looking after himself."

A burst of fanfare from the chamber orchestra on the lawn signalled the commencement of Gertrude's launch. The exalted spectators turned their attention to Mr Rush, whose raised arms and wide, indulgent smile suggested he intended to draw their attention to himself for what promised to be an elaborate and tremendously smug speech. "Oh, he truly is an appalling bore," Lady Elisabeth whispered.

I covered my mouth to stifle my giggles. The Lady Elisabeth was always a charming companion, no matter the circumstances. "Mind your tongue, Lady, for I shouldn't wish to witness the scolding you would receive, should your Sir Benedict hear you speak thus of his dear friend."

Elisabeth laughed. "It isn't his agreeable companionship but his cunning business avarice about which my dear Sir Benedict natters all the day. He would be hard-pressed to scold one who is speaking his own private inner thoughts. Oh, hello, Knightly."

Xander bowed smartly to the Lady, but his brow was furrowed when he returned to my side to watch the launch. "Why the dreary countenance, cousin?"

I asked cheerfully. "Has the venerable Mr Rush treated you ill?"

"What an absolute fraud that man is," Xander announced in a low, disappointed tone. "It is quite clear to me he had absolutely no hand in the engineering and construction of his acclaimed vessel. When I asked whether he preferred a triple or quadruple burner configuration, he looked at me as if I had been speaking ancient Sumerian."

I raised an eyebrow. "As would I have done."

"Yes, but you are not claiming to have been the innovator of such a brilliant and esteemed aircraft, are you? "

"Yes, well, nor would I do, with you around to recognise my deceit, cousin."

Xander smirked, and Lady Elisabeth leaned towards him with sparkling eyes. "You would do well to steer clear of the devious Mr Rush, young Knightly, lest he set his sights on you as his successive protégé."

"I shouldn't worry too much in that regard, Lady, for my dear cousin would hardly allow the desertion. She is quite jealous of my company and would scarcely permit me another mentor above her."

"I sense you might be taking the mickey, cousin," I said sourly.

"Now, Astrid. Your dear cousin is nothing but doting."

A frisson of incredulity and anticipation shivered along my spine, and I closed my eyes, scrunching my face in exasperation. When I turned towards Agent Asher Key of the Ministry of Defence, however, my deportment was perfectly composed.

"Asher!" My treacherous young cousin spun to shake the hand of the roguishly dishevelled and unshaven man at our backs. Agent Key looked as though he'd lately braved untamed conditions and a few very strong winds. His sharp, strong jaw was rough with stubble, and his tousled dark blonde hair had grown down below the collar of his careless grey suit. Had the Ministry taken to employing their agents as brigands and privateers since last I had been in their camaraderie? I conjectured most uncharitably.

The slightly grotty look suited him, all the same, and my ire intensified. When his cobalt blue eyes fixed upon me with an amused twinkle, I pursed my lips in sheer pique. "By what egregious blunder did you find your way here, Agent Key?" I demanded. "I can hardly fathom what a person of your particular persuasion would be doing at such an event. I would not have taken you for a man of spectacle and skill."

His eyebrows travelled upwards into his untidy fringe. "Astrid!" Lady Elisabeth scolded, sounding scandalised. "I hardly think that is an appropriate way to speak to someone in such a position of favour with the Ministry."

Curiously, Asher's brows drew together for an ephemeral instant, but he squared his shoulders to face me sternly. "Now, Astrid." His voice was a low, honeyed purr, and irony seeped from every syllable. "Is that any way to treat an old friend?"

"Need I remind you that we are not, in fact, friends?"

"Why, I was under the impression that, after our charming reunion and subsequent shared defeat of a nefarious terrorist, not to mention the slight mishap with the unspecified former national landmark several months past, we had reached a sort of concurrence."

My lips twitched, but I remained resolute. "I admit we might have been working in accord for a brief time, owing to a temporary common agenda, but that is hardly the thing. You must admit, your sudden appearance at such an exhibition is unexpected and thus worthy of inquiry."

Asher smirked, flicking his fringe negligently from his eyes. "Be that as it may, it is hardly necessary to inquire in such an uncivilized manner, is it?"

I sighed. "Perhaps it was not entirely essential. Still, you haven't answered the question, have you? What are you doing here, Ash?"

He smiled, and his eyes slipped away to watch the breathless release of Gertrude's erstwhile anchor. Rush waved to his enraptured audience like a king upon his steed, and the envelope filled with hot, hissing air. "Off he goes," Lady Elisabeth observed dryly. "And good journey to him. I shouldn't be too eagerly anticipating his return to terra firma."

Xander snorted, and I smirked, watching the vessel rise slowly and peacefully into the air. For a moment, I pictured the outrageous craft plummeting downwards upon the breathless crowd and winced slightly. It did not, however, and in scant moments, it was merely another brightly coloured globe in the cloudless blue sky. I had not realised Asher was at my side until he spoke so close to my ear, I practically jumped.

"And where is your most cherished confidant, Dr Ramsey, this fine day, Astrid? I haven't glimpsed him in the crowd. Surely this is the sort of event which he might be expected to attend."

As if they sensed a storm in the air, the Lady Elisabeth and my young cousin moved away from us, to better view the Gertrude as it drifted towards the horizon. My response, however, was flawlessly even. "He's gone off."

Asher raised his eyebrows, and his eyes glittered suspiciously. "Gone off?"

"He's accepted a post with a contractor, devising his own defence weapon. He left for Wales a fortnight ago."

"A dreadful place." His lips quivered slightly, and my eyes narrowed. "Now that his master is gone, he is the master, then?"

"Yes, well, it would seem as such. He requested Xander join him as his assistant, but, I am pleased to say, my cousin refused."

"Ah, he remains devoted, does he? And such an opportunity, I shouldn't wonder, despite the locality."

"Yes, well, my cousin long since chose the life of an adventurer, rather than the humdrum existence of a lab rat. I reckon someone such as yourself can understand such a choice."

His mouth twisted into a smile. "I understand all too well. I, as well, would choose to remain by your side. Were I young Knightly, of course."

"Of course."

"I suppose your doctor's sent you a telegram a night, bemoaning his devastation over your indefinite division?"

My mouth tightened, but I lifted my chin. "We have not spoken," I responded coolly.

"Oh? Did you have a particular falling out?"

I narrowed my eyes. "Do not trouble yourself over it; it is none of your concern."

"No, of course it isn't," he replied cheerfully. "And how uncouth of me to ask such a question of a lady."

"Ash, why are you here?" I demanded wearily.

He lifted his chin. "Astrid, your country needs your specific expertise in a very grave matter."

I rolled my eyes. "My country? Cor, Ash. My country never pays properly, and I often find myself unnecessarily placed in the clutches of an injudicious tribunal, despite my invariably righteous intentions."

He snorted. "That is gross exaggeration."

I raised my eyebrows archly. "You mean to say the Ministry has forgiven me my previous trespasses and intends to contract me in a legitimate way?"

He sighed, and his eyes slid charily away. "You are too perceptive by half, Astrid. No. In truth, they are still a bit cross over the Parliament building you destroyed last spring."

"That was, in fact, Dr Ramsey, if you'll recall."

"While I am perfectly content blaming him for the transgression, the Ministry, being somewhat less magnanimous than I, has failed to make the distinction."

"Bah. Trifles. So, why, then would you possibly seek to enlist my services?"

"You'll agree to help me, then?"

I narrowed my eyes. "How can I possibly know to what I will agree before I've any idea what you're about?"

He sighed. The orchestra struck up a lively, cheerful tune, and the crowd around us, so enlivened by the sight of the adventurous Mr Rush lifting into the air on a dubious journey of self-discovery, began a jaunty caper. I spun to watch Xander bow to the Lady Elisabeth. Before she could accept his keen hand, however, her husband, Sir Benedict, appeared out of the throng as though equipped with an internal beacon which set off the moment his wife was in danger of actually enjoying herself.

Appearing slightly disenchanted, Xander returned to the conversation, sensing the taut moment between Asher and me had passed. He wasn't entirely correct in that regard, but at least I wasn't yet considering setting upon Asher with my delicate blue parasol. "Have you two sorted each other out, then?" Xander asked with a hint of hesitation.

I smirked. "Not quite as I would have liked, I'm afraid."

Asher's expression was sullen. "This is hardly the place to speak of such grim matters, Astrid."

"Grim matters, indeed?" Xander repeated, his eyebrows arched in interest.

"Let us endeavour to discover a more ideal location for the remainder of the conversation, shall we?" I said brightly, looping my arm through Xander's.

Asher scowled deeply, and Xander was hardly insensitive to the man's ire. He was indeed clever, my young cousin, and this time I cursed his acuity. "Oh, Astrid, must I accompany you? I had hoped to speak to Mr Rush's assistant, whom I am certain is actually responsible for the construction of the Gertrude. I was highly curious to hear his opinions on some of the newer innovations in air transportation–"

"I am sure your cousin can do without you for an evening, can't you, Astrid?" The challenging twinkle in his eye piqued my temper.

I lifted my chin. "Of course. I hardly require a chaperone."

"You don't mind, Astrid?" Xander asked keenly, and I sighed.

"Go on, then."

He bowed to us both and spun sharply on his heel, striding away as though he could scarcely endure another moment in our company. Asher smiled and offered his arm to me. "Shall we, then, Astrid?"

I glared at him and ignored his arm. "I am at your service, Agent Key."

He snorted. "Right."

* * *

Had I the leisure time to endlessly ponder the ideal locations in which the sort of shadowy, mysterious men that conduct covert, whispered discussions regarding national security and general political intrigue might meet, I still could not have imagined a place so completely and utterly dull. The unmarked club in which Asher and I sat, sipping tepid tea without sugar or milk, could only have been the fancy of someone with an absolute lack of innovation and imagination.

The walls were a dreary grey; the tables and chairs were a dull, hammered steel, arranged in such a fashion it was impossible to hear even the slightest murmur from the nearest table. These tables were, even in the late afternoon of a clear, sultry summer day, filled with small parties of two or three men. The occupants of each of the tables were of the same variety of drab, featureless government official. The entire space gave the impression of flat, boring anonymity. I marvelled at how many covert, whispered discussions of potentially interesting political intrigue were occurring at that very moment. The atmosphere was such, however, that I was anxious to be shot of it, and it seemed unlikely the conversations would prove any less insipid than the men conducting them.

I rolled my eyes at Asher. "Honestly, Ash, have you no imagination at all?"

He raised his eyebrows, peering over the lip of his teacup. "I beg your pardon?"

"Do they give you a list of all the places like this when you enlist in the government's service?"

"It is a place to speak where we won't be overheard."

"Could we not have simply taken a walk, or something like? I mean, this place is completely banal. It hardly suits a lady of my taste for flash and pageantry."

He snorted. "That is, of course, exactly the point. It is a place I could ensure we would remain anonymous."

I raised my eyebrows. "Ah, but I suspect, even in such a prosaic place as this, I will not go unrecognised."

He smirked. "As true as that certainly is, this is the sort of place in which people fail to notice who is meeting with whom, you see."

"Had I known you were so uncomfortable being seen in my company, I would not have agreed to this interlude."

"Astrid, I did not bring you here to quarrel."

"Well, I shouldn't think you would need to; we manage to quarrel quite magnificently, regardless of the venue."

"Astrid..."

"All right, then, I did agree to this audience. I am, as they say, all ears."

He smirked. "This place isn't typically patronised by agents of the Ministry. I didn't want them to know I was meeting with you."

"Is that so? And you gave such an impression the Ministry and I were on the path towards reconciliation."

"If you don't mind terribly, I do not have all night to listen to your cheek. I did have a reason to seek you."

"I should hope so. What is this urgent and pressing matter that necessitated your interference in one of my few agreeable indulgences?"

He laughed. "Agreeable indulgences? I know you well, Astrid, and you cannot dupe me. You were dreadfully bored."

I lifted my chin defiantly. "Strictly speaking, I was only marginally bored. I find the Lady Elisabeth's companionship to be most enjoyable."

"You never were in the habit of making things easy on a man."

"I have no idea to what you might be referring. I am quite good-natured, by all accounts. Everyone says so. It's all I can do to hush them, so terribly do they

10

bring me to blush."

He swiped a hand across his face, and I smirked. He had dragged me here in the middle of a comparatively pleasant and very rare day of ease; he could not rightly expect instant capitulation. "Can we just get on with it?"

"It was not I who digressed that time."

"I will not be led astray again, I assure you." His face changed abruptly, and I snapped to attention. Regardless of the tension between Asher and me, he rarely presented a tiresome proposal. After spending the last fortnight idling away in Darby Manor, lamenting the unexpected absence of interesting companionship, I was anxious to hear what might prove a very appealing diversion, indeed. "Are you acquainted with Professor Coffin?"

"Julius? Of course."

Asher did not seem caught out by my response. "Do you know him well?"

"No, not well. He was a friend to dear Nathaniel. They shared a particular interest in the history of science in ancient civilisation. We were never close, owing to a lack of mutual interests, but I have been in his company many times. Has he fallen the victim of some terrible crime?"

Asher sighed. "No. It is worse still. I believe he is the culprit."

"Julius? But he's only an old scholar with a head for naught but science and history. What crime could he possibly have committed? Has he failed to pay his taxes?"

Asher did not rise to the mocking of my tone. "No, it is far more ghastly, Astrid. I believe he has committed murder."

For several moments, I did not speak, for I had no response that did not sound utterly incredulous. "Ash..."

His cobalt eyes burned with an impassioned intensity. "Yes, I had anticipated you would be sceptical, but I assure you, Astrid, I am in earnest. I have evidence that Coffin has been involved in the disappearance of no less than ten victims."

"Ten? Come now, Ash, but how could he have gone on so long without the might of the Met descending upon him?"

Asher frowned. "He has, thus far, drawn his victims from the unremitting pool of unmentionables, not of polite society, and no one of consequence notices the disappearance of a few criminals, prostitutes and runaways."

I considered. "What evidence have you?"

"He was witnessed with one of the victims, a prostitute, just hours before she disappeared from the East End."

"Witnessed by whom?"

Asher's brow furrowed. "Another prostitute. The witness claims she saw him take the woman away in a hansom, and she was never again seen."

"But surely the Met investigated the accusation?"

"Hardly. A man in that part of town might expect to remain anonymous. In fact, the witness did not recognise or even see his face. It was only the description of his carriage which caught my notice. As no body was discovered, the sighting of the carriage was simply dismissed as the ravings of a drunken ladybird. No one even investigated the disappearance. It is not uncommon for a lady such as the victim to disappear, and it is not the custom of the Met to waste valuable resources on such things."

"Ah, I do understand the dilemma. How can one even know she disappeared and did not simply go off somewhere? People do."

"Yes, and had it been the only disappearance of the kind, it might never have drawn my curiosity. However, the Met has been plagued by similar reports spanning the last several months of ladybirds and brigands going off in a carriage and never being seen again."

"Upon hearing the ladybird's account of the carriage she saw, you began to investigate Coffin?"

"Yes."

"But there was only one account of his carriage being seen, yeah? How can you know he is responsible for the other disappearances?"

"I do not begrudge you your scepticism, Astrid. I have been unable to convince anyone else of my suspicions."

"The evidence as it stands is anecdotal at best. There is no proof the disappearances resulted in murder."

Asher's eyebrows drew together. "No, there is no proof, not as yet. But I am convinced of it."

"But how can you be? There is nothing in what you've described that convinces me of anything of the sort."

"That is not all there is, Astrid."

"You have my full attention, Ash. I have never known you to make wild and unsupported accusations of respectable members of society."

He snorted bitterly. "Ah, if only my superiors at the Ministry and the inspectors at the Met valued my convictions so highly. But that is another matter. There is yet more sinister intelligence to impart."

"I assure you, I am most eager to hear what more you have discovered."

His lips turned up slightly at the corners. "Suspecting that Coffin was involved in these appalling happenings, I began to investigate his circumstances. It came to my attention that the professor has been petitioning the court once every few weeks for the release of prisoners sentenced to transportation into his care."

"Once every few weeks? But what does he claim to do with them? "

"I do not believe a thorough inquiry was made into that matter. He is a wealthy and highly respected member of our finest society. If he claims to wish to offer them sanctuary or rehabilitation upon his lands, it is of no consequence to the court."

"Once released to him, these prisoners disappear?"

"They are never seen again."

"But if they are labouring upon his lands or performing some duty for him, of course they would not be seen by open society."

"No, but I have spoken to one of his people inside: a scullery maid upon whom I prevailed to provide me with intimate information regarding his day to day activities. She knows not what happens to the prisoners, but she insists they are not about."

"But she hasn't any idea where they go?"

"No. She is concerned primarily with the care of his daughter, Juliana, and she is not privy to his every activity."

I considered. "Has no one inquired at all what's become of the prisoners?"

"Of course they haven't. Once a man or woman has been sentenced to the Boat, their fate is hardly a matter for public interest. They are the perfect victims; for, as long as they are no longer committing crimes within the city, a satisfactory conclusion of their situation has been achieved."

"Too true, that. All right, I will entertain the notion your conclusions are sound, for the sake of argument. But am I to deduce your superiors are not so credulous as I?"

Asher snorted, and his lips curved into a small smile. "You have never been one to miss the point, Astrid."

"So they see no similar pattern and refuse to investigate the matter further?"

He inclined his head. "They do not believe my suspicions are founded and see no cause for concern."

He averted his eyes cagily, and I gave him an arch look. "But I suspect the matter was not put to rest?" I asked, pursing my lips.

"No. Well, he must be brought to task. A great many men have gone missing and no one has even bothered to notice. I cannot allow him to continue killing."

"Ash..."

"Regretfully, I was not as subtle in my inquiry as I might have been."

"Ah, that comes as no great revelation to me, I assure you. You have never been one for delicacy."

He chuckled. "The scullery maid outed me. Coffin lodged a complaint with my superiors."

"You were scolded quite sternly, I shouldn't wonder."

"Yes, well, they have ordered me, in no uncertain terms, to leave off. Coffin's family has long been friends with the royal family, and his brother, Silas, is a highly respected member of Parliament. He is protected from the very top, and my superiors would not have his feather ruffled."

"Yet you persist." I sipped the drudges of my tea, finding it quite cold and tasteless. I made a disgusted face, placing the cup on the saucer before me. I did not speak for several moments, arranging my skirt carefully around my legs and fingering the broach on my breast. Finally, I glanced up at him with an ingenuous expression. "And for what, then, do you require my services? You are still an agent of the Ministry. Surely you possess resources I do not. I am an adventurer, sir, not an inspector. I do not investigate murders."

His eyes slid away again, and I narrowed my own at him. "Well, I did tread upon the toes of my superiors one too many times this time."

"What, exactly, does that mean?"

"They have suggested I might not be in the right frame of mind to continue my work at the Ministry at the moment."

"Ash..."

14

"They have suggested I take a holiday. And I have done, per their insistence."

"You mean you are rogue from the Ministry?"

"Well, I am on leave, anyway. I haven't exactly gone rogue. It's not as if I've been sacked. Exactly."

"Ash, you are an unmitigated ass! If I am arrested for you again, I will be very put out."

"Don't be so dull, Astrid. You won't be arrested." He considered a moment. "I think."

"Are you mad? You cannot defy your superiors in such a fashion. You will lose your position."

"I am sure once I have solved the mystery and proven Coffin's responsibility in the murders, it will sort itself out." He reached across the table, seizing my hand in his own. His dark blue eyes burned with earnestness. "Please, Astrid. It is important."

I sighed deeply, for he was a difficult man to rebuke when he smouldered so. "But how might I be of help?" I asked resignedly.

His smile was brilliant, and he did not release my hand. Instead, he caught it up between his own, pressing it keenly. "Coffin will be leaving for his summer holiday in the Isles of Scilly within the fortnight."

I smiled. "Ah, yes. On his celebrated private island."

"The Isle of Jules."

I snorted. "Of course. He invites me to his annual retreat each year, in honour of Nathaniel and their cherished friendship before his death. I have never accepted, for I find it to be a most pompous and utterly dull prospect."

He did not speak, but his wicked smile left me in no doubt of his intentions.

"Oh, no," I sighed.

"Oh, yes, Astrid."

"You wish me to accept his invitation."

"Yes..."

"And bring you along so you can badger him further?"

"You've sussed it. You always were quite clever."

"Ash, that would be highly inappropriate and ungracious indeed."

15

"Inappropriate? Astrid, when have you ever concerned yourself with that? This is just your sort of thing." He pressed my hand to his heart, and his eyes were wide with supplication. "Astrid, please. This is of the utmost urgency."

I sighed. "Asher Key, do not think I do not recognise the mischief in your twinkling eye."

He smiled. "Come on, Astrid. What else have you to do?"

"I will have you know, I am highly sought for my expertise and services."

"Indubitably. However, I was informed by your young cousin that you were not currently engaged."

I narrowed my eyes. "When did you speak with Xander?"

"I met him at Mr Rush's launch prior to approaching you. He was most eager to impart your plans for the summer, which were, I understand, none."

"Oh, that boy. He will have some explaining to do."

"Do not blame the young man; I am a very dangerous and persuasive agent of the Ministry, after all. He is quite clever enough to know not to refuse me when I am feeling particularly keen."

I scoffed. "He is merely impish. He does seem to enjoy my discomfort."

"Do I make you uncomfortable?" I glared at him, and he smiled. "Astrid, you know you're going to accept. Why continue to keep me in suspense?"

"Oh, you are insufferable. All right. I'll consent to your proposal. I will inform Julius at once of my intention to accept his invitation." I smirked. "You may accompany me... as a member of my entourage."

CHAPTER TWO

The *Juliana* cast an ominous, bulbous shadow across the lush, green lawn of Professor Coffin's London estate. I peered dubiously up at the monstrous, sapphire blue balloon, and my heart lurched. Coffin had spared no expense on the lavish conveyance of his guests to the Isle of Jules. However, though the wicker gondola was large enough for a score of passengers and looked quite comfortable, I had no desire to experience what the other guests, now gathered around the courtyard awaiting the launch, avowed to be a thrilling and agreeable jaunt.

Glancing up into the keen, excited cobalt blue eyes of Asher Key, however, I lifted my chin and steeled my resolve. It was hardly the time for passing apprehensions, and I certainly did not intend to allow Ash to recognise my trepidation. Were I to do, I would surely never hear the end of his smug mockery. I felt Xander shift beside me, and I turned to look at him curiously. His brilliant blue eyes were, too, directed at the monstrous balloon. "Do not bother yourself, Astrid," he said in a low voice. "I am sure it will be most pleasant. There are clear skies and no sign of peril on the horizon."

I glared at my well-meaning young cousin, though I sensed his good-cheer was carefully masking his own apprehension. His assurances had, however, regrettably captured Asher's attention. He turned his head to look at me. "Do you have a particular phobia of aircrafts, Astrid? I hadn't realised." His voice was amused, and I turned my glare upon him.

"I've nothing of the sort, as you well know, Asher. I find travel by dirigible quite pleasing. However, it is the open gondola I find rather unnerving. It's seems hardly secure."

He smirked. "It is very safe, I assure you."

"That is, unless the burner fails, the envelope deflates and we plummet to our deaths over the sea," Xander muttered darkly.

I looked at him sharply. "Xander."

"Forgive me, Astrid; that was highly inappropriate." He sighed, peering up at the vessel in similar trepidation. "It is only that I cannot help but think of Nathaniel."

I sighed, for my own dread was similarly rooted. Asher glanced down at me sharply. "I am sorry, Astrid, I did not realise."

I was slightly caught out by the softness of his tone, and I avoided his gaze. "It is no matter. We have agreed to this dubious adventure. We will see it through."

"Mrs Darby? I had not expected to find you here."

I spun to face the jovial arrival. "Ah, Mr Chesley. It is a pleasure to see you again."

Jasper Chesley was an imposing, barrel-chested man with pale blonde hair and patrician features, still unlined and very fine despite his five and fifty years. His smile was gleaming white as he strode towards our small party, his hand extended. I shook it vigorously, pleased to make his acquaintance again after many months. I had rare occasion to see the gentleman, whose exceedingly successful business took him so often from England and into the less civilised regions of India and the Middle East. In fact, he had spent much time in New Delhi, in particular, and was rumoured to prefer it most strenuously over the climate and culture of London.

"I would not have expected to see you here, Mrs Darby," Chesley continued. "I was under the distinct impression you rarely accept such invitations as these. What brings you to join our humble party?"

"Ah, Mr Chesley, I assure you, I am most inclined to accept such kind invitations as our dear friend Mr Coffin might extend. My resistance of late is attributed entirely to my work. I have simply been otherwise engaged. As you can see, I am most delighted to be a member of your esteemed party."

Chesley laughed. "Is that so, Mrs Darby? Well, you must regale us with tales of your exploits. The nature of your work is often the topic of otherwise dreary dinner parties, and I am anxious to discover which outlandish accounts might actually be true."

I smiled radiantly at him. "Oh, I am quite certain, Mr Chesley, that even the most outlandish are at least a bit true, though I assure you, my life is not nearly as compelling as gracious society would have you believe. I am often called upon to perform the most mundane of tasks, and adventure is not, necessarily, always the thing."

"I must say, I am highly disappointed. I was most eager to make the acquaintance of the infamous Mrs Darby, swashbuckler and romantic figure of lore and legend."

We turned towards the deep, cheerful voice, and my heart fluttered curiously in my chest. I had had occasion to meet men of many countries, exotic men of all colours and nations, but never had I met a man who so easily stole my very breath. I was not, of course, a woman of whimsy or fancy, and though I often appreciated men, I rarely espoused their particular advantage or fine-looks.

This man, however, was of an extraordinary variety, to be sure. Tall and lean, he was a few years younger than me, though he could have been ageless, for his face was like a moving sculpture. His skin was deep, mahogany brown, as smooth and flawless as fired clay, and his long, black hair was unbound in large, silken curls. It was not his handsome face or his utterly roguish appeal that attracted me to him, however, for his coal black eyes were so large and alight with life, it was as if the man were lit from within by a bright, smouldering flame.

"Ah, young Imaron," Chesley greeted the fascinating man cheerfully, clapping him on the shoulder. The young man was several inches taller than Mr Chesley, but he bowed his head respectfully to his elder. "Mrs Darby, this is my dear late Esha's nephew, Imaron."

Imaron inclined his head to us, but his eyes remained fixed upon mine. "Imaron Behari. Pleasure. My sister, Chanha and I have been visiting from New Delhi. Uncle Jasper has been a very accommodating host, indeed."

"I convinced the two young people to join me on this little holiday of ours, though I daresay they would prefer to remain in the city where they might experience more thrilling fare."

Imaron smiled. "He is very humble, indeed, my uncle, for my sister and I dote upon him, and he knows it. We couldn't bear even a fortnight out of his company."

Chesley laughed. "My dear nephew, I see you've heard of Mrs Astrid Darby."

He offered his hand to me. "Of course. Her adventures are legendary."

"You are too kind, Mr Behari, though I am gratified by your indulgence. This is my young cousin, Alexander Knightly, and Agent Asher Key of the Ministry of Defence. With us is Morgan Reinhart, my trusted associate."

The men shook hands heartily. "Agent Key, you say?" Chesley asked jovially.

"I am," Asher replied, and if his tone was slightly chilly, I suspected only I had perceived it.

"Well, how delightful to have one her Majesty's finest with us on our adventure. But is there some reason for your visit, Agent Key?" Chesley's thin lips turned up in a smile. "Have we something to fear on the Isle of Jules? Some treachery for which we should be on the alert?"

I glanced up at Asher in amusement, but his expression was even. "You've nothing to fear, Mr Chesley, I assure you. I am merely enjoying a rare holiday, accompanying my dear friend, Mrs Darby, in a surely futile attempt to keep her out of her particular brand of trouble."

I rolled by eyes, but Chesley turned his attention back to me. "I did not realise you were acquainted with such esteemed persons, Mrs D."

I smirked. "In my line of work, I make all sorts of salty acquaintances, some more savoury than others."

Asher snorted.

"Are you salty, indeed, Agent Key? How delightful our holiday will be then, in the company of such interesting persons."

"Ah, Chanha," Imaron said brightly, wrapping an arm around the woman who had joined our small party. She was nearly as tall as he and slender as a willow. Chanha Behari shared her brother's extraordinarily fine looks, and her deep, brilliant orange sari suited her colour so well, I felt a drab, colourless thing in comparison. Her long, black hair was straight, unlike her brother's, and it was woven down her back in a long braid.

"Do not listen to my friend, Mrs Darby, Miss Behari," Asher said, and he strode forwards to bow over her hand. When he returned to my side, his eyes remained fixed upon Chesley's lovely Indian ward. "I should not wish you to be persuaded so soon in our acquaintance by such careless words."

Chanha Behari smiled, inclining her head demurely, though her gaze was brazen when she met his eyes. "I declare, Agent Key, I am not a woman easily persuaded."

"Ah, but here is Mrs Marlow and Madam Eliot!" Chesley announced, and we turned towards the women approaching our increasingly crowded party.

"Astrid!" Sophie Marlow exclaimed, and I strode forwards to return her embrace. Though Sophie was not as close a confidant as the Lady Elisabeth, she and I shared many things in common. In her mid-thirties and recently widowed as myself, we shared our tragic circumstances, though she was a far gentler woman than me. Mr Marlow had left her in an extremely comfortable position when he had passed. However, the widow Marlow was widely known amongst our small society to be on the perpetual hunt for a new husband.

The widow Marlow was still fresh and youthful, and her long, chestnut brown hair was highly admired amongst our peers. She was, most unfortunately, however, plain of face and somewhat frail of figure. She looked very elegant

20

indeed in her pale blue day dress, nevertheless. As she turned her gaze to him, I understood that her particular fancy had lately fallen upon dear Mr Chesley. Chesley was well-known for his fortune and flawless breeding, but was, I considered with regret, a man as notorious for his refusal to marry again after the tragic death of his beloved wife, Esha, several years past.

Still, I wished the widow the finest of fortune, for I was not unacquainted with loneliness. In good cheer over our reunion, I leaned down to kiss the weather-worn cheek of Sophie's constant companion, Madam Eliot, who greeted me with a disapproving look. I smirked. Madam Eliot, an aging spinster who had never expressed an interest in marriage, was nevertheless highly old fashioned in her attitude, and she looked upon a woman in my line of work as no less vulgar than a scullery maid. After a few sips of strong port, though, Madam Eliot became quite jovial and had even once expressed a secret longing to traipse across the countryside in search of brigands and ne'er-do-wells.

Our rather tense reunion was disrupted by the arrival of Mr and Mrs Charles Prosser, a very good-natured and amiable couple, whose company I rather enjoyed, despite their predisposition towards very public demonstrations of affection for each other. The Prossers were accompanied by a small army of servants and the Ellis', an utterly dreary and rather ill-natured couple whose great fortune alone rendered them suitable for polite society.

The spirits of the party were high, and a well-liveried manservant approached our gathering, bowing low to us. "Sirs, Madams," he said in a reverential voice. He gestured towards the detestable Juliana, and I sighed deeply. It might have been tedious to maintain a bright, cheerful smile in the face of so much socialising, but I was even less eager to approach the dodgy aircraft.

I felt a hand upon my lower back, warm and reassuring, and I turned, intending to deliver a searing rebuke to Asher, whose attention I scarcely required. It was not Asher, however, who conducted me towards the Juliana's gondola. "Mind your step on the way up, dear Mrs Darby," Imaron Behari purred against my ear. I shivered slightly. "Though I daresay you've the grace of a queen."

I rolled my eyes, but I could not suppress the smile upon my lips. "Your flattery is wasted on me, Mr Behari," I told him merrily. "I'm a woman of extensive experience and hardly one to swoon over the gallantry of a young man, no matter how fine-looking he may be."

"You find me fine-looking? I am heartily pleased by your kind accolade." Imaron pressed his hand to his heart, and his eyes twinkled as he smiled down at me. "I shall have to endeavour to be more creative in my flattery, then."

I laughed. "You will forgive me if I fail to wish you luck in your endeavour."

"Luck will hardly play a hand, Mrs Darby."

"Don't dawdle, Astrid!" Asher snapped from the gondola, offering his hand to me. When I seized it, he hauled me firmly into the gondola, guiding me carelessly onto the cushioned bench between him and Xander.

I fixed him with an austere glower. "You needn't be so crude, Ash."

"This is serious business, Astrid. We haven't the time to waste on petty flirtations."

"Oh? Then what might you consider your specific attention to Mr Behari's charming sister, Chanha?"

He lifted his chin defiantly. "I was merely being polite."

"Were you indeed?"

"If the two of you could set aside your mutual ire for a moment, you might be interested to notice that Professor Coffin is not amongst the party," Xander announced blandly.

"Is he not?" I said, raising my eyebrows.

"Of course it hadn't escaped my notice," Ash informed Xander sourly. "My attention had been, momentarily, otherwise engaged."

"I can see that," Xander replied evenly.

"Mr Chesley," I said in a carrying voice, drawing the gentleman's rapt attention from his young, amiable niece.

"Mrs Darby?"

"But where is the professor? Does he not intend to accompany us on the journey?"

"Oh. No. Julius has gone off ahead. He left two days prior with his daughter, Juliana. She's been feeling slightly ill, you see, and he thought the sea air would be more vitalizing than the city haze where industry and poverty have rendered the air thoroughly unsuitable for a young, fragile lady."

"Is she very ill, young Juliana?" Chanha asked with an expression of pretty concern. "How very dreadful."

"Oh, yes, she's been looking decidedly pale and sickly these last few weeks."

"She has seemed in ill-health often the last few months," Sophie offered. "She seems very fragile, young Juliana, and she's grown so pale. Such a pretty girl; it seems a dire injustice."

"It is a terrible shame," Chesley agreed.

"Well, let us hope we find her in greatly improved health and higher spirits when we have reached the Isle of Jules," I said gravely.

"I am sure a holiday will do everyone a great deal of good, Mrs Darby," Chesley replied, smiling brightly. "How could it not, indeed?"

I glanced at Asher. "I couldn't possibly imagine."

* * *

The Juliana disembarked upon a fragrant blanket of brilliant yellow daffodils. The still, sparkling blue waters of the Celtic Sea stretched out to our left, glittering in the high, afternoon sun. The lush green hills of St Agnes lined the horizon, but as I allowed Xander to assist me from the balloon, my attention was caught by the expanse of gleaming white sand along the water, and I paused to inhale exultantly the crisp, clean salt sea air.

"Is it not stunning, Astrid?" Sophie asked, sounding slightly breathless. "I have visited often these past several years, and yet I am always caught out by its beauty."

I smiled at Sophie, enjoying the warm breeze for a moment. "It is quite breathtaking," I agreed. "But is that the professor's house?"

Sophie turned towards the inner island, and she nodded happily. "It's magnificent, truly. A wonder. Come, let us go up."

I smiled, and I glanced over my shoulder towards my men. Reinhart was wrestling my valise over his shoulder, and Xander was admiring the vision of the spectacular island. Asher could sort himself out. I threaded my arm through Sophie's and walked with her across a sandy path lined by vibrant palm trees. Over the trees, I could see the terracotta rooftops of the Coffin's summer estate, and I was eager to reach the manor grounds.

A large, thick metal barrier surrounded the perimeter of the house. I raised my eyebrows, but I did not ask Sophie for what reason the professor required such extravagant security measures when he was, presumably, the only inhabitant of the private island. Coffin was awaiting us at the gate, dressed in a careless, un-tucked white shirt and thin brown trousers that swirled around his lean legs in the slight salt breeze.

Julius Coffin was a widower, in his late fifties, and still a man of very robust health. His dark, thick hair was peppered liberally with grey, though this afternoon it was hidden beneath a wide-brimmed straw hat. He was smiling, and his lined, slightly hook-nosed face was ruddy with sun. He waved happily to us when we approached.

"Good afternoon!" he called warmly to the party, stepped forwards to meet us at the gate. "Welcome to the Isle of Jules."

We greeted him cheerfully, striding forwards to pump his hand. "Good afternoon, Professor Coffin," Asher greeted him, grinning hugely.

When Coffin's eyes swivelled to me, I smiled luminously. "I see you've met my companion, Agent Key, Julius?"

He raised a single eyebrow, and his expression was arctic. He inclined his head courteously all the same. "We have not met in person, but we know each other by reputation, I understand." His thin lips turned up in a wry smile. "I have learned much about him in the past several weeks."

"And likewise, Professor." Asher smiled, wrapping an arm around my shoulder. "This is quite a pleasant location for a holiday, I must say. I was so pleased to be welcomed into your party."

Coffin glanced at me, and I lifted a shoulder. He smirked slightly and turned towards the house. "Come. I'd like to show you the estate." We followed him, and after a long moment, he half-turned his head to speak to me. "I was most pleased you finally decided to accept my annual invitation, Astrid. I had wondered why, after so many years, you'd changed your mind."

I did not mistake the inference in his tone, and I smiled. "I regret that your annual retreat has always fallen during a time in which I was otherwise engaged. I was delighted that I was able to accept this year. We are very grateful for your hospitality."

His chuckle was low and wry. "And, I shouldn't wonder, your sudden diversion from tradition is the result of your association with Agent Key?"

"It is highly fortunate he was able to join me. I do enjoy his companionship, and, as you can see, he is in desperate need of a holiday." I turned my dazzling smile upon Asher, and he scowled down at me.

Coffin's voice was amused. "Well, I hope you will find many diversions to attract you here on my island, Agent Key."

"Thank you, Professor. I am certain there will be plenty to occupy my time."

24

As we were speaking, Coffin had led us into a large sitting room. The walls and tall, vaulted ceiling were made of the same thick wood as the exterior of the house, though it was polished to a stunning gleam. The furniture was soft and casual, made of strong wicker and thick, plush white cushions. A wide panoramic window displayed the stunning view of the trees and the beach beyond the manor, providing all the ornamentation the room required.

"Welcome, all. I am delighted to have you," Coffin announced again when we had all clustered inside the dazzling room. His countenance was serene, and I glanced up at Asher, wondering if the he had at all shaken the professor's soaring spirits. "I must caution you not to leave the immediate property or go exploring on the island on your own. There are dangers on the island, some of which even I have not discovered. Many people have gone missing, and I would not wish for any of my esteemed guests to be another of their number."

I glanced again at Asher, and he lifted an eyebrow. "There is much in the house and the grounds to provide you with entertainment and comfort," Coffin continued. "Dinner will be served in the dining room in three hours time. If you wish to enjoy cocktails before dinner, they will be served in the parlour in two hours. One of the servants will show each of you to your rooms." He nodded briskly to us and strode towards the door. "See you shortly."

We watched him go, startled by the abrupt departure, but the other guests were unmoved; perhaps the curt introduction was another annual tradition to which they had grown accustomed. "That was quite a speech," I remarked quietly to my party.

"Indeed. I had no idea the island promised such thrilling possibilities," Asher replied.

"Untold dangers are our favourite fare, aren't they?" Reinhart said, smirking. "And here I thought we would be enjoying a tranquil holiday without escapade or peril."

"Ah, Morgan, such a holiday would never suit your particular tastes, would it?" I asked, nudging him.

He chuckled. "Sometimes, Astrid, a man does require a bit of leisure. I don't suppose there will be time to enjoy the beach in between investigations and intrigue?"

"I am sure we can find the time. There is, after all, a week."

"If I may show you to your rooms, sirs and madam." A young manservant in a crisp white line uniform bowed to us. "Mr Reinhart, Francis will direct you to the servants' quarters."

"Servants' quarters?" Reinhart demanded indignantly.

"Sir? Is that not acceptable?"

"I am no one's servant!"

I caught his arm, drawing him away from the small group. "Morgan, we do need a man there, if you wouldn't mind terribly."

"Astrid, this is an outrage. I am a man of science, not service."

"Yes, of course, Morgan, but it is...well..."

He sighed. "All right, Astrid. I'll do it."

I pressed his hand, smiling gratefully. "It will not be so bad. By all accounts, it will likely be an improvement upon your flat."

He chuckled. "You should not attempt to lift a man's spirits, Astrid, for it is an area in which you are particularly inept."

I laughed. "Yes, I have been told as much before. Learn what you can about Coffin and the island from the servants."

"All right. If one is interested in rumour and gratuitous gossip, there is no more likely a venue. I'll meet you all later."

I nodded. "Thanks, Morgan. See you after dinner."

"Ah, yes, I suppose I'll be dining in the servants' quarters with the others, then."

"I'm dreadfully sorry, old friend. It is the way of things, in such a society. I will have someone send you the best of it."

He chuckled and cuffed me gently on the shoulder. He inclined his head towards Asher and Xander, moving towards the cluster of the other guests' servants. "Mrs Darby, if you'll come this way," the white-linen liveried servant said, gesturing grandly towards the door.

"Of course. Gentleman?" I turned to face Agent Key and my young cousin.

They weren't paying attention to me, however. In the brief moment I had been speaking quietly to Morgan, my companions had been drawn in by the tender wiles of the island's young women. Chanha Behari was looking up at Asher from under her long, thick black lashes, smiling coyly as she murmured to him, and young Knightly, hardly a lad to have his head turned by a woman, was engaged with a young, frail-looking girl of near his age with long, red hair and skin as pale as ivory. Her large, green eyes were shadowed, as though she required a long rest.

I cleared my throat, peering at them with my hands on my hips. "Knightly? Agent Key? If you would, we are waiting," I announced imperiously.

Their expressions were identically shamefaced, and they inclined their heads to the ladies, striding towards me. "Forgive me, Astrid. Chan--Miss Behari was merely impressing upon me the delights the island offers," Asher said, rather too heartily for my taste.

"I just wager she was," I replied sourly, but I turned my gaze upon my young cousin as we followed the young servant up the winding wooden staircase towards the second story guest quarters. "And who was the young woman with whom you were speaking, Xander?"

"She's Juliana Coffin."

"Is she really? That is the young lady of the house, then. She does look ill, doesn't she?"

"Yes, she complained of a slight headache, but she is most eager to make your acquaintance, Astrid. She has heard much of our exploits and finds you a rather fascinating character."

I smirked. "I do seem to have admirers today, don't I, Ash?"

His lip curled. "Your humility and decorum is an inspiration to us all, Mrs Darby."

CHAPTER THREE

My accommodations was a luxurious chamber with a large, four-poster bed swathed in a thick, plush white coverlet and a mosquito net that surrounded the bed like a spider's web. Sea shells and ocean landscapes adorned the walls, but the true beauty of the chamber was the large bay window on the wall across from the bed through which I could view the vast expanse of the dark, blue sea. A slight breeze rustled the palm trees outside the window, filling the air with the softest whisper of leaves.

The splendour of the room was only slightly marred by the appearance of a thin wooden door on the far wall, which adjoined to Asher's. I wondered briefly if the professor intended to punish me for imposing the Ministry agent upon him without warning. It occurred to me he might consider Asher's proximity to be a discreet convenience. I opened my mouth in outrage, though there was no one upon whom to deliver my wrath.

"That man," I muttered, shedding my slightly damp day dress upon the pristine counterpane. "I hardly think it is proper to adjoin an unmarried woman's room to a positively roguish--"

"What are you muttering?"

I gasped, instinctively covering myself with the discarded dress as though it were a mantle. "Asher Key!" I squawked. "What are you doing barging in here without even alerting me?"

Asher rolled his eyes. "Come now, Astrid. It isn't as if I haven't seen you without your petticoats before."

My cheeks burned, but I glared crossly at him. "I hardly think now is an apt moment to make such a proclamation! I had absolutely no intention of you ever seeing me thus again. Get out of here at once!"

He was thoroughly unimpressed by my admonishments, and he moved to lounge upon the coverlet. I gestured wildly at him, but he merely shook his head. I sighed deeply, crossing the room to rifle through my valise for a suitable dinner dress. "What do you think of him?" he asked.

"Julius? He seems rather the same as always. Pleasant, gracious, though I suspect he is not exactly pleased with me at the moment, having brought you along as my companion. I suspect I will not be receiving a return invitation next year."

He smirked. "No, I meant do you think him capable of murder?"

"Anymore than when I first made his acquaintance? I should think not. Of course, it's not as if murderers go around announcing it, do they? They don't wear symbols or curl their moustaches in a particular way. Not that Julius has a moustache."

"You are babbling, woman. Get dressed so you might be able to conduct a conversation in a reasonable manner."

"You are the one who is infringing upon my privacy and personal comfort, damn you, Ash!"

He waved his hand dismissively, but he did not avert his gaze from me, and I glowered at him, striding angrily into the washroom to dress. "You needn't preserve your modesty on my account, Astrid," he called from the bed. "I am perfectly comfortable to conduct our meeting whilst you parade around in your smalls."

"You are uncouth and incorrigible, Asher Key!" I growled through the door.

"I don't suppose you require any assistance in there?"

"I am perfectly capable of minding my own toilette, thank you ever kindly!"

His chuckle resounded through the chamber, and I shook my head, pressing my lips tightly together to suppress a smirk. "I'm keen to explore the island," he announced casually.

"Ah, but did you not hear him warn of lethal and esoteric dangers?"

"Bah. Merely bluster, surely. There is nothing here, on these islands."

"How can you possibly know that?" I demanded, emerging, fully adorned, from the washroom.

Asher sat up, gesturing for me to join him on the bed. I rolled my eyes and perched upon the edge of the small wicker chair in the corner of the room. "I have never heard of such a thing in the Scilly Isles. It's not as if there are head-hunters and primitives."

"Ah, but you don't really know. You've never actually seen any, but that doesn't mean they don't exist, does it? There have been reports of privateers and scoundrels making homes on the uninhabited islands for years. This one might not be any different."

"Aside from the ominous metal barrier and the guards patrolling the perimeter with shotguns and crossbows."

I lifted my shoulders. "Well, we'll have plenty of time to explore the grounds and the surrounding areas for signs of other life." I rose to peer out at the sea below. "It's quite pretty here, and I do enjoy a nice expedition, as you know."

His lips curved into a smile. "I remember."

I turned towards him. "I would like to take some time to study Julius and the other guests before we go causing any unnecessary trouble."

He nodded and rose from the bed. He paused with his hand on the knob of the door separating our two chambers. "Will you meet me after dinner?" he asked, and his tone was inscrutable.

I considered, eyeing him shrewdly, then nodded. "Yes, all right."

* * *

Our host did not join us for cocktails in the parlour. His daughter, Juliana, however, seemed in high spirits as she enjoyed the rapt attentions of my young cousin and the charming Mr Behari. Young Juliana was a sweet, fragile thing of Xander's age, though her breeding had been infinitely gentler. She was rather pale this evening, in the blaze of the gas-lamps placed carefully around the room, bathing the chamber in a soft, warm glow. Even in the dim forgiving light, the young lady looked sickly and frail, and a delicate tremor passed through her entire body as she held her teacup.

The delicate china clattered almost imperceptibly against the saucer, though her young, virile attendants seemed not to notice. "What do you think of her?" Asher asked in my ear, and I looked up as he joined me on the divan.

I cocked my head to consider the young lady. "She is very well bred. Polite, demure, everything she ought to be," I told him, and I smiled slightly. "I think my young cousin has taken a particular interest in her, if he's willing to compete with Mr Behari."

"Are you troubled by it?"

"Of course not. I have no interest in engaging Mr Behari's attention for myself."

Asher snorted and rolled his eyes. "I was referring to Xander, not the Indian."

"Ah." I smirked. "No, let him have his fun. As long as he is focussed upon the situation, I do not forbid his interest."

"Nevertheless, a conflict of interest at this juncture can hardly be the thing."

"Oh, don't be such a dreadful bore. Allow the young people their flirtations. It isn't Juliana whom you are after, anyway, is it?"

"That does not mean she will not attempt to hinder our cause should she catch word of it."

"Ah, perhaps, but I hardly think a frail, sickly thing as she will have much to do against the might of the Ministry of Defence and the legendary Astrid Darby, eh?"

Asher's lips trembled slightly as if he were suppressing a smile. "Still. I do not entirely approve."

"It is most fortunate, then, that it is I who claim the right to pass judgment upon my young cousin's conquests, isn't it?"

He sighed. "All right. Have your fun. Pray you do not similarly forget your purpose here, Astrid."

I smirked as his attention wavered slightly, his gaze following young Chanha Behari as she drifted engagingly between the small parties gathered about the lounge like a queen greeting her courtiers. "Perhaps you should consider your advice and mind your own wandering eye, Asher Key."

Asher lifted his chin indignantly. "I'm sure I've no idea what you mean. I have every intention of keeping my eye riveted steadfastly upon the professor until I have sorted out just what he's up to."

"Ah, but your eyes are free for the moment, in the absence of the professor. Upon what shall you rivet them now?"

He rolled his eyes. "Do I sense a note of envy in your inference, Astrid?"

"Don't be absurd. I have far better things with which to be getting on than concerning myself where your roaming eye might settle," I replied, turning my nose up

"Agent Key."

We looked up as one as Madam Eliot lowered herself upon the wing-backed chair across from us. Her small, dark green eyes were shrewd, and I raised an eyebrow, awaiting her remarks; she was a lady with whom to be reckoned, by all accounts. Sophie had spent many an evening recounting her spinster aunt's insistent meddling in hushed stage whispers. I was relieved that her attention was, for the moment, upon Asher and not me.

Asher inclined his head to the steel-haired woman. "Madam Eliot."

The old woman's smile was as sharp as a razor, and there was a flush of great smugness upon her stout, ruddy face. "My niece and I have been discussing you, Agent Key."

He raised his eyebrows. "Is that so? And in what capacity did I enter into your conversation?"

"It seems rather odd that you would be here, on the Isle of Jules. Why, I heard just the other evening at Mrs Winifred Reed's that you and Julius are not exactly friendly at the moment." Madam Eliot's tone was even, but her eyes glittered as though she were enjoying a private secret. "A small matter of you accusing him of heinous doings in the poor districts?"

Asher looked completely caught out for a moment, and I laughed. "Asher, do be wary of Wilhelmina Eliot. She seems to possess more intelligence than all the Ministry's best network of informants collectively."

"Indeed, it has been the talk of our small society the last few weeks. Never would we have expected dear Julius of wrong-doing, so great are his works of charity and so righteous is his bearing. What is it, exactly, that you purport he's done?"

"Madam, I assure you, I know not how you have come upon such information, but perhaps you misunderstood. Why, Professor Coffin is very widely respected amongst my peers. I should not wish to falsely accuse anyone of misdeeds," Asher replied blithely.

"Indeed, Madam, why would Julius have welcomed Agent Key to his private estate, were the two men at such odds?" I interjected, smirking slightly.

Madam Eliot considered. "I must say, it is a mystery. However, I have heard tell from many reliable sources. Your shocking allegations have been discussed many times over in different circles of our small society."

"Well, Madam, surely you, of all people, might well know how rumours are spread."

"So it is merely rumour then, you say, and unjust?"

"Certainly, I would not dare suggest a lady such as yourself would engage in baseless gossip. However, it has been my experience that many small, trifling misunderstandings can be blown quite out of proportion. Would you not say, Madam Eliot?" I asked, smiling brilliantly at the spinster.

Her brow furrowed slightly, and she lifted her chin. "Well, I shouldn't wish to think you were involved in this, Astrid. Always toeing the line of modesty and decorum."

I smirked. "Well, I do enjoy a good wind-up, and so, it seems, do you," Her dark, malachite eyes narrowed, but I returned her gaze with a supercilious smile.

Before she could rejoin with a sharp remark, Mr Chesley approached our tense party, holding a tumbler of a dark amber liquid. He had dressed for dinner, in what I had come to regard as the traditional island livery of white linen. Mr Chesley was well-suited to such attire; it flattered his deeply tanned skin and overlong, sun-kissed hair quite marvellously. "Ah, and what are you three looking so tense over? This is a holiday. No need for such dreary miens."

Madam Eliot opened her mouth to speak, but I cut her off gaily. "Ah, Mr Chesley, do join us and regale us of tales of the Isle of Jules. I understand this is not your first time visiting this island paradise. Tell us, does the good professor always impart such a dire caveat upon his party in the introduction?"

Mr Chesley's laugh boomed across the room, and several of the other guests turned their heads to sight the source of the din. "I say, it was quite histrionic, wasn't it? No, my dear Mrs Darby, this is the first time he's made such ominous proclamations, but it would not have been the first time I'd heard such things about our little getaway."

"Oh?" I leaned forwards in my seat. "And what have you heard, then, Mr Chesley?"

His words had drawn the attention of several of our number, and our party improved with the additions of Sophie, Chanha and Imaron Behari and the Prossers. Chesley seemed buoyed by the enlarged crowd, and his fine face was vivacious as he continued. "Well, two summers past, I understood three of the guests' servants went missing on the island."

"Missing, you say?" Mr Prosser asked, his brow furrowed. "How do you mean?"

"They simply disappeared, is what I mean, Charles. I mean, they went off one day and they were not seen again. They were warned, of course, not to leave the grounds or go wandering around the island, but they must have done."

"You have spent many summers here, have you not, Mr Chesley?"

"In truth, my dear Astrid, this is only my third. Still, I do consider myself rather an authority on the island, being the most senior of us."

"I beg your pardon, uncle, but it is dreadfully uncouth of you to rob Madam

33

Eliot of that honour," Imaron Behari said grandly, smiling widely at the old spinster as though he had paid her a great compliment.

I snorted into my hand, and Asher nudged me. Madam Eliot opened her mouth as though she were uncertain whether she had been highly insulted or flattered. Finally, she smiled at the young, dark man. "Just so, Imaron. I do beg your pardon, Madam Eliot," Chesley said, his lips quivering as though he were suppressing a smile.

Imaron's gaze flicked to me, and he winked. "But do go on, uncle. I believe Mrs Darby was just beginning to settle into your tale, were you not, Mrs D?"

"I was indeed, Mr Behari. Do go on, Chesley. I am most eager to hear what became of the missing servants."

"Well, nothing became of them, far as I can tell. They were, as I said, never seen again."

"Was not a search party sent for them?" Chanha asked.

"Come now, Chanha, the men could hardly risk their lives to seek a few servants who could not abide the rules of the house, could they?"

"And what do you think happened to them, Mr Chesley?" Asher asked. His expression was bland, and his tone was even, but I recognised the gleam in his cobalt eyes.

"Oh, I haven't the slightest idea, and Julius has never offered an opinion on the matter," Chesley replied, as though it were little concern.

"It could be a tribe of murderous gypsies or brigands," Imaron interjected, his dark eyes twinkling merrily.

"Or cannibals," Madam Eliot added, and we all turned to look at her, slightly aghast. "What?"

"Or privateers gone aground," Charles Prosser said keenly, caught up in the excitement of the speculation.

"Has anyone seen anything to suggest we aren't alone on the island?" I asked.

"No," Chesley replied, his shoulder slumping in disappointment. "Once their servants disappeared, no one seemed to want anything more to do with the island outside the grounds. It seemed more sensible to heed the professor's warnings."

"Do you think it might happen again?" Chanha asked, fluttering her hand over her breast as though feeling slightly faint.

I rolled my eyes. "Who could possibly say, my dear niece?" Chesley replied. "It might do, if one is foolish enough to stray from the house."

I exchanged a significant glance with Asher, who looked as though he had much to say. "Are you not frightened to be on the island under the circumstances?" Sophie asked breathlessly. "Why, it gives me the shivers just thinking what might have happened to the poor gents."

Chesley reached across his nephew and patted the lady's shoulder soothingly. "Ah, do not fret, dear Mrs Marlow. I am certain you are perfectly safe, provided you remain in the company of so many strapping lads."

Chanha lifted her chin defiantly. "Uncle, you do do us ladies a disservice. We are perfectly able to mind ourselves. We need not the protection of strapping lads, as you say."

Chesley chuckled. "A tigress, my dear niece," he informed us all. "I do pity the brigand or gypsy who dares attempt to lay a hand upon her."

"Ah, but such talk is hardly appropriate for a party," Mrs Prosser announced. "Surely there are more fitting topics with which we might entertain each ourselves."

"Too true, Mrs Prosser," Imaron replied genially. He turned his gaze to Asher and me. "But I have heard much about the two of you and something about...Big Ben?"

Asher snorted, and I blinked innocently. "I've no idea to what you might be referring," I replied carelessly.

"You cannot fool me with your blitheness and innocent smiles, Mrs Darby. I am well aware of your reputation, and I will not be dissuaded from wheedling the information from you eventually." He winked at me again. "You may as well just give it up now."

I laughed. "Oh, yes, we are all most eager to hear what occurred. It was all over the Times for weeks," Chesley added. "Do tell, you pair."

"I'm afraid, Mr Behari, that I am honour-bound to hold my tongue on this matter. Why, carelessly divulging such secrets of extreme national security would hardly befit a woman of my profession. I'm sure you understand."

"Oh, now, Astrid, I'm sure the Ministry wouldn't mind terribly if you mentioned how you, however inadvertently, aimed a death ray at our beloved Big Ben, thus rendering it nothing more than gears and timber," Asher said, nudging me convivially. "The story was, after all, in all the papers. Did it not simply elevate you and your entourage to hitherto unimagined infamy?"

I glared at him. "Oh, yes, you must tell us all about it," Chanha said, her dark, almond shaped eyes glittering keenly. "And you were there, too, were you not, Agent Key? I did hear you were the commanding officer at the scene."

"He was there, indeed, Miss Behari. Why, his utter inability to stop the destruction of the tower was likewise sensationalised for all to read in the Times and other publications of its calibre. My infamy, I'm sure, Ash, is nothing to yours."

He laughed, but Chanha Behari's supplications were not to be answered, for one of Coffin's men swept into the parlour, ringing a small, tin bell with a dramatic flourish. "Sirs, Madams, dinner is served in the dining room. Master Coffin would request your attendance directly." He bowed smartly to us and spun on his heel, striding out of the parlour without waiting to see if we had risen to follow.

"Well," I said brightly. "I suppose our tale will have to wait until a more auspicious moment, Asher."

He rolled his eyes. "I shall endeavour to suppress my extreme regret."

* * *

The twinkling stars of the clear, tropical sky above the thick, green palm trees outside the villa's dining room created a serene, beautiful backdrop for the extravagant dinner before us. The walls of the dining room were clear glass, and the whole of the grounds could be glimpsed below. An opened pane allowed the sultry salt air to waft into the room, and it seemed as though we were dining directly under the stars, in the midst of this tropical paradise.

Though Imaron and Chesley had lamented the waste of a thrilling dinner on the patio outside the villa, surrounded by the music of tropical birds and the buzz of jungle wildlife, Julius had assured us most unequivocally that we would not wish to dine in a swarm of ravenous mosquitoes. Though I did enjoy the occasional summer picnic in the beauty of the outdoors, I preferred to remain in the safety of the indoors where my flesh would not present a tender feast for the hungry insects.

Our meal was a colourful spread of soup, seafood and exotic delicacies to which our bland English palettes were unaccustomed. Nevertheless, I rather relished the spicy shellfish and rich coconut soup. My companions, too, must have enjoyed the offering, for they exclaimed delightedly over each course and complimented Julius' exquisite taste. They were in high spirits, buoyed by the balmy air through the glass and the cocktails of the previous hour, and their conversations were lively and cheerful.

I did not join in the joie de vivre as I savoured the thick, slightly tangy soup on my tongue. Nevertheless, my lips curved into a smile as I watched my cousin and the young Coffin girl through the stunning bouquets of exotic flowers across the polished wood table. Xander and Juliana seemed keen to continue their engrossing conversation of earlier, and they spoke in jubilant murmurs to each other regarding what seemed to them to be the most fascinating theories of modern science.

I was not surprised to learn the young lady shared an interest in science with my young cousin, as her father had always displayed a similar keenness, which he had shared most often with my dear Nathaniel. Juliana's father, too, watched the young people beside him with an indulgent smile, and I wondered if Julius saw a bit of his old friend in my dear cousin, as I so often had in the years following Nathaniel's tragic passing. Though Xander was not a perfect match for Juliana, their breeding being slightly incongruent, my young cousin did stand to inherit the bulk of the Darby fortune upon my demise, and it could not be said he wasn't an extraordinary young man.

Julius' expression remained tolerant as Xander launched into a thrilling tale of our adventures in Greece several months past, in which we had outrun a murderous historian. We had been engaged by the small museum in Athens at which the historian, Mega, had formerly been employed and from where he had stolen the small, ivory statue of the goddess Ceto, which he believed in his madness could speak to him. Intent upon wresting from us the statue, which we had, though an intricate series of awesome deceptions including bonfire parties and a strange ritual dance, stolen from him, he had pursued us relentlessly across the Balkan Peninsula.

"Mega was upon us, but as we leapt upon our waiting catamaran with the statue tucked safely in my vest pocket, he attempted to pursue, missed the hull and was swept away by the hostile waters of the Aegean Sea," Xander informed Juliana with a theatrical flourish.

"Oh!" Juliana exclaimed. "But was he quite all right?"

"You ask if he was all right? He was attempting to murder us, Miss Coffin!"

"Yes, but he was quite mad, wasn't he, and he surely didn't deserve to die, did he?"

Xander sighed as if her tender heart had thoroughly ruined his tale. "Well, perhaps he did not, but it could hardly be helped. He was, after all, chasing us."

"Do not let my cousin disquiet you, dear Juliana," I interjected, smirking. "Mega was never seen again by us, but he washed up upon the shores of Cape Sounion, quite alive. However, by the time he'd managed to leg it back to Athens, the statue had been restored to its former home, and, to his certain dismay, the law was awaiting him. He was sentenced to the gaol for his theft and treachery, but he lives still, and he is, by all accounts, quite well."

Juliana laughed, but Xander rolled his eyes at me. "Perhaps someone should record your exploits, Mrs D," Mr Chesley put in. "Surely, your experiences are the stuff of adventure novels and penny dreadfuls."

"To be sure, Mr Chesley," I replied blithely, "many a journalist and biographer has approached me for an exclusive consultation, but I much prefer the quiet life." Beside me, Asher snorted into his glass, but I ignored him, lifting my chin with dignity. "I have been recording my memoirs, and when I have finally passed the mantle of head adventurer to my prodigious young cousin, I may present them at last for public perusal."

"Ah, I am certain with your charm and flair for the dramatic, Mrs D, it is a thrilling chronicle, indeed," Imaron Behari stated, and his smile roused a small flutter in my chest. He was too handsome, to be sure. A man like that had no place in polite society; he was certain to cause naught but trouble.

"Juliana, you look pale," Julius said suddenly, drawing my eyes from the young Indian gentleman. "Are you feeling all right?"

Juliana smiled, but her hand shook almost imperceptibly as she raised it to her forehead. "I'm feeling quite cheerful, Father, but I confess I am somewhat faint."

"The excitement is far too much for your delicate constitution, my dear," Julius said, his brow furrowed in grave concern. "I will have Mr Bray prepare something special for you. This spicy cuisine does not suit your condition."

Juliana's hollowed cheeks flushed slightly as though his particular attention embarrassed her, but she inclined her head obediently. "Thank you, Papa."

Julius yanked on the small, brass bell pull at his shoulder, and a tall, austere-looking manservant with shortly-cropped dark hair and pale, translucent blue eyes entered the room with a brisk stride. He was dressed in a crisp, white linen suit, and although the light, careless fabric rustled softly in the balmy breeze wafting through the dining room, he looked dour and rigid. He leaned down to allow his master to murmur orders in his ear and nodded curtly. "Of course, sir. Right away."

He spun on his heel and strode out of the room as smartly as he'd entered, leaving the spirits of the table slightly diminished after his grim appearance. Juliana lowered her head, her pale cheeks pinked with the heat of her blush as she endured the sudden attention of the party. Taking pity on the poor thing, I said brightly, "My dear Julius, I am simply breathless over the wonder of your lovely island retreat. Is there much to do besides admire the beauty of it all? Have you many activities planned for us, or are we to fend for ourselves and invent our own diversions?"

Juliana glanced up at me and smiled, and I winked at her. The party's attention turned to Julius, and he inclined his head. "Yes, of course. Forgive my dismal efforts as your humble host thus far. We've many activities planned for the week. You saw the beach as you arrived, of course. The waters are very warm this time of year and quite well suited to swimming or other water sports in which you might wish to partake. You'll find, I'm sure, that our library is quite extensive and well stocked with any sort of reading you might wish to do—"

"Library?" Imaron asked archly, but he smiled around the table. "Come now, Professor, but who would wish to read when a tropical paradise awaits us outside these walls?"

Julius smiled. "Ah, yes, I am sure a man of your youth and virility would much prefer the more energetic games. For those of you who, like young Imaron, enjoy a bit of sport, the grounds offer much by way of activity. There is a firing range, lawn tennis, all the space and accoutrements for any sport in which you might wish to indulge. I am certain you will find my modest hideaway most pleasant and restful, indeed."

"Oh, I am most eager to explore the grounds and the house," I told him gaily.

His glance was sharp, but his features smoothed instantly, and he inclined his head to me. "I am sure exploring is your particular fancy, Astrid. You may wander freely on the grounds, as you wish, and through the rooms in the house, but mind you all, do not enter the basement past the servants' quarters."

I raised an eyebrow but Chesley laughed heartily. "Come now, Julius, with all the pleasures this paradise has to offer, why ever would we wish to enter the basement?"

Julius chuckled. "Right. Of course you wouldn't. It would hardly be civilised, crawling through the bowels of the villa, but for our more—inquisitive guests, I must caution you, the area has fallen victim to severe weather damage this winter, and it is not fit. A person could injure themselves, should they get a mind to explore it."

"I am sure we can find enough diversions to keep us from the tedium of exploring a perilous basement," Imaron said, grinning.

Julius smirked, but I glanced sidelong at Asher. He raised an eyebrow, but he remained otherwise silent, which I thought was much unlike him. I wondered what he might be playing at, but I was sure I would soon see; Asher Key always had some sort of trick up his clever little sleeve. The appearance of Mr Bray, however, distracted my attention from my devious companion. The manservant placed a tray of steaming vegetables and lean, broiled meat before Juliana, bowing low to her.

"Miss Juliana," he said in an unexpectedly low, gentle voice.

"Thank you, Eli," she said, smiling up at him.

He straightened, turning to Julius. "Will there be anything else, sir?" he asked, and his voice was not as gentle now, as though his affection was for Juliana alone.

Julius waved his hand. "No. Thank you, Elijah. I am deeply appreciative of your care to my darling Juliana."

"Of course, sir." He was gone as quickly as he'd come, and the party was left again in dampened humour.

"Are you very ill, Miss Juliana?" Xander asked.

She smiled at him. "Yes, I seem to be, I'm afraid. I've been feeling quite out of humour for some months," she told him, and her tone was even, despite the sad words. "The doctors have been unable to suss out what ails me. We've tried leeches--dreadful, I assure you--modern medicine and all, but I've not improved. Some of them think it might simply be in my mind. A bad humour."

Xander's brow furrowed in indignation. "That is not very scientific."

She laughed. "Well, I cannot lend all my thoughts to science, especially when it seems to be little help to my condition."

"But such talk hardly befits a celebration, my darling," Julius said, his tone slightly sharp.

Juliana ducked her head, lifting her fork to spear a bit of meat. "Of course. Sorry, Papa."

Xander's eyes followed her keenly as she ate, but Asher shifted beside me, and my attention snapped to him instantly. Asher Key was all cheek and cleverness, but when he set his mind to an inquiry, he was an intractable foe. He was, despite his less venerable qualities and our tenuous armistice, a highly amusing ally. "Professor Coffin, your warning upon our arrival was quite provocative," he said smoothly, and it was not what I had expected him to say. My lips turned down in a slight pout.

Julius glanced at us, and his mouth curved into a smile. "Yes, well, I did not mean to alarm any of you, but the island is home to local dangers."

"Like the East End?" Leticia Prosser interjected.

Julius chuckled. "Perhaps not quite like. I made my villa on the island some six years ago, but much of its geography remains a mystery to me. I was drawn to the beauty of the sea and the pleasant weather, but it is largely a wilderness still. I have not had occasion to plumb the depths of the islands mysteries, and had I years, I don't know if I could discover them all."

"We've heard many stories, Professor," Madam Eliot said, her lips drawn into a thin line. "Stories of privateers and brigands and such."

"Why, Madam Eliot, pray, do not present our posturing as fact," Chanha Behari scolded gently. "We were merely having a laugh."

"Privateers and brigands?" Julius asked, raising a dark eyebrow.

Madam Eliot lifted her chin defiantly. "Well, we did hear of the servants who went missing. And there has always been talk of the Isles of Scilly being home to such sinister elements."

Julius' smile wavered slightly. "Yes, unfortunate business, the missing servants. As I said, it is best not to leave the grounds, lest you place yourself in needless peril."

"You still have no idea what became of them?" Asher asked evenly.

Julius glanced at him, but his expression remained mild. "No, sadly. It was dreadful business, indeed."

"Ah, but some say there are ghosts on these islands," Imaron announced with a flourish.

"Ghosts?" Sophie Marlow exclaimed, and her mouth quivered as though she were unsure whether to laugh or scoff at the suggestion.

"Oh, yes," Imaron continued, his eyes twinkling wickedly. "I have heard many ghost stories. Some of the island people claim they're the ghosts of people who've washed up from sea or have been murdered by pirates."

Julius scoffed. "Come now, young Behari."

But the others seemed delighted by the prospect. "Could it be so?" Mrs Prosser asked, peering at her husband.

Mr Prosser rolled his eyes. "Leticia always did love a good spooky story. But there are no such things as ghosts, my darling."

"There could be," Madam Eliot announced, startling us all. "My cleaning girl claimed she saw one once."

"Bah, Madam Eliot, it was merely a wind up," Chesley told her cheerfully. "There's no documented evidence of the existence of ghosts. What say you, Knightly? You're a man of science. What do you think?"

Xander smiled. "I have seen many strange things these past years. I could hardly say what I think on the matter."

"Truly, Mr Knightly?" Juliana asked, looking aghast. "You believe such a thing could exist?"

"I believe, Miss Juliana, that there are many unexplainable things in the world. Why, until very recently, science was considered no better than witchcraft. I am open to the possibility there is more to the universe."

Juliana smiled, but she turned her gaze to her father. "Well," he said, as if settling the matter. "It could be ghosts as well as anything else."

"You've not explored at all?" Asher asked, and his tone suggested he didn't entirely believe this.

"I have no need, Agent Key. I have all I desire and need here, on the grounds."

"Still, you must have some spirit of adventure?"

Julius laughed. "I regret, in my youth, perhaps, but in my maturing age, I do not." He wagged a finger at us good-naturedly. "And I caution you all not to develop one. Remain on the grounds."

"Ah, but Professor Coffin, we have a Ministry of Defence agent and the legendary Astrid Darby in our party," Imaron said. "Surely we could protect ourselves from brigands and a few ghosts. We could organise an expedition into the wilderness, learn for posterity's sake what lies beyond the grounds."

"No!" Julius barked, and we all turned to him in surprise. "Do not do so. I forbid it." His expression smoothed instantly, however, and he smiled again. "Forgive me. I assure you all, if there are ghosts wandering the island, you would not wish to encounter them."

"Speaking of ghosts..." Imaron said with what I was coming to regard as his characteristic cheeky grin. "Why don't we play a little game?"

"Oh, what sort of game?" Juliana asked keenly. "I do enjoy games, and I play them so rarely."

"It is a tradition in New Delhi."

"A tradition, brother?" Chanha asked, raising her dark, elegant eyebrows.

"A murder mystery."

"I'm certain you just made that up!"

"Hold your tongue, sister. I certainly did not," Imaron replied indignantly. "Just because you aren't invited to the sorts of parties where people play games and actually have fun doesn't mean it isn't a tradition among more jubilant spirits."

Chanha laughed, and Leticia Prosser leaned forwards interestedly. "A murder mystery, you say?"

"Oh, yes."

"Is that strictly appropriate?" Madam Eliot asked

"Oh, don't be so literal, Aunt. It's only a laugh, isn't it?" Sophie said gently. "But how do you play?"

Imaron sipped his red wine and grinned at her. "I am so glad you asked, good lady." He leaned back in his chair as if settling in for an elaborate tale. "One person, of course, will be the murderer."

"How do you decide?" Chesley asked, his eyes sparkling.

"We'll draw slips of paper or something like," Imaron said, waving his hand.

"One marked with an X," Sophie agreed keenly. "X for 'murderer.'"

"Yes, all right, an X," Imaron agreed. "Very good. And once the murderer has been designated, we'll all split up. Like Hide and Seek. And the murderer will pursue us all, waiting to kill us when we least expect it."

"But how does he kill?" Chanha asked.

Imaron considered. "The murderer will say...'I've killed you.'"

"Not very creative, is it?" Charles Prosser put in.

"Well, it doesn't have to be creative. It just has to do the job. We're not animals."

43

"All right, go on."

"The murderer must be sneaky. You have to touch your victim to kill them because if you don't, and they escape you, they'll tell all the others who you are, and the game will be over. Victims, you can try to escape the killer, if you wish, but they will chase you, so you'd better be light on your feet."

"What happens once you are killed?" Juliana asked. She was riveted upon the dark, handsome man's smiling face. Xander seemed not to notice, however, for he, too, seemed involved in Imaron's elucidation.

"You have to stay where you've been killed, and if someone finds you, you have to give them a clue to figure out who the killer is."

"But it mustn't be a good clue, otherwise it will all be over too soon," Chanha told him.

"Oh, it must be good," Imaron replied gravely. "But it must be clever."

"Like...he's wearing a hat, or something?"

"Well, yes, except none of us are wearing hats, and if one of us were to put one on, we would know right away who the killer was, wouldn't we?"

Chanha rolled her eyes. "Well, for example, Imaron. No need to be shirty."

"All right, yes, for example, then, but it's not a good one."

She scoffed and tossed her long, black hair. "Once one of us solves it, how will we alert the others?" Xander asked blandly. "We can't very well go tearing through the house shouting about it."

Imaron considered a moment. "I have a solution," Julius announced, drawing our eyes to him. "We will place a bell at the foot of the stair. Once you believe you've discovered the killer, you ring the bell."

"Yes!" Imaron exclaimed, as though bolstered by our host's implicit acquiescence. "And when you hear the bell, you must stop what you are doing at once and come to the stairs."

"It does sound highly amusing, but what will we get if we win?" Chesley asked, clapping his nephew on the shoulder.

"Oh, but we're against Astrid and her young cousin, and Agent Key!" Sophie exclaimed mournfully. "They will solve it straight away."

"Ah, dear Sophie," I said, smiling brightly. "I can't say for my cousin or Agent Key's honour, but I promise I will endeavour to remain as ignorant as possible to the last."

Sophie giggled, and Asher pressed a hand to his heart. "I, too, promise not to use my unfair advantage and extensive experiences to thwart you all."

"I promise no such thing," Xander announced. "I intend to win. And what will it be that I will be winning?"

"Well, we will have to watch out for you, then, young Knightly," Chesley said, shaking his finger at Xander with a grin. "Whoever the killer is, be sure to kill Knightly first to give us all an advantage."

Xander laughed. Imaron waved his hand to draw the party's eyes back to him. "If you win...then we all must do whatever you wish."

"Whatever we wish?" Chanha asked, her eyebrows raised. "That is quite ambiguous, brother. Why, there are many things I can think of for each of you to do for me."

Imaron chuckled. "I am sure there are, dear sister, but that is not what I meant. The winner may select the activity in which we all must engage."

"Well, those are not very high stakes," I remarked.

"Mrs D is right. That is not a very good prize at all," Leticia Prosser announced.

Imaron shook his head, as if we could not be bothered to see reason. "All right, then. The winner will have...breakfast in bed! Each morning for three days. And the exposed murder must bring it to them."

"Ah, but that's not so fair to the murderer, is it?" Juliana said.

"Well, they'd be a murderer, wouldn't they? It's the very least punishment," Xander told her soothingly, and she covered her giggle with her hand.

"But the murderer may win, too," Asher said. "If they kill everyone before anyone can solve it. The murderer may be particularly clever, and once they've killed everyone, they can ring the bell and reveal themselves."

"Ah, very good, Agent Key," Imaron said. "So? What say you all? Shall we play?"

CHAPTER FOUR

Imaron grinned wickedly and lifted his glass in salute before swallowing the contents in one gulp. "Everyone ready?" He brandished the hat in which Juliana had placed several slips of blank parchment and one fated 'X.' "Miss Juliana, will you honour us by selecting first? We trust that you have fairly distributed the blanks."

She glanced at Xander and smiled shyly. He winked at her and gave her a gentle push towards Imaron. Imaron bowed low, raising the hat to her. She reached gingerly into the hat, swirling her hand around in the slips of parchment a moment before drawing it out, clutching the slip. She moved to open it, but Imaron closed his slender, mahogany hand around hers.

"Not yet, Miss Juliana. Shall we all wait to look together?" Imaron held out the hat. "Who's next, then?"

We stepped forwards to await our turn at the hat, and when we were all similarly clutching our slips, Imaron faced the group, holding up his hands. "Everyone ready?"

My slip was blank. Asher leaned over to catch a glimpse of it, but I covered it with my hand, digging my elbow into his ribs. "Ow! How uncharitable of you, Mrs Darby."

"I do not abide cheaters, Agent Key. For shame."

He chuckled. The other guests eyes eyed each other cagily, but their expressions were keen, and it was impossible to tell which one of them might be our murderer.

"All right...everyone...go! But mind!" Imaron called at our backs as we started towards the door, and we all turned back to him. "The killer must wait a full minute before he--or she--commits their first murder."

"Oh, I don't relish the idea of wandering the house on my own," Chanha purred, gliding towards Asher and me. "Agent Key, would you be so obliging?"

He looked down at her, startled, as she held out her hand. "Miss Behari?"

She smiled. "Would you be my escort for the game?"

"Ah, the young lady wishes to cultivate an unfair advantage for herself," Madam Eliot said disapprovingly.

Juliana laughed. "Well, then, I too intend to have an advantage. Mr Knightly, would you be so kind?"

He smirked and offered his arm. "Of course."

Imaron shook his head exasperatedly. "Mind you, people, you can pair up, if you wish, but at your own peril, for you may be the first to die if your partner bears the 'X.'"

I smirked, but Chanha lifted her large, glittering eyes to Asher. "You won't kill me, will you, Agent Key?" she asked, pressing his hand to her heart.

"Miss Behari, were I to do, it would be a dreadful waste, indeed," Asher replied gallantly.

Chanha giggled, and she clung to him as they exited the room side by side. Sophie leaned to speak low to me. "Would you like to pair up with me, Astrid? I know you promised not to cheat, but you could give me pointers."

I patted her hand, smiling graciously at her. "Sophie, why not ask Mr Chesley? He is, after all, without a lady to escort."

Her fair cheeks coloured slightly, and her hazel eyes darted towards the widower. "Do you think it's proper to ask?"

"Far more proper than Miss Behari's supplications, I shouldn't wonder."

Sophie giggled. "Yes, it does seem highly vulgar to secure the hand of a man another woman fancies."

"Another woman—surely you don't mean me, Sophie."

"No? But I thought you arrived together. As companions."

"As travelling companions, yes, but nothing more. I assure you, I do not fancy Asher Key." My gaze drifted towards the door, but I could no longer see Asher or his lovely, exotic companion. "No, indeed, I do not."

"Forgive me, Astrid. I only thought...well, I think I shall take your advice before Mr Chesley has gone off." She squeezed my hand and hurried towards Chesley. I did not wait to ensure she had secured his companionship but strode smartly out of the room.

I sighed, pausing at the foot of the stairs. I considered briefly ringing the bell and bringing the pairs of players right back to where they started, but it was a petty, fleeting idea which would amount to nothing more than my ejection from the game. Indeed, it was a most fortunate stroke of luck that I might wander the halls quite freely, without drawing unnecessary attention to my search. If Asher was off dallying with a young lady, I may as well accomplish something towards our objective. I certainly hadn't forgotten it in the batting of a dark Indian eyelash.

I crept warily though the darkened halls of the villa, careful to avoid being caught out by the killer, for my search would be most abruptly and vainly ended. There was no one in the library as I peeked my head inside, looking around. The light was dim, illuminated by a single gas light on a library table made from a rough, white surface that might have been bone.

I swept up the light, guiding it along the shelves of books, but a soft noise outside the door captured my attention, and I froze. I heard a soft, incomprehensible murmur outside the door and moved towards it lightly, soundlessly. After several moments of listening at the door and hearing nothing more, I peered out into the hall.

Sitting crossed-legged on the floor and wearing a slightly shamefaced expression was Imaron. I laughed. "Mr Behari, have you been killed?"

He glanced up at me and chuckled wryly. "Can you believe it? So soon in my own game?"

"Ah, how far the mighty do fall, Mr Behari."

He shook his head. "Too true, Mrs D. I am quite red-faced."

"Come now, don't be so hard on yourself. So, what's my clue, then?"

"Clue?"

I crouched down beside him. "Now, it was your rule, Mr Behari. Once you've been killed, you're to give a clue. A clever one."

"Right. Yes. All right." He considered for a moment, then looked up at me with a very cheeky grin. "You'll never guess who it is."

I raised my eyebrows. "Is that my clue?"

"Yes."

"That is the worst clue I have ever heard. You're not quite as audacious when you're dead, are you?"

He chuckled. "It does shame a man to be disenchanted before a woman."

I laughed and rose to my feet. "Well, this has been fun, after all. Thanks so much for the clue. I hope you'll have a better one for the next player that comes upon you."

Imaron grinned, but he hung his head. "I only most heartily hope it isn't my sister. I would never hear the last."

"Don't be so sure I'm finished, either." I winked at him and continued through the corridor, rounding the corner towards the guest quarters.

Someone seized my shoulders from behind, yanking me abruptly into the room at my right. I struck out at my assailant, but Asher chuckled, propelling me backwards into the wall and trapping my hands against my chest. I tossed my head and shot him my most vicious glare.

"Asher!" I hissed. "What the hell are you doing?"

"Me? What are you doing?"

"I was playing the game!"

He shook his head, rolling his eyes. "When you could have been better dedicating your time to sorting out what Coffin is about?"

"Me? What about you? Running off with some woman because she flashed her big, exotic eyes at you. Where is Chanha, anyway?"

He shrugged. "I gave her the slip. She wasn't much interested in playing the game, anyway."

"I just wager she wasn't," I replied sulkily.

"Astrid, are you jealous?"

"Don't be ridiculous. Jealous of what? It is not my business with whom you entertain yourself."

"Is it not?"

I rolled my eyes. "What are you doing here, anyway?"

"Looking for you."

"Well, you've found me. What do you want?"

He bent towards me, smirking. I flinched, but he ignored me, leaning in to murmur in my ear. "I've killed you, Astrid."

"What?! What? You absolute ass!"

He grinned and stepped away from me. "Chanha reacted far more gracefully than you." He paused at the door, and his chuckles echoed in the room when he had gone. I stomped my foot and dropped gracelessly to the ground, crossing my arms over my chest to await the next unsuspecting player. I grumbled to myself, wrinkling my nose in sheer pique.

It was in just this way Xander and Juliana found me, stumbling inelegantly into the room. "Astrid!" Xander exclaimed, his blue eyes twinkling with amusement. "Have you been killed?"

I felt much as Imaron must have done. "Yes," I replied sulkily.

Juliana giggled. "Oh, I can't believe it. How could someone sneak up on you, of all people?"

I lifted my shoulder petulantly. "It happens on occasion. Besides, you wouldn't expect who it was."

"Is that our clue then?" Xander asked. "Because we already got that one from Mr Behari."

I snorted. "I had expected he would have come up with a better one by now."

"Well? What is it? Nearly everyone's dead by now, and we have to solve it before he gets to us, too," Juliana told me earnestly.

I smirked at her. "All right. Here's your clue. The killer is…a complete and total ass!"

Xander snorted, but Juliana's face lit up in sudden realisation. "I know who the killer is!"

* * *

"Astrid!"

I sighed, but I was gratified at least that the old cad had advised me prior to barging into my chambers. "Asher. How are you feeling after your grim defeat at the hands of a sickly young girl?"

He chuckled, and he lowered himself into the chair beside my writing desk. "Ah, Astrid, no need to work yourself into a state over my feelings. I was well pleased to admit defeat to young Juliana. As long as I was able to revel in the great pleasure of trouncing you first."

I glared at him. Lifting my chin haughtily, I gathered up my deep blue skirts to perch on the edge of my bed, facing him with my hands folded primly in my lap. "Well, at least you will pay no penalty for your crushing failure. Julius was quite adamant no one visit his daughter's chambers to deliver breakfast."

"As well he should be. It is not exactly appropriate, wager or not. Anyway, I haven't come to discuss the game."

I sighed. "No, I didn't presume that you had. So, what is it then? Ghosts? Privateers? Cannibals?"

He rolled his eyes at my scornful tone. "Now, Astrid, there is no need to be a sore loser. I was a very ingenious killer, after all. There is no shame in your loss."

I snorted. "Get on with you, Asher. Why are you disturbing me at this hour?"

His expression was serious when next he spoke, and I understood the jesting had drawn to a close. "The basement."

"Oh, I thought you'd be drawn in by that little temptation. I shouldn't wonder Julius did, as well, and so it might be a clever ruse to lure you into a treacherous snare."

"He seemed quite adamant we steer clear of it. If it was simply an elaborate deception, my interest remains captured."

"All right. Perhaps Morgan can further investigate. He is rather plucky, and if Julius was in earnest and it is badly damaged, Morgan will be well up to the challenge of navigating it safely."

Asher sighed. "Yes, that is all true, and it would be the most prudent course, but I would like to see it for myself."

"And so you will do, if he reports there is something to see." His pinched expression suggested he was not entirely satisfied with this. "Julius is already cognisant of our motivations, I shouldn't wonder. If we're discovered creeping around in areas we've been forbidden to enter, we will be hard-pressed to remain out from under his and his servants' watchful eyes."

He puffed out his cheeks, but he nodded. "Right. If we aren't given access to the house, we will learn nothing. All right, I concede to your plan. For now."

"Ace. I'll instruct Morgan directly." I sighed, shifting upon the bed to lean comfortably against the headboard. "Ash, do you suspect there is something out there on the island?"

He lifted a single eyebrow. "I think our game of earlier may have gone to your head, Astrid."

I rolled my eyes. "It's nothing to do with your feeble representation of a killer. I am not suggesting the island is overrun by ghosts. It could be something else out there."

His expression was stern. "Or it could simply be Coffin, indulging his baser impulses."

"You are determined to condemn him, but he strikes me not at all as someone with a murderous nature."

"You can never tell such things, Astrid. Don't be so pedestrian."

"Nonsense. You yourself are a supporter of the idea of instinct and gut," I declared archly. "Have you not said you can read the character of a man in an instant and know what he is about?"

"Coffin is no ordinary man."

"You cannot make such outlandish claims and then mitigate them when it suits you. Do you or do you not have a knack for reading a man?"

He lifted his chin. "I have, yes, and Coffin strikes me as someone very odd, very not right."

"All right, I will endeavour to trust your instinct in this matter, as I have so far done. Nothing will sway my determination to assist you in your duty." I rose from the bed, and, with a flourish, I turned down the counterpane, spinning to face him.

His chuckle was low and his eyebrows ascended suggestively. "What are you about, Astrid?" He rose abruptly, stalking across the room towards me. "Are you suggesting, perhaps...?"

My jaw dropped open in outrage. "Of course I wasn't, you foul, reprehensible man!" I seized a pillow from the bed and struck him soundly with it. "I was merely attempting, in the politest manner, to suggest perhaps it is time we both returned to our respective chambers in order to begin our investigation afresh in the morning." He raised his hands to ward off my pillow assault, but his smirk suggested it had hardly caught him out at all. I sighed, dropping my arm. "I am quite fatigued from the day's events so far."

He rolled his eyes, striding forward to wrest the pillow from me and toss it back to the bed. "It is only eleven in the evening. Wouldn't you rather explore the house a bit?"

"I would not. Surely there are more appropriate times to be sneaking around the house."

"When will we have such liberation? In the day, Coffin and the servants will be about meddling in our investigation." He gave me an imploring look, which caused my stomach to roil slightly in uncertainly. "Come on, let us wander a bit. Clear our heads and see if there is anything of interest to discover."

I sighed. "I would rather not." But my response was weak.

He smirked. "Ah, but you will. You can never resist a chance to spy." He nudged me gently. "Come on, Astrid…"

"Oh, all right."

"Excellent. Come along, then."

"Ash—" But he caught my hand, dragging me bodily from the room.

Most of the villa's doors were closed, behind which our fellow guests were idling or already asleep. We wandered through the empty rooms but found little more than guest bedrooms or recreation rooms filled with sporting equipment or card tables. The house was larger than it had seemed from the pathway, the rooms endless, dark. However, none of them were in any way incriminating.

Asher sighed in disappointment, closing the door on another balmy guest room decorated in sea shells and ocean landscapes. Julius had spared no expense on the comfort of his guests, and his villa was breezy and stunning, everything a tropical haven ought to be. It did not at all resemble the sort of house in which a serial murderer might holiday. "There's nothing."

"What did you expect?" I asked archly, turning a corner into a dark corridor. "Tools of the trade? Axes, knives, crossbows?"

His breath escaped in a huff. "Well, of course not, but I thought there might at least be something more interesting than sea shell sconces and frosted glass windows."

I snorted, but my chuckle broke off when I realised I did not recognise the area of the house in which we found ourselves. "Do you know where we are?"

"Near the library, isn't it?" Asher spun in a circle, frowning. "I thought we just came from there."

I carefully opened one of the doors, peering inside. "No, no library. Just more guest rooms. Do you remember this one?"

He sighed. "They all look the same to me. We might have seen it a dozen times already."

The hallway was filled with similarly nondescript rooms, as the other hallways before it. "Can we find the stairs?" I mused. "What floor are we on?"

"The second, I think. We didn't climb any stairs."

"Yes, we did. We climbed one flight round the back of one of the halls. Remember? It was behind a closed door. That was…" I spun in a circle. "Over here?"

"This house is a veritable labyrinth of doors."

"And which to choose?" I thought I recognised one of the doors, a heavy, pale oak with large, brass handles. "This one might lead back to the stairs."

I pulled it open, peering into the darkness. Asher barrelled in behind me, propelling me forwards into a soft, cramped space. "What are these?" Asher demanded, batting at the hanging fabric around us.

"Coats. This is a closet. Cor, Asher, you've pushed me into the wall."

He flailed out his arm in the pitch blackness, thumping it against the wall near my head. I dodged to the right to avoid him, but there was no more room to move in the small, warm wardrobe. "Oh, this is just brilliant."

"Turn back round the way you came and open the door!" I snapped, but I felt him shift in the darkness, and his breath was upon my face. "Ash..."

"Where are you, Astrid? I can't see you."

"You're right on top of me! Can't you feel me?"

He chuckled low in his throat, and his hand struck out in the darkness. He moved forwards so I was pinned between him and the wall. "Ah, yes, now I can."

"Asher, you absolute cad! If you do not move away from me this instant--"

Light flooded the closet, illuminating the coats hanging around us. I shoved at Asher, who held up his hand to shield his eyes from the gas lamp glowing in the doorway. The light bobbed slightly in the darkness, and Julius Coffin's tanned face appeared before us, his eyebrows raised. "Ah, Astrid. Agent Key."

"Julius," I sighed, pushing Asher towards the door.

"I thought I heard someone moving up here. What are you two doing in this part of the house?" he asked mildly, a slightly cold smile curving his mouth.

"We seem to have gotten turned around."

Julius chuckled. "The hour is quite late."

"Yes. We fancied...a late night stroll," I replied gaily.

He did not look as though he believed this declaration, but he stepped away from the door, gesturing us out of the cramped wardrobe. "Perhaps your rooms would be a more appropriate location for a liaison, yes?"

My jaw dropped in utter outrage. "I beg your pardon, sir; nothing could be further from the truth!"

Julius' lips pursed slightly, as though in disapproval--or perhaps to suppress a smirk. Oh, Asher would be soundly taken to task for this little mortification. "Far be it from me to refuse my guests anything or judge them in any way."

I glared at Asher. "We would be most obliged, then, sir, if you would simply direct us back to our rooms. I am most eager to be returned to my bed for a comfortable night's sleep." As I stepped past him into the hall, I dug my elbow into Asher's side. "Alone."

Julius inclined his head and beckoned us. "Come along, then." He did not speak for several moments as he guided us effortlessly though the labyrinthine corridors to our chambers. He turned to face us, raising an eyebrow. "I suggest, in future, you remain in your beds. You never know what sort of thing lurks in the night."

I paused with my hand upon the knob. "Like ghosts, perhaps?"

Julius smiled. "Perhaps. Or perhaps something like them. Good night, Astrid. Agent Key."

* * *

I rose from bed late the following morning, having always enjoyed a nice lie in when the opportunity arose. If there was any place in which one was expected to idle, it was an island paradise, and, accordingly, I lingered over my toilette. My venerable housekeeper, Mrs Randle, had attended to every detail of my packing, and the clothes with which she had provided me were of a thin, gauzy material that flowed well and swirled around my legs.

Mrs Randle, despite her otherwise unerring meticulousness, however, had failed to account for the effect of a balmy, tropical climate upon my long, curly blonde hair. To my deepest consternation, this it morning resembled the coat of a small, fluffy toy dog with more conceit than manners. I sighed, laying aside my comb in resignation. There was nothing to be done for it; I wove it into a long braid down my back and placed a wide-brimmed straw hat upon my head.

Well...I considered, cocking my head to study my reflection in the vanity mirror. The floppy hat covered the halo of delicate blonde frizz around my temples, and the sun had improved my colour some.

Breakfast was a casual affair, and the members of our party wandered into the dining room at their leisure. I was not surprised to learn I was not the only late riser of the bunch, and I shot Asher a sour look as he entered a step behind me. "Good morning, Astrid," he greeted with a far too brilliant smile for so soon upon my waking. "I trust you slept well after our little tryst in the wardrobe?"

"Tryst in a wardrobe?" Chanha Behari exclaimed, entering the room arm in arm with her uncle. "I say, to what have you two been getting up?"

I glared at Asher. "Agent Key was simply jesting. In very poor taste, I might add," I replied through clenched teeth.

Asher chuckled. "Ah, do forgive me, Miss Behari. I had not realised any gentle ladies were in the room."

"I assure you, Agent Key, I am not so gentle as my uncle would have others believe." Chanha winked at Chesley, and he guffawed appreciatively, guiding her with what I considered wanton jostling towards the bar laden with a spectacular breakfast array.

I ignored them all, piling my plate with eggs, sausages and toast. I avoided the black pudding, for which I had always harboured a particular dislike, having once experiencing the horror of its preparation. "How did you enjoy the game last night, Mrs D?" Chesley asked as I joined them at the table.

"I'm not sure it's the sort of thing Astrid enjoys," Asher said, before I was able to reply. "Losing, I mean."

I glared at him. "Well, you did lose, as well, didn't you, Asher?"

Chanha lifted a finger and waggled it at Asher. "That was very ungallant of you, killing me like that last night, Agent Key."

"Well, your brother did warn you. You took a great risk going off with me like that."

She smiled. "Well, I do enjoy a good risk now and again." Her dark eyelashes fluttered. "Though I did die, after all. It was worth the risk."

I rolled my eyes, and Chesley's brow furrowed slightly. "Chanha," he said gently. "Do eat your porridge before it cools. We've a long day of sun and excitement ahead of us."

"Oh, yes, I do enjoy the beach. Have you spent much time at the beach, Agent Key?"

He smiled. "I have had some occasion to visit the beaches of Europe."

"And which did you find to be the most enjoyable?" she asked.

Asher considered, and his eyes slid to me. I rolled mine and turned back to my sausages, spearing one upon my fork with rather more force than was strictly required. "You remember the shores of New Caledonia, Astrid?" he asked, a sly note in his voice.

I shot him a dangerous look. "I remember rescuing a young virgin maiden from a ceremonial bonfire, if that is to what you are referring."

"Really? Is that what you remember?" He smirked, and I scrunched up my nose, returning my gaze to my plate.

"Have you two been acquainted long?" Chanha asked, picking delicately at her own plate.

"A number of years," I replied evasively. "We have worked together many times."

"Ah, I suppose in your respective lines of work, you often cross paths?"

"Yes, well, it is usually the result of some gross misconduct on Mrs Darby's and her associates' parts," Asher put in, and I suspected he was purposely baiting me now.

"Indeed, it is other times attributed to the utter failure of the Ministry to complete their task and mine and my associates' subsequent successes at the same, which often resulted in my unjustified scolding or imprisonment."

"Indeed, I hear you are often the centre of criminal investigations, Mrs D," Chesley said, chuckling. "Whether it be as consultant or the subject, no one ever seems to know."

I smiled, but I did not respond to this. "So, what has the good professor planned for us today?" Asher asked, smirking sidelong at me. "The beach?"

"Oh, we are welcome to find our own leisure today," Chanha said.

"Is the shore strictly within our bounds?"

"Of course. What sort of man with his own personal island would restrict the very reason to have inhabited it in the first place?" Chesley replied, smiling.

"And the weather is so lovely today," Chanha sighed. "I do think I will have a swim."

"Miss Behari, I look most forward to seeing you in the water," Asher told her, and I curled my lip around my spoon.

She tittered. "And I, Agent Key, look most forward to you joining me."

My salvation from their shameless flirting came in the form of Xander and young Juliana, who entered the breakfast room together, chattering animatedly and resembling life-time chums. "Oh!" Xander said. "Astrid, I had not realised you were awake. I had assumed you'd have a lie in."

"I did," I replied. "It's over now. Are you just coming down?"

"Oh, no. We've already enjoyed our breakfast."

I raised an eyebrow. "We have?"

His cheeks pinked slightly, and I smirked. "Juliana and me."

"Ah, yes, of course. And how are you this morning, Miss Juliana? You're looking rather well."

"I'm feeling much better, thank you." She glanced at Asher with a smile. "And I am relieved you were not in charge of my breakfast this morning, Agent Key, or I might be positively faint with hunger."

He laughed. "Ah, my dear, I assure you, were I responsible for your repast, per the rules of the game, I would have been extremely prompt in its delivery. Seeing as how your father dissolved our agreement, I am, as they say, off the hook, and do myself enjoy a lie in."

Juliana smiled. "Well, your lie in may have ruined Papa's plans."

"And what plans are those?" I asked, leaning back in my chair to sip upon my cooling black tea. "I understood we were responsible for our own entertainment today."

"Ah, well, I insisted he prepare an activity for us all, as we had so much fun last evening together. He's arranged a picnic on the beach this afternoon. The weather is very nice, and there is much sport in the water, if one is not satisfied with simply wading into the waves or lying in the sun."

"Ah, the sun," I murmured mournfully. "It does not well suit one of my fair and sensitive complexion."

"Oh, but you'll attend, won't you, Mrs Darby? I am sure I can provide shade for you. I myself am rather sensitive to the sun's heat. I pink most immediately, but Papa does ensure I am well-protected. Won't you join me?"

I sighed. "Of course. I'll just...gather my bathing things, then."

Asher rose from his seat as well, and he inclined his head to the others. "I shall see you all on the beach, then." When the door closed behind us, he glanced around for a moment to ensure our privacy then said, "It would be a good time to explore the house, with everyone on the beach."

"Yes, but I do not expect our absence will go unnoticed, especially since we promised Juliana we would attend."

He sighed. "Too right."

"Ah, but Morgan may have something for us. Shall we visit the servants' quarters?" His eyebrows lifted, and his lips curved, but I held up a warning finger. "We will not be attempting to jimmy our way into the basement this morning, if that is what you are thinking. We have not the time for such adventures, with a shore side picnic looming in our future."

"You make it sound positively ghastly."

"Ah, I do enjoy a nice picnic, but I don't relish the thought of facing Julius after our humiliating discovery in the wardrobe last evening."

He laughed. "Oh, Astrid, I had not taken you for a lady prone to embarrassment, though I do very much like this side of you."

I glared at him. "I simply prefer our host not believe we were creeping around the villa searching for a dark, private place in which to...well."

He grinned. "Well? And of course he didn't actually think that, Astrid. Don't be daft. He knew precisely what we were about, didn't he? After all, what sensible people with adjoining rooms sneak about a house in the middle of the night when they have two perfectly inviting beds in which to...well, as you said."

I rolled my eyes. "Inviting, indeed. Come on, then. We're supposed to be gathering our bathing things to meet the others on the beach. Juliana will be after us if we aren't there within a reasonable time."

He smirked, but he did not persist in provoking me as we found our way towards the small, stone staircase behind the dining room. "Perhaps Reinhart has gleaned something from the servants that might actually make this day worthwhile," Asher muttered. "I didn't come here to dally all day at the beach with my target."

"Oh, and here I thought you were more interested in dallying all day at the beach with the young Miss Behari."

He chuckled, but he did not respond, for we stepped onto the stone floor of the kitchen. It was a stroke of quite good fortune that Reinhart was already there, but so thoroughly occupied with feeding a young, pretty blonde maid a large, red strawberry was he that he failed to notice our arrival until I paused behind him. I cleared my throat, crossing my arms over my chest to give him an extremely ironic look.

He smirked and patted the young lady on the bottom as she fled, blushing and giggling, from the room. "Morgan," I scolded, but my lips quivered as I suppressed my smile.

"What?" he asked innocently, popping the remains of the strawberry into his mouth.

Asher chuckled. "I see you're making the best of being chucked down here with the servants."

"There are a good number of ladies with particularly loose morals among the maids, I do say."

"Morgan, you are shameless," I complained.

He grinned. "I expect you've come to hear what I've discovered?"

"Naturally. We didn't install you down here so you could have your wicked way with all the servant girls," I replied. "Have you learned anything?"

"Yes, actually. A good deal, in fact. And I'll have you know, it's certainly not all the servant girls. Some of them are rather...homely."

I rolled my eyes. "Well, what is it, then?"

"Servants talk a lot. Did you know?"

"Morgan..."

He smirked. "Come on. We'd better go somewhere we won't be overheard by Mr Bray. The man's all ears, and he moves like a phantom." He led us back up the stairs to the corridor outside the dining room. He tilted his head at me, and we followed him towards the French doors at the end of the hall.

They led to a large, canopied veranda, surrounded by verdant, green palm trees and the soft, perpetual hum of insects. Reinhart gestured us down the veranda stairs, towards a wall of bushes on the side of the villa. "Is there any particular reason we are meeting in the midst of a swarm of insects?" I demanded, batting my hand in the air around my face.

"Yes. Even the gardener only comes round a couple times a week. You want to know what I found out, or would you prefer to complain a little longer and risk being discovered?"

I sighed. "All right, get on with it."

"What do you know about the basement?" Asher asked keenly. He seemed thoroughly untroubled by the gnats buzzing around him, and I wrinkled my nose in irritation; how did he always manage to maintain his equanimity?

Reinhart raised his eyebrows. "No one's allowed in there."

"Right. Julius said it was damaged by a severe storm this winter and unfit."

"There was no storm, not that any of them mentioned, anyway. There is no other damage to the house or the grounds to indicate it was hit by anything more than a heavy rain or two. They are forbidden to enter the basement by Mr Bray."

I raised an eyebrow. "Has he offered any explanation for this?"

"No. He doesn't explain much, him. He's the professor's closest companion; he spends a lot of time with him. Whatever Coffin's up to, Bray's probably in on it."

"And it's probably murder," Asher muttered.

I sighed. "Morgan?"

Reinhart shook his head thoughtfully. "I don't know. They are very good at keeping things secret. Bray spends most of his time shut up with Coffin."

"Anything more conclusive?" Asher asked.

"No. Not yet. Not on that score. He is the key to Coffin, though."

"You're sure?"

"Yes. You know Juliana is very ill?"

"Yes. She stated at dinner no surgeon has been successful in diagnosing her symptoms," I said, frowning.

"Right. Well, Mr Bray must have some treatment for her."

"Yes, he does. At least, we saw him bring her a special meal last evening. I don't exactly know how that is a treatment, unless they're slipping something in it," Asher said, scowling.

"Well, they might be," I mused. "Afterwards, she seemed quite better, and she is almost rosy this morning."

Asher frowned. "But what does this have to do with the investigation?"

Reinhart considered, then shook his head. "I don't know. I don't know that it does. But the servants are talking about it. They worry about Juliana. "

"But not about their master being a brutal serial killer," I deduced.

He chuckled. "No, not about that."

Asher sighed. "Is there anything else might help prove what Coffin and Bray are getting up to?"

Reinhart shrugged. "I don't know if it will prove anything, but I have learned a few things about the island."

"An ideal setting for disappearing servants, I shouldn't wonder," I remarked, smirking.

"Yes, actually, it is. There are a lot of whispers about what sorts of things are with us on the island."

"Such as?"

"Some of the servants think it's haunted."

"Haunted, of course. And half the guests as well," Asher sighed.

"Servants are traditionally more superstitious than their masters, it's been said. They believe there are ghosts here, and some of them even think it is a haunting that is afflicting the young Juliana."

"Oh," I groaned.

"Don't be so flip, Astrid. You never know what sorts of things there are out there," Reinhart said, frowning.

"Morgan, you know I lend no credence to such things."

"Well, perhaps this will interest you: Juliana's mother died under very mysterious circumstances."

I glanced at Asher, who raised an eyebrow. "What circumstances?" Asher asked.

"Well, most of the servants were not in the professor's employ when she died, but Bray was, and he is very sensitive about it. He never speaks of it."

"Then how do you know they're mysterious?"

"That's the mysterious bit, isn't it?"

"Are there no records of her death?"

"Sure there are," Reinhart replied, rolling his eyes. "But servants don't exactly have the resources to obtain them, do they?"

"Hm." I glanced up at Asher. "Is there a telegraph on the grounds?"

"I'm afraid there is not."

Asher cleared his throat. "Well, we can probe that particular mystery when we're back in England. I hardly think it's relevant to the investigation at hand. It isn't as if the ghost of the girl's dead mother is murdering all those convicts, is it?"

"Well, there's no actual evidence so far that Julius is either," I replied mildly.

Asher opened his mouth to retort, but Reinhart held up his hand. "Will you two please belt up? Now is not the time for your incessant bickering. There's more."

"Ah, more than a haunted girl and the ghost of her dead mother?" I asked superciliously.

"Yes. More than that." Reinhart gave me a stern look, and I sighed petulantly. "There have been stories about servants who've disappeared. None of Coffin's people, of course, but some of the guests' men."

"Right. We know about that. There seem to be many rumours circulating around this place, isolated as it is," Asher muttered.

"Well, if Coffin didn't insist on inviting that absolute hag Madam Eliot, his secret might actually remain his own."

"Well, not for long. We are, after all, here to expose him as a murderer for the world to see."

"Mm. Fair point."

Reinhart rolled his eyes, but he continued as if we hadn't spoken. "None of the servants who were with them has any idea what happened to them. They just disappeared in the night."

"Ventured out onto the island?" I said.

"They think they must have done. Or been lured out by the calls of the island phantoms."

"I respect many people's opinions, Morgan, but on this point, I have to object. The superstitions of an ignorant army of servants are hardly worthy of attention," I told him, scowling.

Reinhart's expression was cold when he replied, "Now, Astrid, don't be patronising. There are all sorts of documents and evidence to suggest and confirm the existence of ghosts."

Asher sighed. "Could we possibly soldier through one conversation without unnecessary debate and banter?"

"And who is asking that, then?" I demanded, outraged. "Don't be ridiculous, anyway. There is no conversation in which banter and debate aren't necessary."

Asher pinched the bridge of his nose, and I smirked. "So are you seriously suggesting, Reinhart, that we operate under the assumption that it is ghosts haunting the island that are actually responsible for the servants' murders?"

"Of course not. No one ever said they were killed."

"What?"

"Well, I mean, no bodies were ever discovered."

"Well, Morgan, that is hardly the issue," I told him, nettled. "They were never seen again. We can rightly assume they are, in fact, dead."

"Well, you might assume that," Morgan replied in a leading sort of way, and I narrowed my eyes at him.

"What are you on about?"

"Well, some of the servants have other theories."

I groaned. "Oh, this should be brilliant. Go on, then. What are they?"

His amber eyes glittered. "Vampires."

Asher and I groaned together this time. "Reinhart," I complained. "Not this again."

"What? Well, it's as likely as ghosts anyway. Or wendigos."

"Excuse me, I will have you know, the wendigo is a scientifically proven theory--" Asher began.

"Asher, do not even start. There is no scientific evidence that the wendigo is a real creature," I snapped.

"Not a creature, not exactly. I mean, it's just a person, right, but they've been possessed--"

"Enough of this. Morgan, you couldn't come up with a single sensible theory?"

He frowned at me as though he were disappointed in my narrow-mindedness. "Well, there may be more people on the island."

"What people?"

"A tribe of hostiles. Privateers or shipwrecked people gone native."

I sighed. "Of course. Yet another wild theory straight from the ridiculous rumour mill. Has anyone ever seen any of these tribesmen?"

"Well, no, but that doesn't mean they aren't out there. The servants say the island is much larger than it seems while within the grounds. It's not impossible there's a tribe of people out there that have made it their home, as Coffin has, is it?"

"Well, no," I agreed hesitantly. "It's not impossible, but it's highly unlikely."

But Asher narrowed his eyes in thought, tapping his chin with a long forefinger. "I want to see proof of this tribe." He straightened suddenly and nodded. "Reinhart, we'll have a go. We'll explore the island when night falls. We'll slip out under cover of night, and no one will be the wiser."

Morgan held up his hands, stepping away from Asher as if he had presented him with a venomous snake. "Oh, no. Sorry, mate. I'm not going out there when there could be ghosts or vampires."

I stamped my foot. "Morgan, there is no such thing! You are being ridiculous. You're spooked as a schoolboy."

"You may think whatever you like. You might be able to lure me out there during the day, but I am not stepping out of here after nightfall. Whatever's out there, it's sinister. Six people have gone off at night and never been seen again, and until I know what it is that got them, I'm not risking going the same way."

Asher sighed. "Reinhart, I had taken you for a man of science, not a man of superstition and silliness."

Reinhart smirked. "They are not mutually exclusive."

A din near the front of the house drew my attention, and I sighed. "We have a picnic to attend."

Reinhart snorted. "A picnic. You two. Quite the crack investigation team. Do you hope to uncover a conspiracy beneath the sandwiches?"

I grinned. "Let's hope it isn't regarding spoiled dairy. We will look in on you a bit later."

"I think I'll just return to the kitchen. There's a very pretty maid who seems to think I'm something special."

I rolled my eyes. "Did you tell her what a coward you are?" Asher asked, but he smirked. "Afraid of bumps in the night?"

"Now, Ash, no need to be unkind," I chided, tugging on his arm. "Come on, we had better join the others, lest our host suspects we're snooping about again."

"Though he might just assume we're locked up together in another wardrobe engaged in forbidden congress."

"Asher Key, I am a lady of class, distinction and piety. I am sure no one would suspect un-virtuous behaviour on my behalf. It would be an insult to suggest any different."

Asher rolled his eyes. "If you must say so." He turned to Reinhart, who looked utterly bored. "Reinhart, see what more you can learn from the servants. Something is going on on this island. Whether it is ghosts, vampires or head-hunters, I intended to find out what it is."

Reinhart inclined his head and, with a flick of his hand in a sort of salute, he was off. "Ghosts," I muttered at his back. "I ask you."

CHAPTER FIVE

The shores of the Isle of Jules were serene and peaceful, and a warm, balmy breeze wafted over the picnickers as we lounged on the large quilt spread with a wide selection of finger foods and cold shrimp. The young men were frolicking in the water, splashing around in the gentle waves and calling to the ladies upon the shore, imploring us to join them in the skylarking.

Chanha Behari was the only lady willing to brave the waters, and the rest of us remained on the blanket beneath the cool shade of a huge, white parasol. "She is a rascal, that one," Madam Eliot complained, turning up her nose as Chanha emerged from the water beside her brother, her long, black hair dripping with water and her flowing pink bathing gown clinging to her enviably pert figure. Asher's head turned as if on a swivel as she passed, and I rolled my eyes.

"Don't be so hard on her, Aunt," Sophie said, though her voice sounded slightly meek. "She's young and doesn't understand our customs."

"A lady of breeding always understands what is proper," Madam Eliot replied. "And the little imp was educated in Britain; she is not ignorant to the appropriate image of a young lady. She merely turns her nose up at our gentler sensibilities."

"I say, Madam Eliot," I said, smiling brightly. "Perhaps you are merely feeling most potently the loss of your youth and see in young Miss Behari a particular liberation and beauty of spirit which you yourself quite covet."

Madam Eliot's mouth dropped open, as though she intended to crossly rebuke my observation, but she would not assassinate the young lady's character in the presence of her brother. Imaron lowered himself upon the blanket beside Juliana without bothering to towel off. He was sopping wet and smelled of the ocean's salt, and my eyes were drawn quite unconsciously to him; he was his sister's equal in grace and beauty, to be certain, and the thin, white bathing clothes accentuated the flat, tanned muscle beneath. I had not spent near enough time in India, I decided, and resolved to visit again at the earliest opportunity. It did evidently bear children of advantage, charm and, I thought wryly as Imaron flipped his hair, showering us with a spray of salt water droplets, cheek. Perhaps not, then. We squealed dutifully, and the young men laughed, joining us on the blanket and tucking into the lunch quite voraciously.

"Oh, I do enjoy a good swim," Chesley announced, sweeping his hands through his pale hair with a flourish. "The sea air is just what I needed to revitalise myself after so many long months in London meeting with dreary businessmen and sycophantic solicitors."

"You're looking rather fit today, Juliana," Chanha told her, lounging beside Asher on the blanket.

"Indeed," I added, sipping upon the cool lemon water Julius' men had provided for our luncheon. "You're looking positively rosy."

She smiled. "Thank you. I am feeling in much better humour and health today. My father declares the sea air is quite good for me. The soot and smoke in the air of London is quite harsh on my delicate constitution."

"Miss Juliana, your health may be tenuous, but your constitution is anything but delicate," Xander told her gallantly, and I smirked at him.

She laughed. "You are very kind to say so, Mr Knightly."

"Speaking of your father," Asher said, his tone blasé, "does he not intend to join our little picnic?"

"Oh." Juliana smiled. "No, he prefers to remain indoors. He claims he is quite caught up in one of his experiments."

"That is a shame," Sophie said. "He has hardly attended us, has he?"

"Oh, I assure you, Mrs Marlow, he is most concerned with your comfort. He is a slave to his work, I'm afraid. I am sure he would prefer to be spending the day in leisure with all of us, but his experiment has reached a very delicate juncture. He cannot leave it."

"Well..." Imaron began, smiling. "It is a shame that he could not join us, but perhaps some advantage can be taken of his absence."

Juliana's expression was wary. "What advantage is that, Mr Behari?"

He smiled. "Well, we have been hearing some rather startling rumours about your island, haven't we all? Perhaps you might be just the lady we need to settle it."

"Oh, Imaron, not this again," Chanha said, rolling her eyes. "It is hardly the thing to continue harping upon something so ridiculous."

"Now, Chanha, I do not discourage your amusements, no matter how ridiculous I believe them to be, do I? Allow me my entertainment." He turned his charming smile back upon Juliana, and her cheeks pinked slightly under his dark gaze. "What say you, Juliana?"

"Rumours, you say?"

"Oh, yes, the most disquieting rumours, indeed. Such of vampires and ghosts that walk the island when the night falls, searching for hapless victims who wander too far from the house."

It appeared, I thought, Reinhart was not the only superstitious fool in the bunch.

"Ghosts and vampires? Did we not already broach this topic at dinner last evening?"

"Oh, indeed, but then you were under the watchful eye of Papa Coffin. Now, however, we may all speak just as we like."

She smiled. "Mr Behari, I am beginning to believe you speak just as you like, regardless of whom is listening."

He laughed. "Ah, the lady does have me sussed, doesn't she?"

"And anyway, it is just silly. The servants talk entirely too much, and they often speak of things most civilised and educated people understand are merely superstition and fantasy."

"Oh, they are likely drawn to the novelty of it all. Besides, it must get utterly dull here, with so little of importance required of them. So, if the rumours of ghosts and vampires are only the fancy of a faction of bored servants, what do you think is out there, beyond the house?"

"My father does discourage gossip," she murmured, avoiding Imaron's twinkling, mesmerizing eyes.

"Well, it is quite fortunate he isn't here, then, isn't it?"

She sighed, but she looked around at the lot of us, whose eyes were riveted upon her. "Well...I have heard my father talking with Mr Bray."

"Have you now? And what have they been saying?"

She shook her head. "I didn't understand it all. It was strange, but I think there may be others on the island with us."

"Others?" I asked, glancing at Asher, who raised his eyebrows.

"Ghosts? Vampires?" Imaron pressed.

Juliana laughed. "No. Not, ghosts. I don't believe in ghosts, Mr Behari, and nor, I am certain, does my father."

"Ah, do you not? How dull your thoughts must be."

"I beg your pardon, but my thoughts are very interesting, indeed. However, there is no scientific proof that ghosts or vampires exist."

"There is no scientific proof for many things," Xander added thoughtfully, and she shook her head at him as though he had spoken a grave betrayal.

"Come now, Miss Juliana, you must have seen some very odd things, indeed, especially here on this mysterious island," Imaron added, nudging her gently.

She smiled. "Well, perhaps I have, but nothing that cannot be explained with science or...my particular ailment."

"They really don't know what could be ailing you?" Chanha asked, her expression troubled.

Juliana smiled, but she shook her head. "Ah, the symptoms, they are quite recognisable, are they not?" Imaron asked.

"Are they?" She looked very interested in this, and leaned forwards to hear his reply.

"Oh, yes. Why, could it be, perhaps, the soft kiss of the un-dead?"

We all laughed, but Chanha tossed a grape at her brother in sheer pique. "Imaron! Don't be preposterous. There is no such thing as vampires."

"Now, my beloved sister, how could you possibly know that? There are all sorts of things in this world we know nothing about."

"I am dreadfully bored of this."

He grinned. "In our country, there are many stories of creatures like vampires. Some say the souls of men who died a violent death remain, searching always for a new body to inhabit and with which to drink the blood of the living."

"Those are ridiculous fairy tales. Merely superstitious folklore meant to keep children in their beds at night. As are the rumours about the island. There is nothing out there," Chanha replied, glaring at him.

"Ah, but it suits the young lady well, doesn't it?" Imaron said, gesturing towards Juliana.

"It certainly does not," Xander told him, nettled, but Juliana was smiling.

"Do not speak of it anymore," Chanha said in a low voice.

Imaron's face fell slightly, but he inclined his head to his sister. "My dear, Chanha, I do not wish to upset you." He raised an eyebrow then, smirking. "But, mark my words, when one of your servants fails to turn up in the morning to run your bath, you will think on it again, and you will consider what I have proposed."

She lifted her chin. "I am absolutely certain I will not."

The atmosphere of the picnic declined steadily after Imaron's reckless remarks. "Well, the sea air does fatigue me so," Madam Eliot announced. "Juliana, you should not remain in the sun long; your father would have our heads if you return to the house red from the sun."

Juliana smiled. "Yes, Madam Eliot, I should return to the house. I, too, am feeling somewhat weary from all the excitement. Perhaps I should take a short rest."

"May I escort you back to the villa?" Xander asked, and she smiled, allowing him to assist her to her feet.

"A fine mood you created, Imaron," Chanha chided her brother gently.

He smiled unrepentantly. "I cannot be held accountable for the affects of the sun."

"You speak very rashly at times, my dear nephew," Chesley told him, clapping him on the shoulder, though his eyes twinkled, belying the reproach.

I rose as the party quickly dissolved, dusting the sand from my skirt and turning towards the house. I paused when Chanha spoke behind me. "I am a great lover of literature, Agent Key," she said, threading her arm through Asher's. "Do you enjoy reading at all?"

"I have been known to partake of a novel or play now and again," he responded, smiling, and I rolled my eyes.

"I have a firm mind to visit the library this afternoon. I understand Professor Coffin has a remarkable collection of books of all types. I myself am particularly interested in the history of ancient civilisations. I am told it is one of the professor's special areas of study." She smiled. "Would you care to join me?"

Asher smiled and opened his mouth to reply, but I caught his eye, giving him a sharp look. "Far be it from me to refuse a lady, Miss Behari, but I am otherwise engaged this afternoon. I am very sorry. Perhaps another time?"

Chanha smiled. "That isn't a clever excuse to evade being bored to death by the study of ancient civilisations?"

"Yes, it is that exactly, though I might not call it especially 'clever.'"

She laughed, but she glanced at me as Asher stepped away from her. "Don't worry, sister, I have not abandoned you, despite how fervently you might have wished it," Imaron announced, wrapping an arm around her shoulders to lead her away from us.

I shook my head at Asher. "Honestly, Ash."

He grinned. "What?" He seized my hand, dragging me towards the house. "You were the one who interfered with young Miss Behari's afternoon plans."

I scoffed. "Asher Key, exactly what do you think you're doing? I will not be dragged bodily through the wild like a woman beat about the head by a caveman."

He chuckled, but he did not release his hold on my hand. "Astrid, I am thoroughly convinced something is not right here."

"Yes, I understand that. You would not otherwise have engaged me in this convoluted scheme to investigate our host."

"That isn't what I mean. Well, it is, but specifically I meant the rumours. The missing servants."

I paused, looking at him incredulously. "You believe there are ghosts and vampires on this island, preying upon unwary servants?"

"No, of course not. I am not an idiot. Besides, not all the murders occurred here. The majority of them occurred at home. There aren't ghosts and vampires stalking Coffin's convict labourers there, are there?"

"Well, I should certainly hope not, though I might be more easily convinced when faced with the darker alleys of the city."

"Shall we attempt another search?"

I groaned. "Asher, our last search resulted in nothing more than wasted effort and humiliation."

"Why, Astrid, one might think you did not enjoy our little interlude in the wardrobe. Come now, it is daylight. We will have a much easier time navigating the labyrinth of corridors and stairways. We could leave breadcrumbs to remember our path."

"And Mr Bray will be behind us clearing them up, I shouldn't wonder."

He chuckled. "Now you're getting the idea. Come. Don't be tiresome."

"Oh, all right. Do you suspect you will find evidence of the missing servants therein, now that daylight is upon us?"

"I doubt it. Coffin has not gone this long without discovery by being careless or a fool."

"Then what do you hope to accomplish?"

"I told you last night. I want to find something. Anything that might help." I sighed. "Astrid, I hired you to help me catch Coffin. Are you going to do it, or should I have called someone with a bit more mettle?"

"Oh, all right." I smirked at him. "Of course I am. I am merely unable to keep from galling you."

He rolled his eyes. "What else is new?"

Our exploration of the house was more leisurely that afternoon, and, though we met our fellow guests in search of their own recreation in various areas of the house, our scrutiny went thoroughly unnoticed. "Do you mean to enter the guest quarters, as well? If so, now would be the time. Though I suppose we might come upon Madam Eliot in the midst of a kip. It would be a shame to interrupt her beauty sleep."

He snorted. "I'm afraid it's far too late for that for her."

"That is very callous of you, Asher. She is but an aging woman lamenting her squandered prime."

"She has the disposition of a spiteful Papillion."

I chuckled. "She does, at that. Well, perhaps you would, as well, if you had abstained from the companionship of a lover for as long as she has."

He smirked. "Oh? Would I? And is that what's becoming of you, then? You have grown remarkably spiteful since our particular association was so abruptly severed."

I glared at him. "And here I was under the mistaken impression we had reached an understanding."

"Not about that."

I pressed my lips together in a tight line. "It would behove you not to go opening up old wounds, Ash, should you wish to remain in my good graces. I have accepted this assignment despite our complicated past. It is best left there, in the past."

He sighed. "All right. No, then, I don't intend to search the guests' quarters then. They aren't under suspicion."

I considered. "Though I would like to see what Chesley is about."

"What are you talking about?"

"Well, his attachment to his young female ward is slightly inappropriate, do you not think?"

He lifted an eyebrow. "I had not really noticed."

"Really," I said dryly.

"Now Astrid, you wouldn't be jealous of another woman's attention to me, would you?"

"Of course not, Ash, why would I be anything of the sort? It's nothing to do with you. I simply think there is something not quite right about his attention to the siblings both."

"Yes, well, he is rather doting, and they do practically get away with murder while he's around."

I lifted my shoulders in a shrug. "Perhaps he simply misses Mrs Chesley. She was quite a striking woman. Chanha looks much like her. She is very striking, as well."

He nodded. "Yes, she is that."

"Do I sense a fancy in your tone?"

He snorted. "You sense no such thing. It is merely your imagination running away with you as always."

"I will have you know, I am a lady of firm action and resolve, not fancy ideas."

He shook his head. "I am merely stating the idea of my having a fancy for Miss Behari is highly fanciful."

"Truly, Ash, there is nothing in this house that suggests any villainy."

"Missing servants and the convicts gone mysteriously missing in his charge notwithstanding."

"I suppose there is that. Even I cannot truly argue there is not something off about that."

"Right. So, if you would be so obliging, your incessant nay saying is hardly conducive to a harmonious working relationship. We are supposed to be on the same side."

"I am merely keeping you focussed on the task at hand, rather than the diversions presenting themselves to you at each turn."

"You are playing devil's advocate. Literally."

"Don't be so dramatic. Anyway, I hardly think the implements of Coffin's wickedness are lying about the place in the open."

"Or they are."

"Now what are you talking about?" He caught my shoulders, propelling me into the room outside which he had paused. It was a den of sorts, wainscoted in wood and draped in tartan, but the shelves and racks were stacked with guns of all types: rifles, pistols, shotguns, and breechloaders. There were crossbows and quivers of arrows, even a small, hand-held cannon that looked as if it could level a building of moderate size. Beasts both mundane and as exotic as any I had seen or heard of decorated the walls, their heads mounted upon wooden plaques. "Oh. Right."

"That is an impressive collection of deadly weapons, I do say." He lifted an eyebrow, glancing down at me. "If we're not to leave the grounds, what is all this, then?"

"Perhaps he feels his guests lack the required expertise to hunt these animals. They are not exactly rabbits and wild bores, are they?"

"Or there is something else afoot."

I considered. "Perhaps there really is something else on this island. Though I can hardly envision what." Asher shrugged and stepped forwards to examine the weapons whilst I eyed the animal trophies on the walls with distaste. I reached out, running my finger gingerly along the long, sharp white tooth belonging to an enormous white tiger. "Are you strictly sanctioned to hunt white tigers?"

"Depends upon whom you ask for consent, I expect. There is some very exceptional weaponry here. Nothing to your extraordinary little pistol, but very impressive, nevertheless. Only someone with particular expertise would employ such weapons. He must be a very seasoned hunter."

I glanced at him, smirking. "It only strengthens your conviction of his guilt, doesn't it?"

"Naturally. So..."

I narrowed my eyes at him, for his tone suggested I might not appreciate what next he would say. "What, Ash?"

His expression was utterly innocent. "I want to take a look in the basement."

I groaned. "Julius was quite adamant we should not do. It is damaged."

"And you believed him? Come now, Astrid, when did you become so credulous?"

"I beg your pardon, Ash; I did not say I believed him. I was merely suggesting we should enter into that such trespass with caution."

"Duly noted. Step lively."

I rolled by eyes, but I did not resist as he caught my hand, leading me back into the hall towards the main staircase. We did not encounter any of our fellow guests, but their servants eyed us suspiciously as we snuck past their quarters. I raised my chin and smiled at them brightly. "This was, perhaps, slightly ill-advised. Do you not think Julius' men will inform him we are creeping around down here?"

"Yes, probably, and so we must move more quickly." He tugged on my hand, and I sighed.

Past the servant's quarters, the corridor was dim. The floor was dirt-packed, and dust swirled in the air, causing me to cough slightly. I narrowed my eyes at Asher and waved my hand in front of my face. "Why do your tactics always result in discomfort and embarrassment, Asher?"

He grinned. "Your constitution is not as steady as it once was, Astrid. I do not recall you being quite so petulant in our past dealings."

I glared at him. "In our past dealings I was considerably more naive regarding your flaws, and I am certain you were not so mulish and rash."

He lifted an eyebrow. "My flaws? And what, precisely, do you consider those to be today?"

"The same as they are everyday."

"This area of the house is not among those reserved for guest recreation."

I jabbed a finger in the air towards Asher and spun to face Mr Bray, whose pristine white linen suit seemed to illuminate the dusky corridor. He was garishly out of place in front of the large, rickety wooden door that led, I could only assume, to our prohibited destination. "Ah, good afternoon, Mr Bray," I greeted warmly. "What brings you down here?"

His bland expression did not waver. "I should ask you the same. What are you two doing here?"

I lifted my chin. "We are in search of our man, Reinhart. Have you any idea to

76

where he's gone off?"

Bray lifted a thin, dark eyebrow. "Were you?"

"Are you suggesting that we are not being entirely honest with you, sir?"

"I suspect suggesting such a thing would be an inadmissible trespass upon your virtuous character, Mrs Darby," he replied smoothly.

I smirked. "It would indeed be, sir."

"Well, in either event, it is not safe down here; as my master said, the guests should remain upstairs where there is enough recreation. If you are looking for your man, you might check the professor's laboratory."

"The laboratory?"

"Yes. The master heard of your man's and your young cousin's propensity for science. He invited their input in an experiment with which he has been struggling for many days."

I rolled my eyes. "Oh, I should have known." I spun on my heels, striding towards the stairs. When I did not hear their feet thumping against the packed dirt-floor behind me, I turned to them. "Well? Show me the lab, if you please, sir? Asher, come."

"Of course, Mrs Darby." Mr Bray inclined his head and strode past me without pausing to ensure we were on his heel. "Right this way."

"This is not what I had in mind," Asher muttered as he joined me on the stairs. "This is, in fact, the reverse of what I'd had in mind."

"One must learn to be adaptable to circumstance, Ash."

Professor Coffin's laboratory was situated in the far back of the villa, and I noticed Asher's eyes brighten upon entering the hitherto undiscovered wing. I, however, considered it highly unlikely the professor was hiding the implements of his wickedness in this part of the house, either, else he would surely have instructed his closest man not to lead us anywhere near it. Nathaniel's old friend behaved much as though he had little at all to withhold, in fact.

The laboratory door was metal, and it was dissimilar to doors of its nature I had previously seen in that it was smooth and untarnished. However, odd noises reverberated from behind it. There was a strange, hissing noise, the clink of metal against glass, and then, to my surprise, a low rumbling chuckle that swelled into a chorus of cackles. "Oh, the ubiquitous clamour of mad science," Asher remarked, smirking slightly.

His expression changed, however, when a loud, resonant crash drowned the cackling, and Mr Bray threw open the door in alarm. "Yes! Yes!" Julius exclaimed exultantly, his hands raised over his head.

Morgan and Xander were swathed in white laboratory coats resembling Julius', and they wore thick, bronze goggles to protect their eyes. They were all three stooped to peer at the large, glowing yellow bulb of light in the centre of the wide, metal worktable. "Ah, success!" Morgan said, his grin wide and triumphant.

Xander's eyes twinkled through the goggles like two tiny blue stars, but he blinked, straightening as he became aware of our presence. "What on earth was that crash?" I demanded.

"Ah, welcome," Julius said, grinning. "Come in. We've done it!"

"Done what, exactly?"

"Isn't it brilliant?" Xander asked, gesturing towards the glowing yellow globe.

"Yes, it's utterly remarkable."

"Pay no attention to the crash. Mr Reinhart simply backed into my samples table in his jubilance," Julius told us, but his eyes had returned to the globe. "It is perfectly safe in here. It's phosphorus, you see."

"Phosphorus?" Asher repeated. "But isn't that explo—"

The globe exploded from within, and splinters of glass shot out from it, showering us all. Asher moved so quickly, I was pressed between he and the wall before I had even realised he had caught hold of me. I peered out from around his arm gingerly. Reinhart had leapt forwards, covering the smouldering remains of the globe with a large clothe. "Perfectly safe?" I exclaimed.

"Perhaps we used a bit more phosphorus than was strictly necessary?" Xander asked his cohorts, and they nodded thoughtfully.

"Clearly you three cannot be left together without the supervision of a responsible adult," I said, scowling. I shoved at Asher and stepped around him to face the three pranksters with my hands upon my hips.

"Astrid!" Julius said heartily, striding forwards to seize my hand, which he pumped enthusiastically. "I am much obliged to you for bringing these prodigious young men to me. Their assistance has been most beneficial."

"In creating exploding globes?"

"Oh, no, no. That was a bit of a lark once we completed my actual experiment.

It was, perhaps, ill-advised. Nevertheless, I am overjoyed."

"This was merely a lark? What was the genuine experiment for which you required their particular expertise?" They all three opened their mouths to reply keenly, but I held up a hand. "No. Never-mind. I do not wish to know. I learned long ago it is best never to ask a scientist such a question. I can only assume it is triply ill-advised in this case."

Julius smiled, gesturing us to the door. "Come, let us walk a bit whilst the smouldering remains of our experiment cools. Did you enjoy my little picnic? I hear young Mr Behari's zeal somewhat spoiled the mood."

I smiled. "Ah, the young man is filled with a mischievous spirit. He was insistent upon discussing the rumours surrounding your mysterious island."

"Rumours, indeed."

"It seems all anyone can speak of, doesn't it? There are so many, after all."

"Are there?"

"You are not hard of hearing, my old friend. I am certain you have heard some of the whispers."

He chuckled. "No, I am not hard of hearing. You are so prone to delightful conjecture, Astrid, I simply wished to ascertain exactly to which rumours you were referring."

I laughed. "Well, the matter was put to rest last evening, I find myself continuously diverted by the matter of the missing servants."

"Of course you are. Very grave business, that. Very grave indeed."

"And you truly have yet to solve the intriguing mystery? Why, I myself would have stopped at nothing to determine what dangers lay beyond my grounds."

"I am certain you would. You are very inquisitive, Mrs Darby."

"Many say to the detriment of my otherwise very amiable disposition."

"Oh, no, truly, I find you quite refreshing indeed."

I smiled. "Even when I am inquiring after sensitive subjects?"

Julius lifted an eyebrow. "You assume it is sensitive."

"Is it not?" Asher demanded, frowning slightly.

"I cannot be held responsible for mysterious circumstances, can I, Agent Key?"

"Can you not?"

"Is there something you wish to imply, sir?" Julius' voice was even, but there was a cold glint in his eyes, and I looked between the two men warily.

"Not at all. We are merely inquiring," Asher replied smoothly.

"I must say, Agent Key, Mrs Darby is far more proficient in the art of subtlety than are you."

Asher chuckled. "Perhaps that is why she is the mercenary, and I am a member of the distinguished Ministry of Defence."

"I hardly see the correlation, but if you do say, I am sure it must be so."

"He does say," I told Julius conspiratorially. "Often, in fact. He reminds me each day we are in each other's company."

Julius glanced at us, and his expression was no longer playful. "I warned you all not to leave the grounds, did I not? I cannot be held responsible for imprudent servants who disregard my warnings."

"Can you not stop them?" Asher asked.

Julius laughed. "I am an old man. I have grown quite feeble. Would you recommend I surround the grounds with an electrified enclosure?"

"Perhaps if you just warned them of the specific danger they face, such measures would be unnecessary." When Julius failed to respond to this, Asher added, "Surely you have some idea what became of them."

Julius glanced sidelong at him. "Are you suggesting, perhaps, they were abducted in the night by corporeal spectres or the un-dead wandering in search of fresh blood?"

"Now your tone seems to imply something, Julius," I said, smiling.

"Of course it does not."

"So what is the explanation?" Asher asked. "You know this island better than anyone. Your daughter seems to think there might be someone else on it with us."

"Does she?"

"Could it be head-hunters, privateers or savages, perhaps?"

Julius chuckled. "It would be highly unusual for this particular region."

"Perhaps, but I have heard stranger things," I said. "Do you explore the island

80

much?"

"It is very dangerous, as I said."

"Ah, yes, as is evidenced by the highly sophisticated hunting accoutrements in your study."

He laughed. "You are delightfully insinuating, Mrs Darby." I beamed at him, but he bowed to us, and I realised he had escorted us to the main staircase yet again. "If you'll excuse me, Astrid, Agent Key. I have experiments to which I must return."

"Of course, Julius."

He bowed slightly. "I bid you enjoy the remainder of your stay. See you at dinner."

When he was gone, Asher and I exchanged a glance and spun to descend the stairs side by side. "He is hiding something," Asher declared.

I laughed. "Oh, yes, I am in complete accord. He is a most formidable opponent."

"Astrid, do not enjoy this."

"Oh, Asher, what is the point of doing my job if I do not enjoy it?"

He shook his head. "I am highly uncomfortable about this."

I smirked at him. "Well, it was you who hired me. You will have to find a way to live with the consequences."

* * *

Our evening meal was as elaborate as the previous night's, and I sipped my sweet, spicy shrimp stew with relish. Julius seemed in good humour, despite our impertinent inquest earlier that day. Imaron, too, seemed to be of a particular joie de vivre, and I was unsurprised when he turned towards Julius with a mischievous twinkle in his eyes. I was coming to regard the young gentleman as a very advantageous comrade, indeed.

"Professor," he began, smiling shamelessly, "this afternoon I noticed a very impressive collection of hunting paraphernalia and trophies in your study."

I glanced sidelong at Asher and smirked, but I was more interested to view Julius' reaction to this. He was smiling. "Yes." He glanced at me and Asher. "Have you been speaking with our Mrs Darby and Agent Key?"

"I am not sure what you mean, professor."

"You do seem to have a direct line to their specific curiosity."

"Really." Imaron glanced at us, his eyebrows raised.

"I do take much pride in my collection."

"So it would appear. Do you do much hunting on the island, then?"

"At times, young man, in my youth, I was interested in such endeavours. But now, alas, I am an old, frail man."

"Ah, sir, you are anything but frail. You appear in the height of your health and spirits."

Julius laughed. "You flatter me, young man, but I see through your ruse."

"You are too clever for me," Imaron told him, smiling, but he turned his attention to encompass the table. "I propose we plan an expedition."

"What sort of expedition?" Chesley asked, raising an eyebrow in intrigue.

"To the lands outside the hallowed grounds. A hunting expedition, perhaps."

Julius' smile had faded, but his expression was perfectly still. "There are many exotic and dangerous animals on the island, Mr Behari," Juliana objected gently.

"Ah, but with your father's expertise and our keen youth and enthusiasm, we must be assured of success," Imaron replied confidently.

"I can make no such assurances," Julius told him evenly. "In the past, I have lost many a keen and youthful hunting partner to the unaccustomed brutality of the island's creatures. I cannot allow such an expedition."

Asher and I exchanged a glance. Lost many a hunting partner? "Come now, professor," Imaron urged. "We are men of particular skill and bravery. Why, I know my uncle, Jasper, is a very experienced hunter. And you, Agent Key, must have spent some time in the wilderness, lying in wait for your query?"

Asher chuckled. "Ah, perhaps I have done, yes. But not in the way you are envisioning, I expect. My experience with hunting exotic creatures is trifling at best."

"Anyway, would you not be interested in seeing if the rumours are true?" Imaron continued. "Would you not be keen to explore the very nooks and crannies of the island which may be home to witches, warlocks, vampires and other ungodly creatures of the night?"

"I assure you, young man," Julius said, and now his tone was chilly. "There are no such creatures to be found. Simply venomous snakes, spiders and other dangerous animals which can sneak upon you when you are unprepared."

"Or perhaps a head hunter or two?" I put in, smiling mischievously.

"Head hunters? Oh, could there really be, Professor?" Sophie asked, pressing a hand to her heart.

Julius shot me an inscrutable glance. "Mrs Darby is merely reminding me of the enchanting conjectures with which she regaled me earlier this afternoon. It is nonsense."

"But it could be true. There have been many stories," Chesley added. "Privateers stranded on these islands when their ships ran out of wind or struck the carbon rock. This could, in fact, be one of those islands."

"I have no knowledge of such a thing happening on the Isle of Jules."

"Ah, you are quite adept at subtle evasion, Julius," I told him blithely.

"Father, perhaps it would be good sport," Juliana said hesitantly, drawing our attention to her. She smiled. "Well, if it is what our guests want, I am sure they will not hold you responsible for any adverse circumstances resulting from their insistence."

"The girl speaks sensibly," Asher announced.

"And persuasively, I do hope," Imaron added, smiling.

Julius was silent for a long moment. "I am loathe to refuse my darling daughter anything, as you well know, but I will have to think on whether it is prudent to engage in such a foolhardy venture."

"We are exceedingly foolhardy, Julius," Chesley told him, grinning broadly. "That is, I am sure, my old friend, the precise reason you find us all so amusing."

Julius laughed. "Well, there must be some reason, anyway, for it certainly isn't your humble and retiring characters."

* * *

"Asher Key!" I shrieked, snatching my gown from the bed to cover my state of un-dress.

He rolled his eyes in the doorway adjoining our rooms. "You're hardly a maid, Astrid," he said derisively. "I do have particular knowledge in that area."

"Ash! Is it so much to ask that you desist your course remarks and alert me before bursting into my bedroom while I am in my smalls?" He chuckled, perching on the edge of the bed, and I spun to remain facing him, where the dress clutched to my bosom protected my modesty. "Why have you yet again burst so rudely into my bedroom?"

He sighed, leaning back on the headboard as though he intended to remain. I growled in irritation and wrapped my pale blue silk dressing gown around myself. "I abhor this inaction, Astrid. Any moment, one of our men might go missing, assailed by some unknown foe in the dead of night, and here we sit having tea."

"I wish you had brought some tea. At least it might excuse you."

He ignored me. "How can we just do nothing while this might occur?"

"Well, what would you prefer, Ash? No crimes have been committed here. Not in the last day anyway. There's nothing for us to do."

He scowled. "Until it does and we fail to prevent it." I joined him on the bed, leaning against the headboard beside him. "We are on the brink of discovery, Astrid. I am certain of it. The professor cannot hide all his secrets forever. We will uncover them."

I laid my hand upon his. "You must be patient. You must allow it all to unfold in its proper course."

"That is easy for you to say, Mrs Darby. Your livelihood does not depend upon my success."

I smiled at him. "Ah, but it does."

"How does it?"

"Well, if you're sacked, disgraced and possibly arrested, my affiliation with you will certainly not garner me any respect amongst my clients and peers."

He chuckled, and he squeezed my hand as he rose from the bed. "Good night, Astrid."

"Good night, Agent Key. Close the door behind you, please."

CHAPTER SIX

Breakfast was a lively affair the following morning, for I had risen with the day and had arrived in time to dine with many of the other guests. I nibbled upon the thick, crisp, salty bacon, mindless of the island's dire affect upon my already callipygian figure. "Did you sleep well, Juliana?" Chanha Behari asked, reaching across Xander to brush the young woman's cheek with her knuckle. "You look somewhat peaky, dear."

Juliana smiled, and I tilted my head to study her. She did look drawn this morning; there were dark shadows under her eyes, and there was a distinct pallor to her skin. Her fork clattered against her plate, and she set it aside, as though embarrassed to reveal her quivering. "I confess, I did not. I fell victim to nightmares last night."

"Not about ghosts and vampires, I hope?" Imaron asked, looking slightly guilty.

She chuckled. "No, nothing like that. I was remembering our time in Papua-New Guinea, staying with a small tribe in the Fore villages." Her smile wavered. "They had customs very different from our own, many I did not understand."

"What sorts of customs?" Imaron asked.

"Come now, Mr Behari," I scolded gently. "They are clearly not memories which bring about tranquillity and warm feelings. Leave off her."

Juliana smiled gratefully at me. "Thank you, Mrs Darby. I do not relish speaking of it."

"The morning meal is hardly the time for grim talk," Chesley added, smiling round at the table. "Have some more tea, Miss Juliana. Perhaps it will invigorate you for the coming day's trials."

She smiled, but her hand shook as she held her teacup towards him. Xander took it from her, smiling in a very soft way I had never before seen upon his young, handsome features. Had he come so quickly to develop fond feelings for the young girl? I smirked into my teacup as my young cousin placed Juliana's on the saucer before her.

"Thank you, Xander," she murmured, smiling demurely.

"But Mr Ellis," Chesley said, turning his head to greet Mr and Mrs Ellis as they joined us at the table. "Why are you looking grim this morning? We were just remarking upon the necessity of remaining in sanguine spirits as we break our fast."

In my experience, the Ellis' were predictably a dour and unhelpful presence in any party, but when Mr Ellis spoke, I felt quite shamefaced for my cavalier musing. "I think perhaps the plague of the island has taken one of my young men," he said in a sombre voice.

"Beg pardon, Eugene?" Charles Prosser asked, his brow furrowed in surprise.

"Young Arthur is missing this morning," Eugene Ellis explained as he tucked into his breakfast; his morose thoughts seemed not to have disrupted his appetite, I noticed. "He attends me each morning, but he did not report this particular morning. When I sent for him, Mr Bray informed me he was not in his bed, nor had he been seen all morning."

"Good god, man," Chesley exclaimed. "Have you searched for him?"

"Well, I sent for one of the other servants to search for him," Mr Ellis replied reasonably. "When I heard the news, I called one of my other men to my quarters and engaged him straight away. Antony claimed Arthur was in his bed when the night fell, but he was not when the day rose."

"But did no one hear anything?" I asked.

"No. No one."

For a moment, we glanced at each other glumly, but Imaron, in his characteristic insolence and tactlessness, said, "Well, it is most intriguing, isn't it? Could it be our inquisitiveness drew the attention of the island spirits, who seek now to punish us?"

We frowned at him, but our attention was again diverted when Julius and Asher strode into the room side by side. It was an unexpected alliance, but they did not move towards the buffet table to fill their plates; their expressions were serious as they faced us. "I have heard about your man, Eugene," Julius said in a subdued voice. "I am very sorry to hear it. He has not been seen anywhere?"

"No," Mr Ellis replied, sighing heavily. "But Antony continues to look for him."

"What say you, Professor?" Chesley asked. "Could it be the mysteries of the island have claimed another victim?"

Julius sighed. "I do not believe the young man's disappearance can be attributed to ghosts or vampires, Jasper."

Imaron rose keenly from his chair. "I propose we organise a search for the man. On the island."

Our heads swivelled to Julius, and his mouth tightened. "I do not think--"

"Come now, Professor!" Imaron exclaimed. "You cannot refuse us now. Our man needs his man. Do you not, Mr Ellis?"

"I do need him," Mr Ellis replied morosely. "I can hardly go a morning without his attending to my toilette. He is most indispensable."

"See there. You cannot deny him the chance to retrieve him." Imaron thumped his hand on the table. "I suggest we begin at once."

Julius raised his hand. "If you must venture onto the island," he said resignedly. "Pray, allow me to eat my breakfast before we begin."

* * *

"Mrs Darby, I really must protest," Eugene Ellis said. "An outing of this sort really has no place for a woman, even one of your rumoured proficiencies."

"I beg your pardon, Mr Ellis," I said coolly, hefting a shotgun over my shoulder. "I do suspect I have far more experience of this sort than someone such as yourself."

He stiffened. "With all due respect, Mrs Darby, I highly doubt that."

"Mr Ellis, I have hunted panthers in the jungle and lions on the savannah. And you?"

Mr Ellis hesitated, scowling. Julius chuckled, stepping between us. "Mr Ellis, Mrs Darby is no ordinary woman. I suggest you avoid engaging her in a battle of wits. Or any other sort, for that matter."

"Indeed, my good man," Chesley added from across the study. "If we are to launch a search, we might gladly rely upon Mrs Darby's expertise."

"Thank you, gentleman. I am gratified by your faith in my abilities." I nodded curtly to them, tucking a handful of shotgun shells into my side bag. "Shall we get on?"

Then men followed my lead, selecting their weapons of choice. Asher did not holster the pistol he selected from the rack on the wall, and Julius slung a large, heavy wooden crossbow over his shoulder. Imaron's dark eyes twinkled keenly. He approached the collection of exotic weapons, reaching eagerly for the large, shining bazooka beside the lion's head trophy. Julius chuckled, laying a hand on Imaron's arm. "Young man, that weapon is not for amateurs. You had best take a rifle."

Imaron sighed deeply, but he accepted the ivory-gripped rifle amiably enough. "You are entirely no fun, Professor."

Julius laughed. "I assure you, sir, you will be thanking me later."

The small search party marched resolutely over the path away from the villa, through the field of lush, brilliant yellow daffodils bordering the house. "Be mindful of the forest," Julius ordered us gravely. "It may not appear as a jungle, but it does contain dangers."

"How dangerous can it be, Julius?" Chesley asked jovially, clapping him on the shoulder. "I see only clear skies, temperate weather and a canopy of palm trees ahead."

Julius smiled tightly. "Do not allow its serenity to fool you, Jasper. Be mindful."

I glanced at Asher, but his cobalt eyes were as keen as young Mr Behari's, and he appeared eager to plunge through trees. "We will remain constantly on alert, Julius," I assured him cheerfully and threaded my arm through Asher's, tugging him towards the wall of trees.

We trudged through the forest silently for a few moments, until the last sounds of our fellow searcher's rustling through the trees nearby had faded away. It was serene in the forest, as Julius suggested, and I found it hard indeed to believe the silent, dew-moistened leaves and lush greenery around us could bear such cryptic dangers. "Ah, Asher, we are alone at last."

He looked at me, and his mouth turned up in a wicked smirk. "Do you have some plans for me among these trees I did not anticipate, Astrid?"

I rolled my eyes. "No. I have merely been eager to inquire as to what you believe has come of the missing servant. Interesting, is it not? That one of our own men might go missing at such a time as this, under a cloud of rumour and suspicion?"

He frowned. "You know what it is I believe happened to him."

"Yet there is absolutely no evidence Julius is at all involved in the disappearance. Why, were he, it would be terribly risky, considering the talk amongst our fellow guests and our presence here. I do not believe for a moment he is oblivious to our true motivations."

"But that alone suggests his guilt, does it not?"

"I do not see your reasoning."

"He is the obvious suspect, is he not, being the only link between the missing people here and at home?"

"Certainly, and thus it seems unlikely he would strike while under such suspicion."

"Or perhaps he knows we believe him too clever to act at such a risky time."

"Ah. Still, it would be the act of a very desperate man, and he does not seem so desperate, does he?"

"I do not think him desperate, no. But perhaps he simply cannot help himself. The instinct to kill, once surrendered to, is a yearning difficult to resist."

I sighed. "That is a wild conjecture."

"There is something sinister afoot, Astrid, even you cannot deny this."

"Indeed, I do not deny it. However, I am yet convinced of Julius' guilt in this matter. Circumstances suggest, however, that there is certainly something sinister on this island."

Asher sighed deeply. "Do you not think him guilty, Astrid?"

I paused. "I learned long ago to trust your instincts, Ash."

He frowned. "Yet you do not in this matter."

"I do. Yet I remain unconvinced. It is not that I do not believe there is something afoot and that he is somehow involved. It is simply that my knowledge of my late husband's old friend belies your assertions. He is intelligent and gentile. It is difficult to make sense of how he has changed so dramatically since our last meeting."

He considered. "Do you not think these rumours and insinuations that something is with us on this island may be nothing more than an elaborate ruse?"

"It is certainly possible. If Julius did not start the rumours about the island, perhaps he is encouraging them, in his own way. It does add a bit of mystique to his retreat, as well as creating doubt as to whom is truly responsible for the missing servants."

Ash glanced at me archly. "It is doing that, isn't it?"

The sudden gunfire rent the silent serenity of the forest, and Asher caught my shoulders as though to shield me from the blast. I rolled my eyes and thrust him from me. "Step lively, Asher!" I ordered.

We pelted through the trees in the direction of the din. "Are you not now grateful you did not bring the bazooka, Mr Behari?" Julius asked wryly as we approached the small circle of men.

Imaron's rifle was still smoking, and his characteristically cheerful face was ashen. "Misfired, sir?" Mr Prosser asked dryly.

Imaron shook his head. "I...No, I thought I saw something moving in the woods. Someone moving."

"Someone moving? And you considered it prudent to shoot at them?" Chesley exclaimed. "My dear Imaron, it might have been any one of us!"

"No." He blinked at us, and his expression was so haunted, I stepped towards him.

"What was it, Mr Behari?" I asked soothingly.

"Someone different. Small and pale and dressed in black."

I raised my eyebrows. Julius frowned, and for the first time since I had made his acquaintance, he looked utterly bemused. "Are you quite certain?"

"Yes. No." Imaron sighed. "It was very strange."

"But, young Imaron, clearly your overactive imagination is getting the better of you," Chesley told him gently, patting his shoulder. "You need rest. These stories of ghouls and phantoms are surely getting the better of you."

Imaron shook his head. "No, I do not think I imagined it." When he looked at us, his expression was so spooked, I glanced uneasily at Asher. "I believe we should end this expedition at once. There is something else out here with us. Something that isn't right." He took a deep, faltering breath. "Something inhuman."

"But surely you are imagining such a creature," Mr Prosser said tetchily. "There are no inhuman creatures here with us on the island."

Mr Chesley wrapped an arm around his nephew's trembling shoulders. "Come, my dear, I will take you to your room. You need a lie down is all."

Imaron nodded. "Yes. Yes, I would like to lie down. Thank you, uncle."

We watched them trudge away. Imaron's shoulders quaked slightly as he moved, and I raised an eyebrow at Asher. "Ash? What say you?"

He nodded curtly. "We will continue the search," he said resolutely.

"Perhaps it truly isn't safe out here," Julius told him in a subdued voice.

"Perhaps not, but if we spy any small, ghoulish black clothed figures, we will attempt to capture them and ascertain exactly what they might be," I informed him resolutely.

Julius frowned. "As you wish, Astrid. But I beg you, be careful. I do not know what happened to Mr Ellis' man. If this creature is anything to do with it, you may join him."

"We are better equipped for such things than a servant, I am confident," Asher replied. "We shall return to the house in time for lunch, to be sure."

Julius inclined his head. "I do pray that you do."

Asher tilted his head at me, and we turned away from the perplexed party. "Do you think he truly saw something?" I asked Asher as we continued through the trees.

"Perhaps." He frowned. "Or perhaps young Behari simply carried himself away with his own wild conjectures."

"It is possible. However, he did appear rather spooked, did he not?"

"He might have seen something. I doubt it was a pale little man in black, however."

"No, that does not exactly sound like a creature known to be indigenous to the archipelago."

There was no sign of any such creatures as we burst through the trees on the other side of the island. The expanse of the Celtic Sea lay before us, and we paused a moment on the sparkling white shore. "It is quite beautiful here," Asher remarked. "It is truly a shame our holiday is disrupted by missing servants and our murderous host. We might have had occasion to enjoy ourselves." He glanced down at me. "It has been long since we enjoyed leisure time together."

I sighed. "Ash..."

"Do you remember Fiji?"

"Yes. We ensnared a very dangerous renegade and successfully returned him to London to receive his just punishment. Your Ministry actually thanked me for that one, rather than cite me for destruction of property and obstruction of justice, as is their custom."

"I mean after that."

I lifted my chin. "No." I turned from him, striding along the sand.

After a long moment, he caught me up, but he did not speak as he walked beside me. He paused, however, as we stepped over an outcropping of dark carbon rock on the border between the sand and the daffodil fields. "Astrid."

I glanced at him warily, though his tone indicated he had discovered something of interest, rather than intended to further discuss our previous acquaintances. "What is it?"

He crouched and reached between the rocks. "It's a fork."

"It's what?" I snatched the small, bent tin utensil from his fingers, holding it up to examine it. "It is indeed."

"And what might have been a plate. There's a mug, as well, and some rubbish."

"In the rocks?"

"Just here. As though someone hid them or stored them here to keep them from the tide."

I lowered myself beside him, poking through the detritus. "That is odd indeed. Someone clearly camped here at one time."

"Yes. Maybe there is a tribe of savages here, after all."

I glanced at him sharply, but his eyes twinkled. "Rubbish. A tribe of savages who shares one tin mug? Perhaps Julius occasionally enjoys a night in the open sea air under the stars. Perhaps he's camped here before."

"Perhaps. Or perhaps it was a shipwrecked pirate or a sailor lost at sea."

"Lucky they managed to rescue this dining set," I replied superciliously.

He chuckled. "I suppose we could ask the professor if he often finds occasion to sleep under the stars and dine with arcane utensils on the shore. Though that would take all the fun out of wildly conjecturing, wouldn't it?"

"It would indeed. Still, it is interesting, isn't it? Perhaps the owner of this set is the creature Imar—"

"Astrid, did you hear that?"

I paused, listening, and I did hear the rustle in the trees beyond, as though something large and ungainly was plodding through the woods. He seized my hand, yanking me abruptly to my feet, and I ran with him towards the noise, readying my shotgun as he drew his pistol.

We did not discover a ghoul in the trees, however. For a moment, the forest was silent, and then the leaves rustled again, and we spun to watch a large, red fox emerge from a thicket. Asher raised his pistol instinctively, but I caught his wrist. When it spotted us, the fox darted away, disappearing among the dense coppice once again. Asher sighed. "It was merely a fox?"

I frowned uneasily. "I don't know. The noise we heard before…"

He glanced at me. "It seemed louder."

"Yes."

He lifted an eyebrow. "Perhaps the rumours are affecting you, too, Mrs Darby."

"Of course they aren't. You noticed the incongruity, as well. It sounded as though a much larger animal were plodding through these trees. Are there many large animals indigenous to the islands?"

He shook his head. "No. Perhaps we heard Imaron's ghoul."

I rolled my eyes. "I find that very difficult to believe."

He smirked at me. "For a moment, you looked quite spooked yourself."

"I assure you, Asher, I am quite in control of my faculties." I frowned. "All the same, perhaps we should return to the house. There seems little to discover in the woods, after all." I raised my eyebrows at him. "Perhaps the island's secrets are revealed only when night falls."

"No, I don't think so. I noticed what looked like some small caves near the shore. We were coming upon them when we were so diverted."

"Caves?"

"Well, they might have been. They might simply be crevasses in the rock face. Nevertheless, care to take a look?" When I sighed, he smirked at me. "Are you losing your mettle so soon, Mrs Darby? Afraid to run afoul of ghosts, vampires or demons?"

I rolled my eyes. "Don't be ridiculous. In any case, it's daylight. I understand vampires only walk at night."

"Ah, so they say, but what do we really know about vampires?"

"That they aren't real."

"Now, Mrs Darby, with all the things you have seen in the world: cursed masks and human sacrifice, can you really discount the existence of a creature who feeds on the flesh of humans?"

"Blood."

"What?"

"Vampires feed on blood."

"Ah, so they do. Well, then, perhaps the remains of their victims lie in wait somewhere here on the island, awaiting a proper burial."

"Oh, you may have convinced me Julius is up to some sinister misdeeds, but I certainly can't comprehend the idea that vampires are running amok on this island snatching servants from their beds."

"So what do you think Imaron saw?"

"Perhaps the missing servant. He's probably been out all night wandering about lost in these woods. We can only hope he's made his way back to his master by now."

"So?"

I glanced at him sharply. "What?"

"Caves?"

"Oh, all right."

"Do you think vampires can live in caves?"

I scoffed. "Why are we still talking about vampires?"

"Well, I was just thinking. If they can't come out in the daylight, they must hole up somewhere when the sun is up. Perhaps there's an entire family of vampires living in one of the caves."

"I don't think vampires have families."

"Do you reckon they change into bats during the day, making it easier to sleep in light-tight chambers?"

"I don't reckon anything about vampires; it is a singularly unproductive use of my time."

"You will be eating your words if we find a family of vampire bats in that cave."

"If we do, I will not reproach you for gleefully pointing out your triumph over me."

"Yes, you will."

I glared at him, but he caught my arm on the border between the sand and

94

trees, gesturing towards a small opening in the carbon rock face. I raised my eyebrows. "It does indeed resemble a cave." I stepped forwards, peering into the yawning darkness beyond the mouth. "Have you a gas light?"

"Yes."

"Really?" He produced a small lantern from a pocket of his trousers. "Honestly, how could you possibly know we'd need such a thing?"

"Madam, I am an agent of the Ministry of Defence. I am prepared for many contingencies."

I stepped towards him. "What else have you in your trousers?"

He smirked and held his hands out at his sides. "You may search me, if you'd like."

I paused and spun back to the cave mouth. "I am certain there are better uses of my time. Give me the lantern."

He handed it dutifully to me. "I've matches, as well."

I lit the small wick inside the lantern and guided the light towards the mouth. The meagre illumination revealed a small antechamber, but beyond was thick, inky blackness. Asher stepped forwards to follow me inside, but I paused. "It truly is a cave."

"Yes. As we expected. What are you waiting for?"

I glanced up at him uneasily. "I would prefer not to enter."

His expression was incredulous. "What? You? Astrid Darby? You're backing out now, particularly in front of me?"

I scowled at him and lifted my head, stepping reluctantly forwards. I ducked to enter the cave mouth. I felt him behind me, but I kept on, moving slowly inside. My breath came in short, shallow bursts in the small, still space, but I pressed on. I would be damned if I did back down in front of Asher Key, but the carbon rock walls were narrow, and the light barely penetrated the endless darkness ahead.

After a moment, he paused, catching my arm. "Astrid?"

"What?" I demanded.

"You don't like the dark, cramped spaces?"

I held up the lantern so he could see my scowl. "Belt up, Ash. I'm perfectly all right."

"You can turn back if you want. I can go in alone."

I lifted my chin, despite the low ceiling. "I have been in more cramped and dirty spaces than this. I am sure I will manage."

He smiled, and he stepped forwards, gently taking the lantern from me. "Why don't I lead, then?" I considered a moment, then nodded. He caught my hand, and, though I was quite averse to admitting such a thing, I felt slightly better.

The cave was not as large as I had feared. We reached the rough, rounded end quite abruptly, and Asher placed the lantern on the stone floor, crouching down to examine what appeared to be a small pile of ashes. I crouched beside him. "Someone's been here?" I asked, surprised.

"Yes. But not very recently. This appears to be the remains of a small fire. It seems as though someone has spent the night here, anyway. Maybe more than one night."

He lifted the lantern, and I rose abruptly to follow the light. He shone it around the cave, as though expecting to find the remains of a body or articles of clothing. There were none, but he paused, tugging on my hand. "What?"

"Astrid, look at these."

I frowned, moving up beside him to see upon what he had cast the light. They were carvings in the rock wall, though they appeared little more than crude squiggles. "What do you think they are?" I ran my fingers along one of the curved symbols.

"It appears to be writing of some sort, though I don't recognise the language."

"It could be Middle Eastern? Or some sort of hieroglyph?"

"Or perhaps the meaningless scribblings of someone trapped here for a time."

"Perhaps. It does appear someone spent some time here, anyway. These must have taken effort to etch. It is not easy carving rock." I looked at him. "Have you any parchment or charcoal?"

"I have parchment and a pencil, if that will do for you."

"Yes." I snatched them from him, rubbing the pencils across the parchment to capture the embossed images of the symbols.

"Ah. Very clever."

"We can study them at our leisure later. Can we be off now?"

He nodded, and he moved ahead of me towards the cave mouth. The lantern light bobbed ahead of us, and I took a deep breath, anticipating the crisp, fresh sea air. He paused, however, abruptly, and I collided with his back. "Wait."

"What is it?" I demanded tetchily, but he ignored me, bending down. When I caught what had attracted his attention in the lantern light, I gasped. "Ash?" He reached forwards, but I caught his hand. "Don't touch it."

"Astrid, it isn't going to harm me. It's a skeleton. I assure you, he is already quite dead."

"It might be a woman."

"It hardly matters, considering it is now merely a pile of old, brittle bones." He shrugged me off and picked up one of the bones, examining it in the lantern light.

"How did we fail to notice it on our way in?"

"We're lucky we did not tread upon it. I was not looking at the ground at the time."

"Asher Key, it is disrespectful to look that gleeful in the presence of the long dead."

He glanced up at me. "These bones prove someone died here."

I sighed, crouching down beside him. "Is there more?" He cast the light around the floor, rising to retrace our steps through the passage. He turned a corner, and I was plunged in the darkness. "Ash!"

The light reappeared around the corner. Asher's face was sheepish in the flickering light. "Sorry, sorry. No, there doesn't appear to be anything more. But this is enough to bring back to the Ministry."

I pressed my hands to my hips. "Asher, do not get ahead of yourself. Have you any idea how old these are? Who they could belong to?"

He paused and shook his head. "No. Of course not; there are experts to determine such things. Your carvings may be of help."

"If they are related. These bones don't necessarily prove anyone was murdered, and certainly not by Julius."

"They could belong to one of the missing servants."

"Yes, or a savage or pirate or a shipwrecked seaman who washed up on the shore decades or more ago. If these carvings are related, they are more likely to have been etched by a foreign person, not an English servant."

He sighed, and his lips pressed together. "All right. But this is not a complete skeleton. There are several of the larger bones missing. Where is the rest of it? Where is the rest of the body?"

I shook my head. "I don't know. Perhaps they were carried off by animals."

"Yes, perhaps."

"If you insist upon gathering these remains, please do so quickly so that I might be out of this dreadful cave with haste."

"Right." He peered down at the bones a moment longer then rose abruptly.

"You aren't taking them?"

"What am I to do with an old pile of bones? Hide it in my washroom? If I can prove Coffin has something to do with this, the evidence is best left undisturbed. Perhaps those etchings will give us some clue."

"While I support whatever decision you make, I would prefer to do it quickly so that we might expedite our emergence from this small hellish cavern."

"Ah. Sorry." I inhaled several long, deep breaths of the clean, salty air when at last we had stepped from the cave mouth. Asher glanced at me. "I must say, Astrid, I would never have suspected you to have such a weakness."

I glanced sharply at him. "I would prefer you not make a sport of it, if you please."

"I wouldn't dream of such a thing, Astrid. I am wounded you would suggest it."

I rolled my eyes. "Right." He turned towards me, and the expression on his face was so peculiar, I tilted my head warily. "What? What is it?"

"I have a thought."

"I can see that."

"A brilliant thought."

"Brilliant. Really. Well?"

"Could it be Coffin is hunting something else out here?"

I blinked. "What are you talking about?"

"Well, there was the little camp hidden in the rock, the signs someone spent the night in the cave and died there--"

"It might have been a different person, you know."

"Yes, exactly. Who knows how many there's been?"

"Ash..."

"Why would Coffin leave a small dining set in the rocks when he has all the amenities of his villa? You saw his picnic spread. And, anyway, who spends as much time and money on a holiday home if they intend to sleep on the beach?"

I began to cotton on, and I raised my eyebrows. "All the hunting accoutrements..."

"Yes, Astrid. Perhaps it is more exotic game he prefers to hunt."

"Do you think it is possible?"

"I have heard of many rich man's depraved hobbies. It would not be the first time."

"But hunting humans, Ash?"

"One develops very corrupt tastes when one has all the power and money he could ever desire."

"Is it possible the creature Imaron saw in the woods is one of his prey?"

"Very. It would explain the strange appearance Imaron described and fleeing when he saw the hunters. If it was the servant, would he not have simply presented himself to his master to be rescued?"

"He may have mistaken our appearance as being part of the game."

"Just so. After all, Imaron did fire upon him."

I considered the horrific idea a long moment, and a sick feeling welled in my gut. I glanced at Ash. "Should we attempt to find him? The man in the woods, I mean?"

"It will be a challenge. He is obviously hiding out. If he has been running from a hunter, he will not likely believe we aren't also intending to kill him."

I grimaced. "We cannot allow him to continue running, out here alone in this wilderness. It would be inhumane. We would be as wicked as Julius, doing nothing and leaving him to be hunted."

Asher sighed. "I will help you, if you wish to search."

But another sweep of the island turned up nothing more. I pressed my hand to my forehead in distress. "It is most troubling to think of someone out here like this, fearing the sound of footsteps, left to die from exposure or at the end of a gun."

Asher laid a hand on my shoulder. "I'm sorry, Astrid. But we must get back to the house before night falls or we'll never make it back."

I sighed, but I nodded reluctantly. "I know."

"At least we might have a chance to discover what the carvings are."

I nodded. "Perhaps Morgan or Xander can translate them or at least recognise the script."

"If it is a script at all."

"Yes, well, they might at least suggest how old they are or from where the person--or victim--came."

He tugged on my hand. "Astrid. Step lively. We cannot remain out here any longer, or we may become the quarry ourselves."

I nodded, striding with him towards the terracotta roof of the villa in the distance. "We mustn't speak of this to anyone," I mused. "I am almost afraid to discuss it with Xander. It will distress him deeply."

Asher shrugged. "We will appeal to Reinhart for information. Xander has developed an emotional investment in the situation."

"Yes, I'm afraid you're right. However, I do believe he is positioned to obtain information we could not without his attachment to young Juliana. He will do what he must; he will not allow his emotional investment to affect his duty. Though I do pity the girl for when she learns to what her father is getting up. If Julius truly is hunting humans...and I am increasingly convinced of his treachery, we mustn't risk him discovering we have cottoned on or we will all be in danger."

"There must be more bodies and bones around," Asher mused several moments later as we neared the villa grounds.

"Yes..."

"But there is no sign of them. We have been over most of the island."

"Perhaps he's buried them."

"Yes, but why leave the bones in the cave?"

"That is an interesting point. Truly, the more we discover, the more mystifying it all becomes."

"The point is, he must be disposing of them somehow. And I did not see any sign he possesses a large incinerator anywhere on the property."

I considered. "Well, if he isn't burying them, he's keeping them somewhere."

100

"Right..."

"Oh, Ash..."

"Yes. We must get into that basement."

CHAPTER SEVEN

Xander and Juliana were bent together over a large, ancient text when we discovered them in the library. Juliana's voice was low, but her words were an excited jumble, and I watched them a moment, smiling unconsciously as my young cousin stared, entranced, at the keen young woman. Asher cleared his throat, however, disturbing the sweet, innocent moment. "Astrid?" Xander and Juliana looked up, startled at our arrival.

"Xander, we need to speak to you," I told him. I turned a smile upon Juliana, and she ducked her head, her pale cheeks pinking slightly.

"Of course." Xander rose, inclining his head to Juliana. "Please excuse me, Miss Juliana."

"Of course." She smiled, turning back to the text as Xander stepped into the hallway with Asher and me. "What is it, Astrid? Has something happened?"

"Yes," Asher replied, crossing his arms across his chest as he leaned against the corridor wall. "We just aren't certain of when."

I rolled my eyes. "No need to be cryptic, Ash. Xander, there is something very sinister occurring on this island."

"Yes, I had gathered as much."

"Have you? Have you heard something from Juliana?"

Xander peered around us, pitching his voice low. "She seems to be under the impression there is a tribe of savages with us on the island."

I frowned, and Asher shook his head. "We spent the day searching the land beyond the grounds. There is no sign of a tribe of any sort."

"She seems to believe they are very inconspicuous. Her father often leaves on hunting expeditions in the woods but never returns home with any game. Still, she is sure she can hear the gunshots from the house."

I glanced at Asher, and his mouth tightened into a grim line. "Xander, come. We must speak somewhere we will not be overheard," I said. "We have a theory, and perhaps you may be able to assist with something we've discovered."

His blue eyes glittered keenly. "Oh? I am extremely eager to hear what you believe is going on here, as I do not, despite any leaning towards fancy and superstition, believe in the existence of ghosts or vampires on the island causing the disappearances."

"Yes, Xander, it would be difficult to believe such a thing, indeed. But I am convinced our explanation will be much more sensible."

"I do not know if sensible is the correct word for what is happening here," Asher put in wryly.

"Please, then, enlighten me," Xander said, looking between us keenly.

Chanha rounded a corner, striding towards us. "Ah, Agent Key," she greeted, smiling from beneath her dark, thick lashes. "It is a pleasure to see you all here. Have you come to visit the library?"

"No, we have come to visit Xander," I replied.

She smiled. "I see. Well, as it appears you have something very serious indeed to discuss, I will not interfere." She inclined her head at us and glided into the library.

Asher's eyes followed her, and I nudged him irritably. "This is not the most auspicious location to engage in such a conversation. Let us go to the kitchens so that we may engage Morgan and relay our story once to you both."

"Of course. Allow me to inform Miss Juliana I will be unable to return to our study."

Reinhart was not in the kitchen when we arrived as last he had been, and I was relieved not to find him again in such a compromising position. Nor was he in the servants' quarters. "Did he speak with you, Xander?" I asked, frowning at Morgan's cot. The coverlet was folded in a neat square at the foot of the cot, and his effects were packed neatly in his rucksack.

"No. I have not seen him since this morning," Xander replied. His expression was troubled. "Do you think something has happened to him?"

"This is Morgan of whom we're speaking," I replied, though I was not as confident as my tone implied. "I am certain he is about, likely immersed in some mischief."

Asher turned from us, catching the arm of the young, pretty maid with whom we had caught Morgan in the kitchen our first day as she passed through the servants' quarters towards the kitchen. "Excuse me, miss, have you seen Mr Reinhart about anywhere?"

"Morgan?" She peered between us, bemused. "I haven't seen him since this morning. I met him..." Her cheeks flushed. "It has been several hours since last I saw him."

"Thank you, miss," I said, smiling brightly at her, but she bobbed her head and fled towards the stairs. I sighed, peering grimly at Asher.

"Can he be yet another victim?" Asher mused, frowning.

"I desperately hope not."

"Perhaps Mr Bray has some idea to where he's gotten."

"Astrid, what is going on?" Xander asked in a low voice.

"I will explain, cousin, but I am concerned at the moment with discovering where Morgan has gotten to."

The gravity in my tone impressed him, and he nodded. Mr Bray was in the dining room, supervising the staff as they laid the settings for dinner. "Mr Bray," Asher greeted, striding forwards purposefully.

Mr Bray turned to face him, his expression arctic. "Agent Key. To what may I attribute this interruption of the evening preparations?"

"Have you seen our man Mr Reinhart about?" I asked, and Bray turned his nearly colourless blue eyes upon me, lifting his eyebrows.

"Mr Reinhart, Mrs Darby? I regret I am not in charge of your servants; I am in charge of Master Coffin's. I cannot be expected to keep track of everyone who is brought here," Mr Bray replied coolly.

"He has not been seen since the morning, and we are very concerned," Xander explained earnestly. "Can you help us, please, Elijah?"

I blinked, glancing at Asher. Mr Bray's expression softened slightly, and he inclined his head. "I am sorry I have not seen him, Alexander." He considered a moment. "I will inquire as to if anyone might be aware of his whereabouts."

"Thank you, sir."

"Incidentally, have you looked in upon the laboratory? The master was quite pleased with your man's gift for science. Perhaps he is there, with the master."

"I had not considered it. I had assumed they would have called upon me to join them."

Mr Bray's thin mouth turned up in a small smile. "You were quite otherwise engaged this afternoon, young Xander. Perhaps they wished not to disturb you."

Xander's cheeks flushed slightly, but he inclined his head. "Thank you. We will inspect the laboratory at once. If you hear anything, will you tell us?"

"Of course." Mr Bray turned back to Asher and me, and he eyed us warily. Finally, he bowed neatly and returned to his work, dismissing us entirely.

"I am most uncomfortable with this development," I remarked as we strode quickly towards the laboratory in the furthest wing of the house.

"Worry not, cousin," Xander said bracingly. "Morgan is highly resourceful and clever indeed. He is also highly inquisitive. He may simply be on the trail of some break in our case."

"Let us hope you correct in thinking," I murmured, and I pounded upon the laboratory door. "Julius?"

His hair was wildly mussed, sticky with some strange, yellow substance that caused it to stick straight up in several directions. He shoved the goggles from his eyes to the top of his head and blinked at us in confusion. "Xander? Astrid, what it is?"

"Is Morgan with you?" I asked, peering around him into the laboratory. On the worktable, test tubes and beakers filled with bright, toxic-looking substances hissed and smoked ominously.

Julius shook his head, his brow furrowed. "No. I'm afraid I haven't seen him at all this afternoon. Have you misplaced him?"

"We are uncertain," Asher said grimly. "No one has seen him since the morning."

Julius sighed deeply. "Has he too fallen victim, then?"

"To what, precisely?" Asher demanded.

Julius frowned at him. "I know what you think of me, Agent Key, but I assure you, I have no idea where he is or where he might have gone. I have no idea where any of the missing servants have gone or I would myself have recovered them. I have been tolerant of the wild accusations you have lodged against me, but I will not continue to be so tolerant, particularly in my own home."

Asher lifted his chin, and he opened his mouth to speak, but I laid a hand upon his arm. "Ash," I said softly.

"I am most aggrieved that Mr Reinhart too is among the missing," Julius added. "Have you implored Mr Bray to launch a search for him?"

"He has agreed to do so," Xander replied.

"Thank you, Julius," I said, inclining my head at the scientist. "Come, you two. Let us continue searching. Perhaps he is merely off conducting an investigation of his own, and we are simply making more of it than there is. It does seem highly unlikely he might be felled by an old man or anyone else that might be wandering the island. Perhaps we should wait until nightfall and ensure he is safely tucked into his bed."

My optimism was in vain; Reinhart did not appear in the kitchen or the servant's quarters before dinner, and the party was grim as we sat down to the evening meal. "Imaron," Chanha said abruptly, shattering the morose silence of the table. "Uncle Jasper tells me you had rather a fright in the woods this morning."

Imaron glanced up at his sister, startled. His face was still slightly pale, and there was no evidence of his characteristic cheerfulness. "Yes. Indeed I did, sister."

"I reckon you've some wild tale of ghouls or phantoms with which to regale us this evening?"

Imaron's expression was grave. "Chan, I cannot say for certain what it was I saw, but I assure you, I am in no spirits to make jokes."

Chanha raised her eyebrows. "You? What did you see out there, Imaron?"

The attention of the table was riveted upon the young India man, and he sighed deeply. He was a different man than the keen, cheeky charismatic gentleman whom we had met upon our arrival. His expression was haunted as he looked around at us. "He was thin and pale and stooped. He moved...not like a man but an animal."

"Did he resemble Mr Ellis' missing man?" Leticia Prosser asked.

Imaron blinked, turning his gaze to her as though he had not even considered it. "I haven't any idea. I've never seen him. Mr Ellis?"

Mr Ellis shook his head. "It sounds nothing like my man. He is young and tall and quite ruddy of complexion. He sounds nothing of the pale creature in black you described."

"Do you still believe it is ghosts in those woods, Mr Behari?" Sophie asked, pressing her hand to her chest. "Could the man you saw have been..."

"He seemed very much real and alive, but I only saw him for a brief moment," Imaron said in a low voice. "I do not know what I believe, but I know we are not alone on the island."

Sophie turned to Julius. "Professor?"

Julius looked up from his soup, as though startled to be addressed. "Mrs Marlow?"

"What do you think of this creature Mr Behari spotted in the woods?"

Julius smiled enigmatically. "I know not what to think, my dear."

Beside him, Juliana's fork clattered loudly against her plate as she dropped it, drawing our attention to her. Her hands and shoulders trembled violently, and she appeared in the grips of a seizure. "Juliana!" Xander exclaimed, jumping to his feet the same moment as her father, who shouted for Mr Bray over his shoulder.

Juliana was not experiencing a seizure, however. Though she continued to tremble, she smiled weakly around at us. "Forgive me." Her voice shook.

Mr Bray appeared at Julius' shoulder, but when he saw the young woman, he needed no command. "I will bring Miss Juliana her dinner."

"Thank you, Elijah."

"It is another symptom of my ailment," Juliana said as her father tucked her quivering hands at her sides to steady her. "I lose control of my hands sometimes."

Xander's eyes were wide and glittering. "Professor, can you not form any idea what is ailing her? You're a doctor!"

Julius pressed his hand to his forehead. "I have tried many times to figure out what is wrong with my daughter, Mr Knightly. I am afraid I have been unable to determine the cause. If I could, I would do something."

"Is there some treatment you are supplying in her dinners?"

Julius' expression was cold when he looked up at my young cousin. "I understand you are concerned with my daughter's health, Mr Knightly, but I would prefer not to hang my family's conditions out for all to see."

Xander deflated slightly. "Yes. Sir, forgive me. I did not mean to intrude upon your privacy. I misspoke."

"Not at all, young man. I should not have reacted so coarsely." He smiled wanly. "We are friends again, yes?"

Xander inclined his head. "Of course."

"Do you think perhaps we should launch another search of the island tomorrow?" Mr Prosser asked abruptly, and the mood instantly shifted.

"No!" Imaron exclaimed, paling.

"I do not think it would do very much good," Chesley added. "We have found nothing of the missing servant, and we covered the entire island."

"Not the entire island, surely," Mr Prosser replied.

"There are caves and crannies in the rock faces concealed by trees," Juliana put in, and her voice sounded slightly steadier. She smiled at Mr Bray as he appeared, placing her special dinner before her.

"We have seen some of the caves," Asher said in a perfectly level voice.

Julius' eyed him shrewdly, but he did not offer a rejoinder. "Well," he said instead. "If you will all excuse me, I am unaccustomed to such activity in my old age. It has been long since I explored my island. Juliana, are you feeling better?"

She smiled. "Yes, Papa, thank you." She lifted her fork carefully, displaying her recovered control over her faculties.

Julius rose to his feet. "Then if you would all excuse me, I think I'll be to bed."

"Papa? You have not finished your meal," Juliana told him fretfully.

"I have had enough to eat, my dear. All I require now is a long, restful night." He kissed the top of her head and inclined his head to us. "I am certain you will all find your own entertainment for the remainder of the evening?"

"I am certain we are all likely to retire early, my old friend," Chesley said in a bracing voice. "It has been a difficult day for us all."

"Good night to you all, then."

"Good night, Papa."

Julius paused in the doorway, turning back to face us. "I urge you all to remain in your beds tonight and not to wander. It will be much safer."

* * *

I was prepared when Asher burst into my bedroom, and I turned to him defiantly. He looked slightly disappointed when he realised I was wrapped securely in my dressing gown. I rolled my eyes at him, perching on the edge of my bed. "I had anticipated you would come."

He slouched into the desk chair beside the bed. "I can see that." His gaze followed me as I sat against the headboard. "There has been no more word about Reinhart?"

"No. He hasn't been seen all day, and he did not return to the servants' quarters when night fell."

"Are you all right?"

I sighed. "I am concerned, of course, but at least we know where Julius is. If he is intending to hunt my associate through the forest, he's given him a head start. And he will likely regret having done."

Asher smiled. "Reinhart is not a man with whom to tread recklessly."

Despite the bracing words, I hugged a pillow to my chest. "Nevertheless, I am most concerned for him."

"I know. You are justified in being."

"I feel as though there is something I should be doing on his behalf."

"We have done all we can. We can go to the kitchen again, see if he's finally returned?"

I sighed, shaking my head. "I have the distinct feeling it will be nothing more than an exercise in effectuality."

Asher rose abruptly, moving to sit beside me on the bed. He wrapped an arm around me, pressing me to his chest. I attempted to lean away from him, but he held fast, ignoring my resistance. "Astrid. I am your friend. At least allow me to comfort you when you are worried for your friend."

I smiled wanly up at him and leaned into him, allowing him to wrap his arms around me in a reassuring embrace. "Without Morgan, how will we determine what those scrawls mean?"

"We will find a way. If he hasn't returned in the morning, we'll search the island for him again. It is not so large. And Knightly can research the carvings from the cave. Perhaps there is something of use in the library." He smiled, stroking a hand over my long braid. "At least we can be certain what is happening on this island isn't supernatural, after all."

I snorted. "That, at least, is a comfort. Though I suspect, for Morgan's sake, it might have been better if it was supernatural."

"Perhaps. But what is more difficult to combat? Vampires, ghosts or a deranged old man with a depraved hobby?"

I smiled. "I wouldn't know. I have engaged none of them in battle."

He laughed. "Nor have I, at that. I suppose perhaps we're soon to find out."

He leaned back, peering into my eyes earnestly. "We will find him, Astrid. I will stop at nothing to return him to you."

"Thank you. I am, at least, willing to admit that if one of my most valuable associates remains astray, there are few others I would prefer to have at my side than you."

He chuckled. "Such benevolent words from you? Is that a peace offering, Astrid?"

"I had thought we had achieved a general accord." I looked up at him in surprise when he lifted his shoulders in a silent shrug. "We have been getting on marvellously well."

"Yes, as partners in this investigation. I could ask for no better a fellowship."

"Well, what more do you require?"

He peered at me silently for a long moment, and my stomach sank when he next spoke. "You still haven't told me why you were so cross with me regarding our previous parting."

I drew away from him, frowning. "Ash, now is not the time."

"Then when?" he demanded. "When will it be the time? If it was not when last we met, when we were battling international terrorists with a death ray designed by your former paramour--"

"Joseph was not my paramour!" I exclaimed indignantly. His expression was dubious, and I lifted my chin. "Well, he wasn't. I mean..."

Asher held up his hand to silence me. "No, Astrid, I do not believe I care to know the specifics of your connection with Joseph Ramsey. I would prefer never to think or speak of him again, truth to tell."

I slid off the bed, facing him with my hands upon my hips. "Ash, now is not the time to talk about the circumstances of our parting. It would be best if we focussed on the task at hand, rather than the past."

He sighed. "Astrid..."

I looked away. "Ash, I would prefer to leave the past in the past, where it belongs. I am willing to go forwards with you and leave it alone."

"What does that mean?" he asked, rising from the bed to face me, his expression serious. "Forwards with me in what way?"

"Forwards with this investigation," I replied reasonably.

"You know that isn't what I meant. You know it isn't that simple."

I frowned. "It is that simple. What happened those years ago is best left there. There is no need to dredge up old cruelties and trespasses."

"To what do you refer, Astrid?" he asked, his tone exasperated, and I blinked at him in surprise. "I tell you, I have no idea what caused you to walk out on me those years ago. I have no idea what has caused you to harden your heart to me." He gripped my shoulders. "We were brilliant together."

I shook my head. "I do not wish to speak of it now."

He shook me slightly. "When, then? I will not allow you to continue holding this taciturn grudge. You will let it out, and you will tell me."

I glared at him, jerking out of his grip. "All right," I replied petulantly. "I will tell you. But not now. When we've found Morgan, perhaps, but not now."

He sighed, dropping into the desk chair. "You will forgive me if I am unable to take you at your word on that, Astrid."

"I do give you my word, Ash," I told him gently. "We will speak of the past when this task is complete. There is no sense tearing down the tentative partnership we have worked so hard to achieve."

He exhaled heavily. "All right."

"What do you think of Mr Bray? He's very odd, isn't he?"

He leapt eagerly upon the change of topic, leaning forwards on his knees. "He must be involved in his master's hobby. Do you think he might be facilitating it?"

"It's a very reasonable conclusion. Surely Coffin is unable to overpower these men himself, despite his good health. He must have help. And Bray seems to be his closest confidante. He trusts him with Juliana's care, and he always seems to be about and aware of his master's location."

"I agree it is unlikely he is unaware of his master's activities. Do you think it is possible Juliana knows, as well?"

I frowned, sitting down on the edge of the bed. "Juliana? No. She is the gentlest of creatures. And she is ailing terribly."

Asher sighed. "Perhaps Xander can extract something from her about Bray, nevertheless. She likely knows things she has been unable or unwilling to put into context."

"Perhaps." I considered. "I suspect Xander will be reluctant to exploit her in such a way, but he will do anything he must to find Morgan. Morgan would do the same for him."

"We will instruct him to find out as much as he is able."

"Ash, what I do not comprehend is, if Julius has such a macabre hobby which could easily be discovered by his guests, why bring us all here? Why not bring only his quarries and alleviate the risk of exposure?"

"I know not. I, too, have wondered the same. It is possible his intentions were to remain virtuous for the length of the holiday, but he simply could not control his impulses. It is too much to consider the disappearances are coincidence."

"Still, that makes little sense. Servants have gone missing in the past. He would be aware of his inability to control his impulses."

Asher shook his head. "I am afraid I have no insight into the man's psyche. I am very well-acquainted with his actions, but I know little by way of his personality."

"It is a mystery to me as well, but we will solve it, Ash. We have never failed in the past; I do not expect this time shall be any different."

"And I intend to solve it before anyone else is hurt." He surged to his feet, startling me. "Astrid, we must get inside that basement."

I sighed. "Ash, must you keep on about that? What do you think you will find down there?"

"Evidence. I am certain. More than supposition and a few bones in a cave. I am convinced we will find all we need to bring him to justice for what he's done."

"Do you expect to find a pile of bodies?"

"Perhaps. Or morbid trophies like those in his study. Something, anyway. Why lie about the storm if not to hide something?"

"I agree. But how do you propose to gain entrance? We tried once already. Bray is like a watchdog, and Julius will have warned him to remain on the alert."

Asher lifted his chin. "Then I will have to exert my authority."

"You authority? What authority? Ash, you were sacked."

"I was not sacked. I am simply on administrative leave. I still have the might of the government on my side, should a crime occur. And a crime—many of them, I suspect—have certainly occurred here."

"You have no conclusive evidence of that as yet."

His expression was incredulous. "Do you really doubt it even now?"

"No, of course I don't. I am convinced, and I am on your side. I am merely cautioning you against imprudence at this sensitive juncture. Julius is aware by now of your so called leave. You pose no real threat to him now."

His cobalt eyes were blazing. "I pose more threat than he might imagine."

I rolled my eyes. "Masculine posturing aside, you cannot simply march up to him and demand to be allowed in. We must use a certain measure of finesse under the circumstances. We will find the proper way to approach it when the time arrives. I am most confident."

He frowned. "I will find something to condemn him. And when I do, the Ministry will regret their doubts. Coffin will be exposed for what he's done."

"I have no doubts, Ash, but we must be delicate."

"Oh, I will be delicate." He spun, striding towards the door. "See you in the morning."

"Ash, don't do anything rash."

He paused, turning to me with a smirk. "I had no intention. But I am going to check the kitchen again. And if the basement door happens to be ajar, well... there is no harm against nudging it a bit further open."

I smiled slightly. "Right."

"Are you coming?"

I sighed. "No. I think I'll leave this one to you."

He nodded. "If I hear anything of Morgan, you will know directly."

I smiled, turning back the counterpane. "Thank you, Ash."

"Good night, Astrid."

* * *

Reinhart had not returned to his quarters the following morning, and I trudged back up the stairs from the kitchen gloomily. Asher was waiting at the top of the stairs, leaning against the wall with his arms crossed across his chest. "I thought you might stop here before breakfast," he remarked in a subdued voice.

"Still no sign of him," I said morosely.

He nodded. "I know."

I sighed, and I took the arm he offered as we walked slowly towards the dining room. "Did you learn anything last night after you left my room?"

"No." His tone was bitter.

"What's the matter? What happened?"

"I encountered the professor."

"Did you? And how did you fare against him?"

"Not well. He must have anticipated my intentions. He was there, waiting for me in the kitchen."

"Did he make a claim as to what he was doing there?"

"Yes, of course. It was very sensible, though it is his kitchen. If he chooses to be there, it's nothing about which to form suspicions."

"Though I am certain that did not prevent you."

"Of course it didn't. Nevertheless, he claimed to be checking up on Reinhart himself."

I sighed. "No news at all, then."

"No. I am sorry, Astrid."

I nodded. "I expected as much. How great is the extent of alienation you managed to create last evening?"

He chuckled. "Well, it could certainly be worse."

"Could it?"

"Well, you could say it was slightly tense."

"If you say you accused him outright of hunting humans for sport, I swear, I will hit you firmly about the head and neck with my valise."

He laughed. "You certainly will not. As often as you threaten bodily harm against my person, I do not remember a single time you laid a finger upon me... in a violent fashion, anyway."

"I warn you, Ash, you do not wish to embark upon this particular vein of conversation at this juncture."

He smirked. "I did not accuse him. I simply insinuated we were on to the unsavoury behaviours occurring hereabouts."

I shook my head. "Asher, if you have ruined my breakfast with awkward tension, I will be very indignant."

"Don't worry. He was quite sanguine, which I believe is a highly inappropriate attitude, considering my specific abilities in the area of investigation. However, his confidence may work in our favour."

"He will not let down his guard."

"No, I don't expect that he will, but I don't expect he has yet, so, generally, it seems a wash."

The breakfast table was as grim and quiet as dinner the previous evening. Sophie Marlow was pale beside her aunt, Madam Eliot, and she barely twitched her lips in a smile when she saw me. "Have you heard anything of your associate, Astrid?"

I shook my head. "I'm afraid he has not been seen."

"No, nor has the Ellis' man." She sighed, pushing her food around her plate with her fork. "Can you do nothing to help, Agent Key?"

Asher's brow furrowed. "I assure you, Mrs Marlow, I will do all in my power to discover what has become of our friend and Mr Ellis' man."

She nodded, but it did not seem as though Asher's assertions had bolstered her confidence. Sophie's expression remained downtrodden as Xander and Juliana arrived for their meal, followed by Chesley and the Beharis. "I have heard nothing of Morgan, Astrid," Xander told me in a low voice as he sat down with his plate beside Juliana.

"Nor have I, I'm afraid, Xander."

His mouth turned up slightly in a half-smile. "I suppose it is too much to think he might return at any moment with a wild tale of his adventures and a cheeky grin."

I considered. "It is unlikely at this juncture, but we will not give up on the hope."

"I am most frightened for us all," Sophie said, drawing our attention back to her. Her skin was pallid, and she pushed her plate away from her as though the scent were nauseous. "I would prefer to be back in London where it is safe."

"London?" Imaron asked, and his eyes twinkled in a characteristic way that suggested he had regained his higher spirits since the previous day's scare. "Safe? You, Madam, must live in a different London than I."

Sophie waved her hand daintily before her face. "At least in my part of

London, none of my servants have gone missing."

"Not for more than a few days on a bender, anyway," Madam Eliot added sullenly.

We chuckled, but it was a tense, anxious moment. "But, Miss Juliana, is there no way to get a message to the mainland?" Sophie asked suddenly. "To have someone retrieve us early?"

Juliana sighed, dipping her head. "I'm sorry, ma'am. I know of no way off the island until the airship arrives in three days time."

"In three days time, all our men might be missing," Madam Eliot snapped.

"What sort of modern man of science has no telegraph?" Chanha asked, her dark, elegant eyebrows travelling up her smooth, mahogany forehead.

Juliana smiled. "My father is a highly eccentric man. This is his asylum from the outside world. He prefers it remain untouched by modern communication. I believe he fears he may be called away from it at any time."

I met Asher's gaze, and his expression was sombre. "Well, we appreciate his need for sanctuary and escape from his bustling life," Chesley said. "But a lifeline would be even more greatly appreciated under the circumstances."

She inclined her head. "I admit, I am in accord, but my father will hear nothing of it."

The table fell silent, but only Imaron's appetite seemed as voracious as it once was. I speared a sausage upon my fork, eyeing it contemplatively for a long moment before returning the fork to my plate, my stomach roiling. I felt Asher shift beside me, and I glanced at him, meeting his small smile with a troubled look. "I reckon we are left to our own entertainment this morning?" Imaron asked, soldiering through the quiet tension.

Juliana smiled wanly. "I am afraid Papa has not informed me of his intentions--"

"Mrs Darby!"

The young, red-haired maid with whom we had discovered Reinhart upon our first visit to the kitchen burst into the room. Her braid was slightly dishevelled, and stray strands of hair stuck out from every angle like a copper halo. I did not know her name, but I rose quickly to my feet to meet her. "What is it?"

She gestured wildly towards the servants' entrance. "Come quickly! We have found Mor--Mr Reinhart!"

116

I glanced at Asher and Xander, who jumped to their feet to race towards the kitchen beside me. Our fellow guests trailed behind interestedly, but I paid them no mind. Reinhart lay upon his cot, but he was in no fit state. "What has happened to him?" Xander demanded.

I knelt beside my associate. His face was pallid, and his hair was wildly mussed. He smelled of the sea and of sand, and his mud-streaked clothes were still damp as though he had been recently immersed in the ocean. There was smeared blood on his collar, as though it had failed to wash away in the waves. His features were slack, but his mouth moved rapidly. The words were jumbled and too soft to comprehend. When I spoke his name, his eyes opened, rolling languidly to me. "Astrid?"

"Morgan, what has happened to you?" I demanded, laying a hand upon his moist chest. "Where have you been? Has someone hurt you?" He squeezed his eyes shut and tossed his head back and forth, as though in the throes of a terrible fever. "Morgan! Who has done this?"

His eyelids fluttered, and he gripped my hand so tightly, I winced. "Step aside, step aside. Let me through, people. I am a doctor," Julius ordered sharply, pushing through the crowd to kneel down beside me. "What has happened to him?"

"I don't know," I replied. "There is blood on his collar."

Julius leaned over Morgan, who moaned softly and squeezed my hand. I glanced up at Asher, who leaned over us, frowning deeply. "Look at this," Coffin said so quietly, I barely heard him over Morgan's muttering.

Two tiny puncture wounds stood out starkly on Morgan's marble pale throat. "What is it?" I whispered, pressing a hand to my mouth.

His expression was utterly grave as he met my eyes. "I really don't know."

"What is happening?" Sophie asked anxiously behind us. "What has gotten to him?"

Morgan opened his eyes, and they glittered intensely for a moment before they rolled into the back of his head. "It was...a vampire."

CHAPTER EIGHT

There was no sound from inside the room in which Julius had had Morgan moved, and I paced nervously outside the door, wringing my hands. Asher sighed, leaning against the wall beside the door. "Astrid, don't fret. Reinhart is alive, which is much more than we can say for the other missing man."

I paused, and my brow furrowed. "Yes, but who knows for how long? Ash, he was so pale."

"Coffin is with him. Despite all else, he is a fine doctor by all accounts. He will not fail to tend him."

"That is, if his intention is to save him," I whispered, and Asher straightened, striding forwards to grip my shoulders. I looked up into his eyes. "What could have happened to him?"

"A vampire," Asher said, his eyes sliding away. "He said it was a vampire."

I scowled at him. "Ash, you can't possibly believe he was attacked by a mythical horror creature."

"No, of course I don't, but something caused him to believe that is what attacked him." I sighed, and he folded me abruptly into his arms. "Morgan will be all right, Astrid."

I leaned into him, inhaling the crisp, woodsy scent of his skin. It was pure and familiar, and I allowed myself to indulge in the comfort of his embrace for a languid moment. He stroked a hand over my hair, leaning his cheek against the top of my head. I sighed, pulling away from him, and, though he resisted a moment, he released me, stepping back as I straightened my skirts.

I took a deep breath, swiping a single, traitorous tear from the corner of my eye. "We must speak with the young maid that discovered him," I said in a deceptively calm voice. "I wish to determine where and how he was found. At least we can attempt to learn what truly happened to him."

Asher nodded, and though his expression was blank, his tone was strange. "It's certainly better than doing nothing at all." He lifted an eyebrow. "At least Coffin is otherwise engaged and will be unable to hinder our investigation."

"Now, now, Ash, there is no honour in besting a fragile old man," I told him, though my smile faltered slightly.

"Fragile he is not," Asher replied wryly.

The young maid was encircled by a throng of concerned older women as we arrived in the kitchen. They clucked sympathetically while the young woman sobbed quite dramatically, and I chuckled as Asher reared back, as though he might flee. I rolled my eyes, suspecting the maid might be somewhat exaggerating her distress. Nevertheless, my voice was soothing as I addressed her. "Miss..." I faltered, realising I had never asked her name.

She lifted her head, and the maids around her stepped aside to allow me to approach. "Marjorie, ma'am," she said meekly.

"Marjorie. You are particularly close to my associate, then?"

Her eyes slid away a moment, but she nodded. "We have become friends since he arrived."

"Are you the one who found him in this state?"

She blinked. "No, I...no. It was Fredrick."

"Fredrick?"

"One of the kitchen boys," she said. "He brought Morgan in from the grounds."

"I see. And where is Frederick now?"

"He is likely resting; he spends the early morning on the shore fishing for dinner, and usually lies down for a couple hours afterwards."

"That is when he found Morgan? When he came in from the beach?"

"Well, yes, I assume so. I am not entirely sure. Shall I wake him?"

I considered. "Yes. Please. Inform him we will not keep him long."

She scurried away towards the servants' quarters, and I turned to Asher, who crossed his arms over his chest. "Coffin's servants appear to be quite safe moving freely through the grounds," he commented wryly.

"Yes, but I suspect they obey orders, unlike Morgan."

He snorted, and we turned towards the door as Marjorie emerged beside a bleary-eyed young man with dishevelled blonde hair and round, rosy, youthful features. "Ma'am? Sir?" he asked, rubbing his eyes.

"Young man, you are the one who discovered our man, Mr Reinhart?" I asked curtly.

Frederick nodded. "Yes, ma'am. On my way back from the shore."

"Where did you find him?"

"On the grounds."

"Yes, we had gathered that, young man," Asher said, lifting an eyebrow. "Can you direct us to where exactly you found him?"

Frederick looked between us anxiously. "Master Julius has ordered us not to leave the house."

Asher smirked, pushing aside his waistcoat to reveal the pistol on his belt. "Young man, I am an agent of the Ministry of Defence. I assure you, you are safe with us, no matter what is out there on the grounds."

Frederick hesitated, but he nodded meekly and gestured us towards the door. We followed him outside, towards the hedgerow in the back of the house. He pointed to a tall, thick tree trunk. The wide, green leaves cast a shadow over the ground beneath, but the depression where Morgan's form had lain was unmistakable. "I found him here," he said.

Asher circled the tree, crouching low to examine the blanket of crumpled leaves. "Did you see anything else?"

Frederick shook his head. "No. Just your man. He could hardly move or speak. I brought him in at once."

I raised my eyebrows. "How did you manage him on your own?"

"Mr Porter, the cook was with me. We carried him inside together."

"I see. Was anyone else with you?"

"No. He and I go to the beach alone in the mornings."

"Ah. So we shall thank him, as well, for your quick rescue. We are in your debt, sir."

Frederick inclined his head. "I do hope he is all right."

"And is able to inform us what happened to him," Asher added.

"He did tell us," Frederick replied, sounding surprised. "He said it was a vampire."

I lifted my eyebrows. "Do you believe that?"

Frederick tilted his head. "I have seen stranger things."

"Have you?" Asher asked, rising abruptly to his feet. "Such as?"

The young kitchen boy hesitated. "We should not be out here. It is not safe."

"I assure you, Frederick, if a vampire attempts to attack in the day, we will be perfectly safe," Asher told him, lifting his chin. "You have the Ministry's assurance."

I rolled my eyes, but the sentiment did not appear to sway the young man. "Frederick!" We spun towards the angry voice to find Mr Bray striding towards us. "What are you doing out here?"

Frederick ducked his head. "Assisting Agent Key and Mrs Darby with their man, sir."

"You should not be outside. You should remain in, as our master bid," Mr Bray told him, scowling. "Return to the house at once."

Frederick bowed, turning to lope sheepishly back towards the villa. Mr Bray turned his pinched, disapproving face to us. "I was in the process of questioning a witness, Mr Bray," Asher said angrily.

Mr Bray raised his eyebrows, unmoved by Asher's dangerous glare. "I am aware of your circumstances and position within the Ministry of Defence at this time, Agent Key. You have no authority here. I am the head of this household."

Asher opened his mouth to retort, but Mr Bray spun smartly on his heel, striding away from us without another word. I glanced at Asher, and he turned his back to me, crouching back down to poke at the leaves around the tree trunk. "He must have crawled here," he said after a long, silent moment, looking up at me.

I raised my eyebrows. "From where?"

"I don't know. The leaves along the path are disturbed. Perhaps it may lead us to where he was attacked."

I nodded and followed him, my head bent to focus on the leaves below our feet. When Asher stopped abruptly in the path, I collided with him. I looked up with my hands on my hips to admonish him, but he wasn't paying attention. "What is it?"

"Storm cellar door," he replied, pointing at his feet, and I raised my eyebrows.

"Perhaps he was attempting to break in when he was attacked."

A flash of gold glinted in the sunlight, and I bent to pick up the long, thin metal prong-tipped wand from a thicket. I held it up to Asher. He frowned. "What is it?"

"One of Morgan's instruments. It's a lock pick."

"That is a lock pick?" Asher eyed it warily. "How does it work?"

"I haven't any idea. My interest in Morgan's inventions is limited mostly to weapons and time-saving devices."

Asher raised his eyebrows, and he took the instrument from me. "I've never seen anything like it before." He turned his attention to the storm cellar, bending to examine the thick padlock securing the doors. "It looks slightly damaged. There are some cracks here near the keyhole."

"It likely emits some sort of static charge; Morgan is particularly keen on lightning devices."

"Is that strictly safe?"

"No. Which is precisely what he fancies about them, I expect."

"There's no way to tell if he actually managed to open the lock; someone might have closed it behind him."

"Well, open it," I suggested.

"What? With this?"

"Yes. Unless you have a more effective method of prying open industrial strength padlocks."

Asher inserted the prongs into the keyhole. Nothing happened, and he looked up at me. "I don't know how it functions."

"Let me see. Perhaps there's a trigger or something."

He rose to his feet, and the prongs suddenly crackled, shooting sparks towards my face. I threw my hands up and took a step backwards. "Astrid?"

I waved my hand at him. "Be careful with it, Ash."

"I'm trying. I can't figure out how it works. Are you hurt?"

"No. Put it down."

He sighed, tossing the wand aside and bending down to examine the lock again. "It doesn't appear to have done anything."

"Perhaps it takes a moment to spark."

"Obviously." Asher considered the lock for a long moment.

He glanced up as quick, sharp footsteps rustled the leaves behind us. I spun, and my stomach sank as Julius approached us, his expression stony. "Bray informed me you were out here," he said coolly. "You should be inside. As you know, it isn't safe."

Asher straightened abruptly, crossing his arms over his chest. His expression was as austere as Coffin's as he faced him. "For what was Reinhart looking in this cellar, Professor Coffin?"

Julius' eyebrows drew together. "I couldn't possibly know what was going through his mind, Agent Key, but it appears he was attempting to destroy my property and trespass in areas forbidden to my guests."

Asher lifted his chin and opened his mouth to retort, but I stepped forwards. "Julius, how is Morgan?"

Julius sighed, turning towards me. "He is resting."

"Can you do anything for him?"

"I am unsure at this time what is ailing him. I am trying to discover it." He sighed, scowling at Asher. "I should be in there with my patient rather than ensuring my rogue guests are remaining out of harm's way."

"And not trespassing upon your private chambers?" I asked cheerfully.

He turned his frown on me. "Just so, Mrs Darby. Now, if you will please return to the house."

We did not move, and I crossed my arms over my chest. "Have you any idea what attacked Morgan, Professor?" I asked.

"If you are asking whether I believe it was, as he said, a vampire, I assure you I am a man of science, not mythology."

"You have spent much of your time with savages and primitives in the wilderness," I replied. "You have developed none of their mystical thinking?"

"I have seen many things, Mrs Darby. But I have seen nothing that could not be explained away by science. There is another explanation."

I lifted an eyebrow. "And what do you think it is, exactly?"

His jaw set. "I am doing my best to find out, and I ask that you not continue to detain me. Lunch will soon be served. I suggest you return to the house."

* * *

"I am unable to determine if we have actually learned anything of use or not," I remarked, striding beside Asher towards the guest chambers.

He frowned. "Of course we have. Reinhart was attacked for trying to get into the cellar. I have been right all along; we must get inside."

I chuckled, but I cut off abruptly when Xander barrelled around a corner, nearly colliding with us. "Oh," he said, blinking in surprise. "I've been looking for you."

"So we see. What is it, Xander?" I asked, raising my eyebrows. "Has Morgan come around?"

"No. I'm afraid not, but I have been in with him, watching the professor attend him."

"Really? He allowed it?" Asher asked, caught out.

"What do you make of it, cousin?" I added.

"I am thoroughly convinced Morgan was not attacked by a vampire."

Asher snorted. "Well, yes. We had worked that out on our own."

"But what did attack him, Xander? Has Julius any idea?"

Xander's eyes glittered, and he nodded keenly. "He's been poisoned."

"Poison?"

"Venom, actually."

"Venom?" Asher repeated, frowning. "From a snake?"

"The puncture is a snake bite?" I added.

Xander shook his head. "No, I don't think so. It's possible they were caused by a hypodermic needle."

"There are two marks. Like fangs."

Xander nodded. "Or made to look like fangs. It is snake venom, all right; the symptoms are unmistakable, but there are no venomous snakes indigenous to this area."

I considered. "Morgan was poisoned with snake venom."

Xander inclined his head. "I believe so, yes. But there is no tissue damage to suggest a snake actually bit him."

"So where did the venom come from?" Asher asked.

"I don't know. It is possible to milk the venom and store it."

"You think someone injected him with snake venom to make it appear as if a snake bit him."

"Or a vampire."

"Or simply to cause confusion," Asher mused. He looked at Xander. "Knightly, you must not mention this to anyone."

"Of course I would not."

I lifted an eyebrow. "Not even Juliana, Xander."

He shook his head. "I understand. I would not wish to distress her with elaborate treacheries potentially committed by her own father."

"Not at least until we can prove it was he--or someone else--and to what end."

"Surely it was he," Asher put in, scowling. "Or his man, Mr Bray. It is as if the storm cellar door possesses a trip alarm; they were upon us instantly."

"In any case, you may be assured of my silence. I am most concerned with Morgan's recovery, and I am as eager as you to discover the culprit."

I considered. "Asher and I will attempt to discover if the venom is being stored in the house. If we can find it, we can learn who used it to poison Morgan."

Xander nodded. "You are sure it is the professor who is responsible for all this?"

"You are not?" Asher demanded, scowling. "Surely you have come round to our point of view by now. I do not understand all this uncertainty."

Xander sighed. "Juliana speaks so highly of him."

"Well, of course she does. She is compelled to do," Asher snapped. "She will not see him as a villain; he is her father. She loves him."

"Surely she does, but she is not ignorant to our purpose here. She is very bright. Very bright indeed."

"Yes, she is," I said firmly. "And so we must be cautious of her, Xander. We cannot allow your attachment to her to cloud our judgment on the matter."

"I would never allow such a thing," Xander replied indignantly. "Astrid, you know me better than to think."

"I have the utmost faith, dear cousin."

"Is there an antidote to the poison?" Asher demanded.

"An anti-venom. Yes. But I do not have the necessary ingredients nor a laboratory to manufacture one. Indeed, we would require the venom itself to determine the appropriate counteragent," Xander explained grimly.

I considered. "Is there a way to manufacture one without the venom?"

"Perhaps. I could research anti-venoms. Perhaps I could formulate something that will replicate the affects. The professor has offered me access to the lab; I could simply attempt to use it without him discovering what I am up to."

I nodded. "If anyone can replicate a counteragent, I am confident it is you, cousin."

He smiled wanly and inclined his head. "I shall endeavour to solve it with haste. If you do discover the venom, bring it to me in the library at once. If I am not there, check the laboratory."

"Right." When he was gone, I looked triumphantly at Asher. "Ah, so, no supernatural creature or head hunters, after all."

"It would appear you have, indeed, been right all along. It comes as quite a surprise."

I rolled my eyes. "Do you think it was Coffin who poisoned him?"

"Well, he does have access to hypodermic needles. But it might also have been Bray. I suspect more strongly it was his man."

"Why?"

"I do not think Coffin would have allowed Morgan to live. Why allow him to be discovered?"

I sighed. "Well, any one of us in the house might have access to needles, if we must consider every angle. We were all given leave to wander freely about the house."

"Though I hardly think it likely Chanha or Imaron Behari or their uncle is responsible." He considered. "Perhaps Madam Eliot. She does seem rather full of malice."

I chuckled. "She does seem to sustain herself almost entirely on bigotry and spite." I sighed. "We remain where we began then?"

"Well, somewhat, but our list of suspects remains firm."

"Why poison, I wonder? Or venom, as it were? It seems to make little sense. It does not at all fit the pattern of behaviour so far."

"Perhaps simply to mislead us. The symptoms are very similar to what is described in the myths about vampires and such."

"That is a very convoluted subterfuge, if that is the intention."

"Yes, but we are dealing with a very depraved individual."

"Certainly, but not a fool, obviously. Something very strange is happening here, and I believe we lack the necessary context to analyse the evidence. Could it be simply to suggest there are natural creatures upon this island that might harm a man?"

"Perhaps. Or Morgan got too close to the truth. If he had simply disappeared, it would easily have been blamed on Coffin. If it were snakes, well..."

"Yes, I can see that. Still, we lack perspective."

"Aye, so how do we place the evidence in the proper context?"

I shook my head, pressing my hand to my forehead. "I have no suggestions." He tilted his head at me, and I sighed. "Oh, but I reckon you do."

He smirked. "We must get into that basement."

"All right. Under the circumstances, I believe delicacy is no longer the thing. I am prepared to risk it."

Though we met no one on our way to the cellar who might have alerted him, Mr Bray was upon the stairs when we reached them, carrying a dish covered with a shiny metal lid. He sighed, crossing his arms over his chest as he peered up at us from the foot. "Hello, Agent Key. Mrs Darby. We seem to be running into each other quite a lot," he said wryly. "You wouldn't be thinking of sneaking down to the basement, would you?"

"Now why ever would we do such a thing, Mr Bray?" I asked blithely.

"I will not dignify that with a response, Mrs Darby. You are guests in this house. Please respect the master's wishes."

"Where are you off to, then?" Asher asked, frowning.

Mr Bray's mouth turned up in an irritated sneer, and he lifted the covered dish in his hands. "I am bringing lunch to Miss Juliana. She is feeling in ill health today."

"The same way Mr Reinhart is ill?"

Mr Bray appeared genuinely surprised by this suggestion. "No, not at all."

"How can you be sure? Do you know what ails them?"

He paused, considering the question. "Juliana's illness began nearly a year ago. Mr Reinhart's illness has had an immediate effect on his health. They seem to be entirely different ailments."

"What has caused Juliana's illness?"

I glanced at him, and for the first time, I wondered the very same thing. "I am not a doctor, Agent Key."

"Your master is."

"I'm afraid he's seen no cause to medically train me, as well."

"Yet you are solely responsible for Miss Juliana's care."

"Not solely. I am instructed by my master."

I raised my eyebrows. "What are you giving her when you bring her special meals?"

He paused. "Nothing. There is no medicine to treat her illness that we are aware of. It is only a special diet recommended by the doctor. It contains nutrients and vitamins not found in a normal English diet."

Asher did not seem interested in this information, but a nagging sensation in the back of my mind suggested it was not entirely in vain. "Let us into the basement, if you please, sir."

Mr Bray scowled. "We have already spoken regarding this matter, and I have lost my tolerance for it."

"If you have nothing to hide, why will you not simply allow us a peek inside?" Asher insisted.

"It is not a matter of anything to hide. It is a matter of safety."

"We do not believe the basement is damaged, Mr Bray."

"It is not my concern what you believe, Agent Key. It is my concern to carry out my master's orders."

"And you do so to the letter, I shouldn't wonder," I remarked.

Bray lifted his chin. "Yes, I do."

"If you will not let us into the room, we will find a way in ourselves," Asher told him resolutely.

Bray smirked. "You are welcome to try. Now, if you don't mind terribly, I must deliver Juliana's lunch."

We stepped aside to allow him to pass us, his head held high. When he was gone, Asher turned to me with a smile. "You heard the man. We are welcomed to try."

I lifted my eyebrows. "I suspect it will not be as simple as you expect."

"That is not going to stop me, I assure you."

* * *

I leaned against the stone wall of the corridor outside the cellar door. "Do you intend to give up any time in the near future?" I asked dryly. "I am growing increasingly bored."

Asher ignored me, bending down to squint at the lock once more. "I have never seen its like. I don't know that even your man Reinhart could have constructed a lock so impenetrable."

I sighed. "But perhaps he has constructed an instrument that might penetrate such an impenetrable lock."

Asher blinked and straightened, fumbling in his jacket for Morgan's pronged wand. "I am not certain I can wield it."

"Just don't wield it in my general direction."

He pressed the prongs into the large, thick lock and waited. It sparked. "Aha!" When he bent down, however, he sighed.

"Ineffective, then?"

Asher scowled. "This is unproductive." He lifted his eyebrows at me. "I don't suppose you have Nathaniel's particular pistol?"

"Of course not," I replied, offended. "We're on holiday."

"We aren't on holiday. This is a job! You did not think to bring it with you? You are never without it."

"I most certainly am. Not every occasion calls for a handheld death ray."

"You did not think this one did?"

"I saw no particular need o carry such an item on this trip. I did not expect to require it. Besides, we can't exactly go round disintegrating doors while you are on administrative leave from the Ministry of Defence. You'd be sacked for certain then, and I do not fancy the gaol or transportation."

He sighed. "All right. Yes, you're probably right. But that doesn't mean I'm happy about it."

"You aren't alone in that sentiment, I assure you."

He fell against the wall beside me with a frustrated sigh. "What now, then, Astrid?"

I considered a long moment. "We must discover the venom. Or the needles that pricked him, at the very least. Xander is looking for a counteragent, but he would have a much easier time if we could provide the actual poison."

Asher nodded. "All right."

"First I'd like to look in on Morgan to inquire if there's been any change."

He nodded, launching himself off the wall and offering his hand. I raised my eyebrows, but I took it, allowing him to escort me to Morgan's room. I knocked lightly upon the door and pushed it open, peering gingerly into the room. Xander was alone, sitting in the chair beside Morgan's bed. "Xander. I did not expect to see you."

He turned towards us, smiling grimly. "Nor I you."

"Have you found anything?"

"No. You?"

"I'm afraid not. We've been at the basement door for the last several moments. How is he?"

I moved inside the room, perching upon the edge of the bed beside my pale, unconscious friend. Asher leaned against the wall behind me. "He is not better, but he is not worse," Xander replied, sighing. "Which is the best to hope for at this stage, with no counteragent. You had no success attempting to gain access to the basement?"

"No," Asher replied flatly.

Xander raised his eyebrows. "To what purpose are you so keen to penetrate it?"

"Asher believes whatever is behind that door is the key to discovering what is truly happening on this island."

"I can't imagine what you think might be behind it."

"I have several ideas, but there is no way to know until we are able to get inside."

"There is nothing in there."

His tone was so certain, I blinked. "How do you know?"

"Juliana told me so."

"If there is nothing behind the door, why are Bray and Coffin working so hard to protect it?"

Xander sighed. "That is a reasonable point."

Asher opened his mouth to continue, but the door banged against the wall, drawing our attention. Julius stood in the doorway, grinning. I shot to my feet. "What is it, Julius?"

"I think I have discovered the source of Mr Reinhart's ailment," Julius announced.

I glanced at Xander, who rose to face the doctor. "What is it?" Xander asked carefully.

"It is poison."

I raised my eyebrows, and my gaze slid to Asher. He straightened, and his expression was perfectly impassive. "What sort of poison?"

"I am most convinced it is snake venom."

"But how can he have been poisoned by a venomous snake?" Asher demanded. "There are no vipers indigenous to the island."

"No, but they do occasionally make it to our shores."

"You think a snake bit him?" I said.

"No. I do not."

We were silent a moment. "Then how do you reckon he was poisoned with snake venom, Julius?" I asked dryly.

Julius sighed, lowering his head a moment, then he looked up, into our faces. "I believe the wounds on his neck are the result of two punctures produced by two separate needles."

I blinked. "Two?"

"Yes, two. Needles of a sort, anyway."

"From where did the needles come?"

Julius hesitated. "Savages."

It was the last thing I had expected him to say. "What?" I said, completely caught out.

He sighed. "We are not alone on this island, Astrid. There is a tribe of savages who inhabit it with us."

131

My jaw dropped, and I snapped it shut, lifting my chin. "There really are head hunters?" Asher said dubiously.

"Yes. I'm afraid there are."

"Then why have you been keeping it such a secret all this time?" I asked.

Julius shook his head. "I did not wish to frighten anyone, but this incident is very characteristic of our interactions with them thus far. They might have used blow darts or another device to poison him from afar."

"With snake venom," Asher added.

"Yes, of course, Agent Key. They are savages. They hardly possess the knowledge and necessary equipment to create complex chemical compounds. The venom is naturally occurring and is very effective."

I frowned. "They must be very prodigious marksmen."

"They are indeed, Astrid. They are especially skilled."

"Have you actually seen these savages?" Asher asked.

"Signs of them," Julius replied. "Glimpses in the trees, but I have never faced them or I too would likely not be here today. We have managed to form a symbiotic existence on the island."

I considered, my brow furrowing. "Could it possibly have been one of them upon whom Mr Behari came across in the forest yesterday?"

Julius inclined his head. "I suspect it might have been. Or it might simply have been in his mind. When one has adrenaline pumping through his veins and an unfamiliar weapon in his hand, the mind plays interesting tricks."

"That aside," Asher put in, "if there is a tribe of head hunters on the island, why did we not see a sign of them when we searched the island?"

"They are clever and skilled at concealment," Julius told him. "They might have been there all the time, watching from the trees and bushes."

"But why not attack any of us?"

"They had no reason to attack. We had not discovered them or disturbed their habitat."

"And where might that be?"

"I haven't located it."

I sighed. "Then why would they attack Reinhart? What purpose could it possibly serve?"

"We have yet to determine exactly what he was doing out there on the grounds that night. Perhaps he came upon them or neared one of their hidey holes."

"But he was on your land."

"Yes, he was, but there is no indication that was where he was attacked. He might have crawled there from wherever the attack occurred."

I considered this a long moment, my mind racing confusedly. Head hunters, indeed? It mattered little to me at the point, however. "So you can cure Morgan?"

"Yes. I believe I can. I am confident he will make a full recovery."

I nodded. "Ace. We'll leave you to it, then."

"Thank you."

Morgan moaned suddenly, and I turned to him, gripping his hand as a convulsion seized him. I looked at Julius earnestly. "Please. Hurry."

"Of course, Astrid. If you'd all leave me to my work."

"Yes. Asher, Xander, come."

Julius' voice stopped me at the door. "I ask that you not share this information with the others. There are already in fear. It would do little good to incite more concern than is strictly required."

"I wonder how much concern is strictly required," Asher muttered, but I nodded to Julius, dragging Asher from the room.

"Head hunters?" Asher demanded incredulously when we had closed the door to my chambers.

I scowled, dropping gracelessly onto the bed. "Well, Asher, you must admit it would explain everything that has happened since we arrived. The carvings, the bones, the disappearing servants, all of it."

"Of course it would!" he growled. "It is a very convenient explanation. Just plausible enough to mislead us, but that does not explain the missing convicts in England."

"No, it does not explain that," I murmured. "Though that too could be attributed to other coincidences."

"Such as?"

"Escape, simply."

Asher shook his head. "Are you leaving my side, Astrid?"

"No. Of course I'm not. I'm merely entertaining the possibility of other explanations."

"Well, don't spend too much time entertaining. We have work to do."

I sighed. "Of course."

"On the bright side," Xander said tentatively. "We are no longer pressed to discover a cure for Morgan on our own. He is in the doctor's hands now. He has identified the poison."

"But if he is the one who poisoned him, can we trust him to save Morgan?" Asher said.

"I do not think he would offer any explanation if he intended to let him die," I replied.

Asher scowled. "Perhaps the entire point was to introduce the confusion of a charade, claiming the existence of savages, and feign innocence by rescuing Morgan from certain death."

"You are so cynical," I complained.

"Madam, I am an agent of the Ministry of Defence. I have seen much to jade me."

* * *

Despite the sombre mood of the dinner party, Julius was cheerful when he sat down to the evening meal. He attacked his food voraciously, turning to us with a wide, triumphant smile. "I am delighted to inform you all that I was able to determine the nature of Mr Reinhart's ailment and offer an antidote. He should experience a full recovery very soon."

"By the time the airship arrives to return us home?" Sophie asked hopefully.

Julius nodded to her. "He may not be completely up to snuff, but he will be much improved. A bit of bed rest when he arrives home will do him very well, I am sure."

"You must be very reassured, Mrs Darby," Imaron Behari said.

"I am very pleased, indeed, to hear such news. I am most relieved Julius was able to discover the cure," I said, inclining my head.

"Was it as the man said?" Imaron asked, his full, sensual mouth twisted into a smirk. "Was it truly a vampire who attacked him?"

"Imaron, no one believes in vampires," his sister said irritably. "It is utterly ridiculous."

"But something attacked him, didn't it? Something is out there on the island with us." Imaron smiled at Julius, and his tone was playful when he said, "I demand to know precisely what that is."

Asher lifted an eyebrow. "Are you concealing things from your guests, professor?" he asked in a low, even voice.

Julius's glance was sharp. "As I have said, there are many dangerous creatures on the island. If Mr Reinhart ran afoul of them..."

"And the others? Did they, too, run afoul of these dangerous creatures?" Chesley asked.

"It is impossible to say what became of them, as they were never discovered," Julius replied woodenly. "But it is a most likely explanation."

"Dangerous creatures, indeed," Leticia Prosser said, lifting her chin. "And what, pray, might those actually be? What precisely do you expect caused the wounds in the man's neck?"

Julius considered a long moment, then opened his mouth to speak. Whatever he intended to say was cut off by Juliana's unexpected eruption of hysterical laughter. Our heads swivelled to her in astonishment. "Juliana!" Xander exclaimed.

The young woman seemed unable to cease the outburst, and she gasped desperately for breath. Julius shot abruptly to his feet, overturning his chair. "Elijah!" he shouted, reaching to seize his daughter's shoulders.

Mr Bray appeared, looking alarmed. "Juliana."

"Take her to her room at once," Julius ordered. "I will be there to attend her."

Bray nodded, grasping Juliana' shoulders and leading her towards the door. Xander rose to watch, his eyes glittering with agitation. Juliana lost her footing in the doorway, and her legs buckled beneath her. Xander leapt forwards, sweeping her up into his arms. Bray glanced at Julius anxiously, but the professor nodded curtly, and Bray led Xander out the door.

When they had gone, we looked at Julius in shock. "Well, I...I hope you will not fault my daughter for her inappropriate outburst," he said in a low, wavering voice.

"But what is the matter with her?" I demanded. "Is it another symptom of her ailment?"

"I am afraid it is. She is often overcome with outbursts of this nature. If you will excuse me, I must attend to her at once."

We watched him go, caught out by the abrupt shift in the mood. Chanha Behari leaned across the table towards us. "Agent Key," she began. "You are an agent of the Ministry of Defence."

"I am indeed, but I cannot fathom what that might have to do with Miss Juliana's ailment," he replied warily.

"No, no. Of course it hasn't anything to do with it. But what do you make of all this?"

"I am not entirely sure to what you refer, Miss Behari."

"Well, to the entire situation, of course: the missing servants, your man's attack, the mystery of the island. Have you anything to offer by way of insight?"

Asher sighed. "I regret I do not. The circumstances are as mysterious as I have ever encountered."

"Could it really have been some animal that attacked Mr Reinhart?" Sophie asked.

"Animal?" Chesley repeated, frowning in confusion.

"Well, Julius did say dangerous creatures. I assumed he meant some sort of animal," she replied.

Chanha brightened. "A snake, perhaps. You saw the punctures on his neck, yes?"

"No, I did not see them, but I did hear of them. He was taken away so quickly I was unable to see them for myself," Sophie replied.

"A snake," Imaron mused. "Yes, it is certainly possible. Of course. The marks, the venom. It all makes such perfect sense, doesn't it?"

"The island is clearly extremely dangerous," Madam Eliot announced. "We must remain indoors, as Julius insisted from the very beginning. As I have been stating clearly myself, haven't I, Sophie?"

"You have, Aunt, yes."

"Your man, too, perhaps, Eugene, fell victim to the killer snake," Chesley told Mr Ellis.

"Yes," Mr Ellis replied dully. "It could only have been."

I glanced at Asher, and his expression was stony. "There are certainly many theories, anyway," he muttered.

Chanha lifted her eyebrows. "You do not credit the theory of a venomous snake, Agent Key?" she asked.

"Oh, it is surely a most obvious and convenient explanation. It must certainly be given due consideration," he replied reasonably.

"But what else can it be?"

Asher smiled, shaking his head. "Nothing. Nothing at all. Indeed, it is the most logical. I am certain the explanation lies thereabouts."

"And so an anti-venom may be given to your man, Mrs Darby," Sophie said cheerfully. "And he will be right as rain in no time."

"Indeed, Sophie," I replied, smiling. "I am certain Mr Reinhart will experience a full recovery, as Julius has assured me."

Despite Juliana's peculiar outburst, dinner was a pleasant affair, and the grimness that had plagued our party since the disappearance of Mr Ellis' man seemed to have lifted slightly. Upon Imaron's suggestion, we retired to the drawing room after our meal for wine, cards and much easier conversation than any in which we had engaged since the onset of all the strangeness.

Asher seemed unable to enjoy the leisure time however, and he rose abruptly from the settee, placing his untouched wine upon the side table. "You will forgive us, but Astrid and I must excuse ourselves," he announced, and I glanced at him, my eyebrows lifted. He nodded to me, and I sighed, placing my half-empty glass beside his and rising to my feet.

"Oh, but will you not join us for a short time?" Chanha Behari asked, her lovely features drawn in disappointment. "The night is young."

"Yes. The night is young, indeed," Imaron said, smiling. "Perhaps we could organise another murder mystery game. That was highly agreeable at the last."

"It was indeed, but I am afraid Mrs Darby and I have particular business to which we must attend," Asher replied, bowing slightly at the waist.

"But what business could you possibly have?" Chanha asked reasonably. "This is a holiday."

Asher smiled roguishly at her, and I rolled my eyes. "Perhaps I will return shortly to join you for a game of cards and agreeable conversation."

Chanha blushed prettily, and inclined her head. Safely out of their hearing in the corridor, I snorted. "Pray tell, Ash, what was that all about?"

"I was merely wishing not to disappoint the young lady."

"Not Chanha. Why have you dragged me out of what promised to be the first pleasant free moments we've had in some time?"

"We haven't time for pleasant free moments, Astrid." He seized my arm, marching me away from the drawing room. "What is Coffin playing at now? If the explanation was as simple as the snake attack he suggested to the other guests, why insist upon misleading us with the story of savages?"

"Well, he did not exactly suggest it was a snake. He insinuated it was exotic creatures; that could refer to savages. It was the rest of the party who extrapolated."

"In any case, there are too many lies and mysteries about at present. Shall we attend to the basement door once more, while they are otherwise occupied?"

I sighed. "Why do I feel as though we continue to engage in nothing but ineffectual efforts?"

"Astrid, we have nothing else!"

"All right, all right. Perhaps Xander can assist in discovering how to use Reinhart's dingus. It is possible we have been wielding it incorrectly."

"I think perhaps young Xander is more concerned with the health of the lady at present."

"Yes, as I suppose he should be. Speaking of health, I would like to look in once more on Morgan."

He sighed. "Yes, of course. Would you care for my company?"

"It will not be necessary. You attend to your mysterious door. I will send Xander forthrightly if he is able to leave his lady's side."

"Right." He inclined his head curtly and spun on his heel, striding smartly away.

When he was gone, I sighed and turned towards the stairway. Reinhart was alone when I arrived in his room. I was relieved to see his colour had much improved since last I had laid eyes upon him, and his slumber seemed untroubled. I smiled, sitting in the chair beside him.

"You're looking much improved, Morgan," I told him favourably. "I really

138

haven't any idea why someone poisoned you, but I assure you, I intend to learn who has done and exact swift justice. When you awaken again, your assistance will be most appreciated."

I sighed, brushing his roguish fringe from his face. "I do hope the doctor has given you the proper counteragent. Whatever caused this, we aren't entirely certain it wasn't him. It is a great gamble allowing the suspect to administer the cure. But Julius is, if nothing else, a very good doctor, despite all. He attends quite carefully to Juliana."

I leaned back against the curved winged back of the chair, considering the young woman for a long moment. "There is something dreadfully wrong with the girl," I mused aloud, and if Morgan heard my words, his restful face gave no indication. "I fear she is not long for the world, and our dear Xander has grown quite unfortunately attached. No one is too young for a broken heart, Morgan, but I had hoped he might live a bit longer without experiencing it. I only wish we could determine the cause of the girl's illness."

I straightened abruptly, smiling down at him. "But it is beside the point at the moment, isn't it?" I patted his hand reassuringly "I am most anxious for your quick recovery, my old friend."

I rose, smoothing my pale blue skirts. "At present, Asher and I have a mystery to solve and a door to break down. I don't suppose you informed my young cousin how to use your extraordinary dingus?" I smiled slightly when he failed to respond. "Right, then. Well, we'll do our best."

I stepped from the room, pulling the door quietly closed behind me. I turned towards Juliana's quarters, but it seemed I was not the first to have thought of it; I heard sharp, rapid footsteps moving in the same direction in the corridor ahead. I followed the noise, but though I expected to find Xander in the hall, when I arrived at Juliana's door, the corridor was empty. I lifted my hand to knock, but before my fist fell upon the thick, wooden door, I heard a door slam in the adjoining room.

Lifting an eyebrow, I moved towards the neighbouring door. From inside the room, I heard an angry grumble and, interested, pressed my ear to the door to listen. "Her condition has worsened, sir." The even timbre of the voice was unmistakably Mr Bray's, and I held my breath, listening for more.

"You think I haven't noticed?" Coffin growled. "I am aware of it."

"The treatments you have proposed seem to be having no effect on her recovery, not anymore. The illness continues to progress; we cannot hope to continue this way."

"I must do what I can to prolong the incubation period! You are my servant, Elijah. You do as I order."

Bray sighed. "Yes, sir, but I am also your friend. And I must protest continuing this course. Juliana should be sent to a special treatment clinic."

"She is unaware of the nature of her illness. I cannot allow others to poke and prod my daughter!"

"But, sir--"

"Enough, Elijah! She is my daughter, and it is my decision." The swift click of his heels suggested one of the men was pacing inside the room. "This holiday was a mistake. I had hoped that the peace and the sea air would do Juliana some good, but it has only put her in more danger."

"You should not have allowed Astrid Darby and Agent Key to accompany us on our journey," Bray said. "It is most incomprehensible, sir. To what end did you invite them?"

"I did not invite Agent Key! Mrs Darby has never accepted an invitation, and in the spirit of my relationship with her late husband, Nathaniel, I was compelled to continue to extend the hospitality. It would have been the height of bad manners to deny them when it was I who bade them join us."

"But can we not simply be rid of them?"

"You know, of course, we cannot. We must endure and make every effort to keep our secrets hidden."

For a moment, the room was silent, and I pressed myself closer against the door. "I did not anticipate the cunning of their associate," Coffin continued after a long pause. "Nor did you, I expect, Elijah."

"Sir, I am most ashamed."

"How did he survive?"

"I did not anticipate his preparedness. He injected himself with some sort of syringe."

Coffin seemed to be considering this, for he did not speak again for another pause. "That would explain how slowly the venom has taken affect."

"But why have you administered him the anti-venom? You could simply have allowed the poison to eventually take effect. It would have done its work in time."

"It was unavoidable," Coffin snapped. "I would have appeared both dreadfully incompetent, which I am not, or highly suspicious having allowed Mrs Darby's man to die." I heard Bray sigh, but Coffin continued. "Our only option is to keep him sedated, at least until a suitable alternative can be discovered."

I blinked, fluttering my hand across my forehead. Inside the room, I heard a shuffling noise, and Coffin spoke again from the other side of the room. "Please, Elijah. Leave me with my daughter. I fear I will have little time left to spend with her, and I find I cherish it more and more, even as she lays unable to realise I am beside her."

"Yes, sir." His footsteps moved towards the door before which I stood, and I backed quickly away, casting about for a suitable hiding place. I ducked into the room behind me. It was strewn with a woman's effects, and I absently assumed it to be Chanha's. I pressed my ear to the door, waiting until Bray's footsteps faded away down the corridor.

When they had, I scurried from Chanha's disordered chambers, moving as quietly as possible past Juliana's door. When I rounded the corner, however, I raced for Asher's door, rapping sharply upon it. He did not respond, and nor did Xander when I knocked upon his. Still in the basement, then, attempting to break down the door. I prayed Bray would not discover them, despite his taunt earlier in the day; the man was a dangerous and treacherous foe. I did not relish the idea of him coming upon Xander and Asher in the act of the break in.

I discovered them before Bray, gratefully, and they looked up at me in shock when I pelted down the stairs to find them standing silently side by side, considering the locked cellar door. "What is it, Astrid?" Asher asked, startled.

Xander strode forwards to meet me at the foot of the stairs, his eyebrows drawn together in concern. "Astrid?"

"I have much to tell you," I said breathlessly. "I have heard many interesting murmurs through the walls."

"Murmurs through the walls?"

"Come. We must go somewhere we cannot be overhead."

CHAPTER NINE

"What is it, Astrid?" Asher demanded, perching on the edge of my bed as I paced before them, extremely troubled.

Xander sat on the desk chair, peering at me keenly. "While in search of you, Xander, I came upon the master and servant having a very heated discussion."

"Coffin and Bray?" Asher asked.

"Yes, of course Coffin and Bray."

"What was the discussion regarding?" Xander asked.

I apprised them forthrightly. When I had finished my tale, I allowed them a moment of astonishment. "I believe there is something more afoot here than a man who makes a sport of hunting men," I said.

Xander's focus seemed to have fallen on other matters. "Is Juliana truly so unwell?"

"I am sorry, Xander. Her father does not believe she is improving."

Asher rose to his feet to pace beside me. "It was Bray after all who attacked Reinhart. "

"Yes, it was indeed. I find I am actually quite astonished."

Asher nodded slowly. "In truth, as am I. I suspected his involvement, but it is something else entirely to have confirmation."

"Clearly Morgan had gotten close to discovering something. Or did discover it."

"But what?"

"The key to it all, I am certain," I replied. "It was a desperate act, indeed. I do not think Bray would have done if he felt he had any choice."

"What is in the basement?" Asher murmured, tapping his fingers against his chin. "Perhaps he had discovered something prior to attempting to jimmy open the cellar door."

"Or he did," Xander put in, and we turned to look at him in surprise. "They may have caught him up in the cellar and carried him up to the grounds."

"Perhaps. Julius is keeping him under sedation to keep him from telling what it was he discovered," Asher replied.

"It is most dastardly," I added indignantly.

"You say he injected himself with something?" Xander asked, his expression thoughtful.

"Yes. With something that slowed the poison. Have you any ideas what it might have been?"

Xander considered. "I could not say for certain. Morgan had many eccentricities and paranoia. He might have been carrying an anti-venom or adrenaline of some sort." His eyes slid away thoughtfully. "Most likely an adrenaline shot, since it slowed the process but did not serve as an anti-dote."

"All right." Asher glanced at me. "Do you think that could be helpful to us in some way?"

"Perhaps. And it may be helpful again."

Xander nodded slowly, understanding dawning in his brilliant blue eyes. "I will look through Morgan's things and see if I can discover something else that may be useful."

"Useful for what?" Asher demanded.

"Waking Morgan up," I replied, as though it should have been quite obvious.

"Waking him up?"

"Yes. Julius is keeping him sedated, but Morgan is cured. We must wake him so he can tell us what it was he learned that caused him to be attacked. If you would prefer to continue focussing your attention on that door, be my guest, but this might be more expedient."

"Ah." Asher was a step behind us when we rushed from the room, crossing the hall to Morgan's chambers. "Do we actually have his personal items?"

"Of course. He would not have allowed us to leave them unattended in the servants' quarters," Xander replied, scooping up Morgan's rucksack from the floor beside the bed in which the engineer still slept peacefully. "Someone might have been harmed."

I snorted, taking the seat beside Morgan whilst Xander rifled through his effects. The floor was soon a jumble of ominous-looking, incomprehensible gadgets, copper wires, clockworks, gears, tubes, goggles, a soldering gun, tools, and bottles of suspiciously glowing substances. "Xander?" I demanded, rolling my eyes.

He shook his head, gesturing at the heap of syringes and corked bottles before him. "It could be any of these. If we inject him with the wrong liquid, it might kill him rather than wake him."

"But you are an avid student of chemistry. You cannot identify them?" I asked, disappointed.

"I am a student of chemistry, not medicine. These are not base elements. They're compounds. It would take a lab and extraction tools to learn what each of these are."

I sighed. "We do not have the time for such delicate work."

"It may be our only option if you intend to use one of these to bring him from his sedation." Xander sighed. "At least we have a laboratory."

"How long will that take?" Asher demanded.

"It depends upon what sort of equipment I can find in the lab. And whether the professor will allow me unrestrained access. If he has become suspicious of my intentions, he may attempt to forbid me."

"It might be best to keep him in ignorance."

Xander frowned, holding the bottles up to the light as though they may reveal their ingredients to him. "Still, someone with medical training might well be able to identify them."

Asher and I exchanged a glance. "Medical training, you say?" I said shrewdly.

Xander looked up at us, his expression completely bemused. "What?"

"Juliana, of course," Asher replied.

"I don't understand."

"She has grown up at the knee of one of the premier doctors in Britain," I said. "I suspect she might be adept at identifying healing medicines, yes?"

He hesitated, his brow furrowing. "She is not well, Astrid. She may not even be awake." He glanced away. "And she should not be involved in this campaign against her father."

"Xander, we may have no other chance to ascertain what is happening before it is too late, we lose Morgan or someone else goes missing," I replied heatedly.

He sighed deeply. "All right. I will engage her assistance. If she is awake." He rose to his feet, tucking the bottles into his waistcoat pocket. "Otherwise, it's to the lab for me. I will, however, do my best to persuade her."

"She need not know why you ask."

He smiled. "She is clever, and she is inquisitive. She will not be easily put off."

"Well, you know her best of us, and you are the cleverest young man I know. I am sure you will find a way to engage her assistance without the unnecessary unburdening of you inner knowledge of her father's sinister activity."

Xander smirked, but he inclined his head before spinning smartly and striding from the room. I glanced at Asher. "This does not seem like the best idea we've ever had, Astrid," he said glumly.

"No. But I have had much, much worse ideas indeed. At least in this case, there is very little risk anyone is going to be caught in the crosshairs of a death ray or destroy a beloved national treasure."

"Yes, you really do have some awful ideas."

* * *

Xander met us in the hall outside Juliana's chambers. He appeared pluckier than he had since the young lady's outburst at dinner, and I smiled at him. "Juliana is awake," he announced.

"How is she?" I asked.

"She is not well, but she is improved. She is still experiencing tremors, but she is no longer laughing."

I sighed. "That was dreadfully peculiar."

"Yes, any ideas what might cause such behaviour?" Asher asked, crossing his arms over his chest to lounge against the wall.

"None at all," Xander replied unhappily. "And she is equally at a loss, I'm afraid."

I considered. "Do you believe her father truly knows what is ailing her?"

"Perhaps. At least, he's prescribed a special treatment regimen. It seems he has some idea."

I was silent a long moment. "It seems more and more as if all of this has to do with Juliana."

"What do you mean?" Asher asked, turning to me in surprise.

"But how?" Xander added.

I shook my head. "I've no idea. Is she willing to help us?"

"I have not been able to speak with her regarding Morgan's tonics. Bray is inside with her."

"Where is Julius?"

"Not with her. Nor with Morgan."

"Is she strong enough to aid us?" Asher asked delicately.

"Yes, I think she will be."

"We must ask her assistance as soon as she is up to it." Asher's tone was still careful, but his eyes glittered keenly.

"Yes. Of course. I am eager to assist in Morgan's recovery."

Juliana's door creaked open, and Mr Bray strode out of the room. We spun to face him, and he paused in the hall, eyeing us shrewdly. He inclined his head as he approached us. "Miss Juliana is asking to see you, Mr Knightly," he said mildly. "You may go in." He glared at Asher and me. "However, I must urge you not to excite or upset her in any way."

Xander glanced at me. I nodded. "You go on, Xander. We shall await you here."

He nodded. "Thank you, Mr Bray." The head servant, however, was already striding away from us towards the main staircase.

I glanced at Asher. "Do you think she will be able to help?" he asked.

I lifted a shoulder. "I think she may. She seems very clever and also quite attached to my young cousin. I believe she will do what she can to help him."

Asher frowned. "You approve of his attachment despite the suggestion the young lady might not live much longer?"

I sighed. "Who am I to speak on ill-advised attachments?"

He lifted an eyebrow, but he did not seem to have a response to this. I was relieved when Xander peeked around the corner of the door, gesturing to us. "Juliana has agreed to help us." He ducked his head, and his cheeks coloured slightly.

I narrowed my eyes at him. "What is it, Xander?"

He gestured, disappearing once again inside the room. I glanced at Asher, and we strode forwards side by side to meet Juliana. She was sitting up in bed, and though she still looked pale and her shoulders trembled slightly, she smiled. "Hello, Mrs Darby. Agent Key."

"You are looking much better, Juliana," I told her.

She waved her hand, but her smile did not waver. "I appreciate your kindness, but I have seen a looking glass. I know what state I am in." She gestured towards the bottles and syringes spread across her counterpane. "Mr Reinhart has quite the collection."

I glanced at Xander archly, and he ducked his head. "Can you determine what the substances in the bottles are?" I asked Juliana.

"Several different things. I am not entirely certain they aren't illicit intoxicants of some sort, but it is hardly my place to judge."

I smirked, and Asher rolled his eyes. "I should have expected as much, I suppose," he muttered.

"Xander tells me your purpose is to wake Mr Reinhart from sedation."

I crossed my arms over my chest, shaking my head at Xander. He shrugged sheepishly. "She is most persuasive."

"Why is it you wish to wake him up? Xander will not tell me."

I considered. "We wish to find out what happened to him. To ensure it will not happen again to another. If it truly was a snake bite or..."

"Or head hunters?" Juliana asked shrewdly.

I raised my eyebrows. "You are aware of the possibility?"

"Yes. My father has tried to hide it from me, but I have heard him talking with Elijah. The only explanation for their whispering is that someone else lives out here on the island." She considered. "I did not receive the impression, however, that there was more than one."

"One?" Asher asked, completely caught out.

"Yes. They speak only of a singular person."

"What have you overheard?

She smiled wanly. "Capturing him."

Asher and I turned simultaneously to each other in surprise. Were we back to the hunter theory, then? Could it be Julius and his man referred to a different quarry? There was so much confusion, I could not make heads of it.

"I, too, would wish to learn what Mr Reinhart knows," Juliana added.

"Miss, it is no such thing for a lady to be doing," Asher said indignantly.

I peered at him incredulously. Juliana's expression was equally stony. "Sir, I am not a child. I am clever, and I know my father is up to something. I want to know precisely what it is." She hesitated, sighing. "I think it might have something to do with me."

"What do you mean?"

She shook her head. "I am not certain. They speak of me often when they think I cannot hear them. I know something is terribly wrong with me, and I know my father is keeping it from me." Xander frowned, but she smiled at him wanly. "I am going to die of this ailment. I know this to be true."

"Do not speak of it, Juliana," Xander told her ardently.

"I will speak of it if I wish," she replied, her chin lifted. "It is my life, and I have the right to know what is to come of it. To form opinions about it and express them."

I inclined my head. "You do indeed, young lady."

"I will help you. But I demand to be there when Mr Reinhart awakens. I, too, want to hear of what is happening in my own house with my own father. I have a right to know."

Her voice brooked no argument, but we hesitated, glancing at each other. She lifted her chin defiantly. "It is my condition," she added.

"Absolutely not," Asher replied heatedly. "It is no thing for a young gentlewoman to be doing."

"Asher, leave off her. She is a grown woman. She deserves to know what is happening to her and around her," I told him firmly. "I would have demanded the same, were I in her position, and I will not deny her now."

"Thank you, Mrs Darby," Juliana said, smiling at me. I winked at her, and she turned her attention to the syringes in her lap. She raised one upon the palm of her hand. It was a sickly yellow colour, and it glowed slightly as though imbued with some radioactive substance. I eyed it warily. "This shot will awaken him."

"How can you be sure?" Asher asked, frowning.

"It is a synthetic adrenaline compound. It will shock his system into waking, but it is extremely dangerous," she warned, her expression grave. "It could cause more harm."

We looked at each other thoughtfully. Xander inclined his head. "Morgan would have wanted us to know what he knows. He would insist we take this risk.

The pursuit of knowledge is his greatest mission."

I sighed. "I fear you are absolutely right, Xander."

* * *

Morgan's sleep was uninterrupted by convulsions or fits, and I sighed, brushing his fringe from his forehead. "Are you sure this is the best course of action?" I murmured, frowning. I peered down at Morgan's face.

"I do not think he will remain awake for long. The shock of waking may be worsening to his condition."

I looked up at Xander in supplication. "I do not wish for him to worsen."

"He will be all right, Astrid. He is strong as an ox and ten times as surly."

I chuckled. "We must do it, Astrid," Asher said. "I will administer the injection. Juliana, hand me the syringe."

She shook her head, curling it against her chest as if to keep it from him. "It is delicate work. I shall do it. I have done it before, after all."

Asher sighed, but he gestured towards Morgan. His jaw was rigid, and I suspected he was chafing slightly under the young lady's audacity; nevertheless, I equally suspected he appreciated a brazen woman, under the right circumstances, if history could be relied upon. As she lifted the syringe, however, Juliana's hand shook violently. She closed her eyes, lowering her hand, and for a moment, it was as if she had deflated.

She looked up at Asher, however, her chin lifted proudly. "I regret I am no longer capable of performing any such delicate work, Agent Key. It is left to you, then."

Xander wrapped an arm around Juliana's shoulders, but Asher took the syringe from her, smiling. "You are still capable of instruction, I reckon, however," Asher said. "Tell me if you please how I should proceed."

She straightened. "The injection must be given in the thigh. It is the safest place, less likely to develop infection and will send the compound directly into his blood."

Asher nodded. He hesitated a moment before pushing aside Morgan's dressing gown. He glanced up at me for a split second before stabbing the needle into Morgan's leg, injecting the toxic-looking fluid. I pressed my hands to my mouth anxiously, but for several seconds, nothing happened. I held my breath, glancing up at Xander distraughtly.

Morgan's entire body jerked, startling us all, and he jolted upright in bed, glancing around with frantic, terrified eyes. When he caught sight of Xander and me, however, his entire body relaxed. "Ah. Astrid. Xander." His voice was hoarse from lack of use, but he seemed quite in control of himself.

"Morgan, I am so glad you're finally awake," I said heartily. "Do you remember what happened to you?"

He was silent for a long moment, as though attempting to recall the previous days' events. His eyes rolled to me. "I was attacked."

"Yes. We know. You said it was by a vampire," Xander told him.

Morgan blinked. "It might have been."

"Why do you say that?" Juliana asked eagerly.

His face drained of colour as he looked between us. "I saw such terrible things. Blood everywhere. Body parts."

"Is he damaged in some way?" Asher demanded.

"I don't know," Juliana admitted fretfully.

"What, Morgan? You saw dead bodies?" Xander asked incredulously.

"Bits of them." His voice lowered to a horrified whisper. "It was the most terrible thing I have ever seen."

Asher's eyes were alight with excitement, but I frowned deeply, fearing my old friend was still suffering from the delirium of the venom. "Do you know where you are, Morgan?" I asked carefully.

"Yes, of course I know where I am. On the Isle of Jules. In my own proper room, by the looks of it. Out of the servants' quarters, am I?" He frowned at me. "I am not delusional, Astrid. I saw what I saw."

"All right. Forgive me. Where did you see this?"

"The basement."

Triumph sparked in Asher's eyes, then he narrowed them. "How did you get in? " he demanded, slightly resentfully.

"The door was ajar that night. I snuck inside."

"And you really saw..." Juliana's voice trailed off.

"Blood everywhere."

"Yes, Morgan, we heard that part," I said impatiently. "And body parts?"

150

"Surely you are mistaken, Mr Reinhart!" Juliana exclaimed, her hand pressed to her chest.

Morgan gestured towards her. "Why is she here? She should not be here. She should not hear speak of such things. She is only a girl."

"I am not a girl--" Juliana began indignantly, but she cut off as Morgan winced in pain.

I pressed a hand to his chest. "It's all right, Morgan. You must rest. Lie back."

"I feel as though I have been resting for days." He made a disgusted face, sniffing at his clothes. "I smell as though I have, as well."

I smirked. "Do you remember anything else?" Asher asked.

Morgan shook his head, lowering himself carefully back onto the pillows. "Just blood. It was dark. I heard someone coming, and I fled."

"You attempted to get back into the cellar?" I guessed.

"Yes. I had not been prepared the first time to explore. I required my lantern and lock pick and..." He glanced at Juliana, then back at us, his expression guarded. "Other items. I went back but found the door locked. My lock pick was ineffective, and I attempted to find another way in."

"The storm cellar door outside," Asher said, nodding. "That was when you were attacked."

"Yes." Morgan raised his chin defiantly. "By a vampire."

I shook my head exasperatedly. "It was not a vampire," I snapped.

"What was it then?" he demanded.

Asher and I exchanged a glance, and Asher's eyes slid to Juliana. This transgression did not go unnoticed. "What was it?" she asked, glancing between us.

"Perhaps it was a snake," Xander suggested weakly.

"Do not treat me like a fool," she snapped. "I know there is something not right here."

I sighed. "It was a needle."

"He was poisoned?" Juliana exclaimed. She shook her head mournfully. "It is dreadful." She looked up at Morgan earnestly. "I am so sorry this befell you in my house, Mr Reinhart. We will learn what is going on."

Morgan sighed deeply, and his eyes began to droop. "Sorry," he murmured. "So...tired."

"Sleep, Morgan," I ordered. "It's all right. We'll be all right for a while without you."

He nodded wearily, but his eyes closed as though he were unable to hold them open any longer. He was asleep in moments. I looked up at the others, tilting my head towards the door. We rose, and I closed the door quietly behind us. Juliana spun to us as soon as we had stepped out into the corridor. "Whatever he saw down there caused this to happen to him," she said intently. "I intend to find out what it is. I intend to find out what people are hiding from me!"

"Juliana, you must not--" Xander began carefully.

"I will! I will not continue to be lied to."

"If there is blood down there, if there are bodies, it is not a thing for you to see!" Asher replied sternly, and I sensed he had reached the limits of his patience with the precocious young woman.

She stepped up to him, her chin lifted in determination. "If I am right in thinking this has something to do with me, I want to know what it is."

"This can have nothing to do with you," he told her, scowling.

"Do not treat me as though I were a child. I will go where I wish in my own home. And if you wish to do the same, you will not bar me from accompanying you." I lifted my eyebrows, my lips curving slightly into a smile. "I can get you into the basement. If you wish to see once and for all what is inside, you will have to take me along with you."

Asher blinked. "You can get inside?"

"Oh, yes. I know where the keys to every room are kept. My father believes I am unconditionally obedient, but he underestimates my inquisitiveness. Until now, it has never occurred to me to attempt to gain entrance, but I think now is the time, don't you?"

Xander's expression suggested he was impressed with her tenacity, but he shook his head. "No. We cannot allow it, Juliana. It would be irresponsible. If the place is actually damaged or dangerous, you are in no fit state to navigate it. If it is something more...your health."

She glared at him. "I am not well. It is true, but I will find the strength. You will take me along or you will continue to try ineffectually to enter the room. And I will go anyway. Without you."

Xander sighed. Asher scowled, but I smirked. "Let us go then," I said, offering a hand to Juliana. "Still, young lady, you will remain in the rear with Xander, in case there are perils."

Juliana sighed, but she nodded. "Let us just get on."

* * *

Juliana preceded us into the kitchen, her head held high, despite the delicate tremor that coursed through her entire body. There were no servants or guests within when we reached it, and the young lady sighed in relief, as though she had anticipated a confrontation. She glanced over her shoulder at us, smiling weakly.

"Have you some sort of trick to open the door we have yet to imagine?" I asked interestedly.

Juliana smirked, climbing atop a small, wooden footstool to lift a dusty pot from the shelf above the water basin. When she stepped down, she held up a large, shiny key. "No. Just the key."

"There has been a key here this entire time?" Asher asked, outraged. "And he's just hidden it under a pot?"

She lifted a shoulder. "Perhaps he believes it is safer than keeping it on his person. Or it is a spare."

"That's oddly convenient," I remarked, following them as they marched purposefully out of the kitchen towards the basement stairs.

Juliana paused in front of the door, and Asher stepped forwards to take the key from her. "With Xander, if you please, Miss Juliana."

She sighed in disgruntlement, but she nodded and stepped back towards Xander, who smiled bracingly at her. Asher looked at me, his eyebrows raised, and I nodded. "It is all come to this," I told him in a low voice. "Get on with it."

He nodded, eagerly inserting the key into the lock and twisting it with gusto. The door opened easily, swinging into a dark, yawning stairwell. Xander handed Asher a gas lamp over my shoulder. Light flooded the well-worn stone steps. "Well?" Juliana asked impatiently, attempting to peer over our shoulders.

Asher nodded sharply, descending the stairs slowly. I rolled my eyes. "Get on with it, Ash."

"Astrid, you truly know how to spoil a dramatic pause."

"This is hardly the time for dramatic pauses--"

The light fell upon the large, white-tiled room, and I nearly collided with Asher as he stopped dead on the stairs. "Xander!" Asher barked urgently. "Get her out of here now!"

"But–" Juliana protested.

Asher half turned his head. "No buts! Go!"

"No, but--" Juliana's supplications were in vain, however, for Xander guided her firmly up the stairs. We could hear her cursing him all the way towards the door.

"I'm sorry, Juliana," he said firmly. "But they would not order it if it were not important."

"Good god, Asher," I said, my voice sticking slightly in my throat.

He did not speak, for there were no words to describe the horror in which we descended. Blood spattered the walls of the otherwise white room. In the centre of the room was a large chopping block, out of which a large, gleaming butcher knife jutted, as though someone had lately stabbed it into the thick, criss-crossed wood. From the ceiling, hung from blood-soaked ropes like sides of beef, were sections of what looked to be...human limbs.

Nausea welled in my throat, but it was not the worst of the horrors in the room. Discarded in a heap in the corner of the room was a pile of raggedly chopped body parts: sections of thighs, arms, torsos and hands.

"No heads," Asher said in a low, deadened voice.

"I think they go in there." I lifted a shaky hand to point towards the large, cylindrical incinerator that filled the far corner of the room. From it, the scent of burnt flesh and hair hung in the air.

"This is a slaughter house."

"Of sorts."

I stepped further into the room, my face scrunching involuntarily in disgust. Blood ran in rivulets across the floor, towards a drain in the centre of the room beneath the chopping block. Asher knelt beside the pile of appendages, a kerchief pressed delicately to his nose and mouth. "These are fresh."

"How fresh?"

He glanced up at me, and his cobalt eyes were remarkably calm, despite the astonishment and revulsion I was certain twisted my own features. "Days. They likely belong to the missing servant."

154

"There is more than one body's worth of pieces there."

"Yes." He sighed deeply. "I don't know to whom they belong."

I shook my head slowly from side to side, pressing a hand to my roiling belly. "What are they doing in here?"

He lifted an eyebrow, rising abruptly to his feet. "Murdering people. Obviously."

"No, it is more than that."

"More than that? What more is there?"

I spun in a slow circle, my brow furrowing in consideration. Asher watched me as I bent over the irreverent heap of limbs, but I grimaced, turning quickly from it. I narrowed my eyes at the incinerator, peering inside. Asher stepped towards me, handing me his kerchief, which I gratefully pressed over my face. "There is something in there," I told him, gesturing towards the incinerator.

He frowned, moving past me to examine the twisted, blackened pile of metal in the burner. He held out his hand to me, rolling his eyes when I peered at it blankly. "The kerchief, if you please, Astrid."

"Oh. Yes. Of course." I handed it to him, straining to catch a glimpse over his shoulder of what he extracted from the incinerator. When he turned, he held it out to me. Though the metal was black and bent, it was still recognisable as jewellery. There were twisted, broken rings, a scorched cross and a clear, brilliant stone that sparkled in the stark, naked light. "These did not burn."

"Is that a diamond?"

Asher held it up to his face, squinting at it. "Blimey." He carefully wrapped the pieces in the kerchief, tucking it into his jacket. "We'll bring these to the Ministry. Perhaps they can assist in identifying the victims."

"But how many have there been?"

His expression was grim. "No way to say. Astrid, we must arrest Coffin and his man Bray at once. Surely they are both involved in this. We will have to secure them until the airship arrives, but then we will bring the full might of justice upon them."

"But why, Asher?" I demanded, troubled. "Why would they do this? It does not make sense."

"They are killers, Astrid. Their motivations rarely make sense to normal people."

"No. I am convinced there is more to all this than that." I sighed deeply and regretted the foul odour that invaded my senses when I did. "Juliana believes all this has something to do with her."

Asher frowned. "But what could it have to do with her? It matters not at this time. When we have arrested them, we will have all the time we require to extract the information from them."

"But can we not wait until we have had more time to sort this out?"

He lifted his chin. "Madam, I may be on leave, but I am still an agent of the Ministry, and I am required by law and duty to act. You may question him when I have had my say."

"And what say is that, Agent Key?"

My blood froze in my veins, and I glanced at Asher, whose expression was suddenly utterly blank. We spun towards the stairs to face Julius. His slender form filled the foot of the stairs, blocking any escape of which we may have conceived. The long, wide barrel of his rifle did not waver as he aimed it towards us. His eyes darted between us, but they were eerily serene.

Asher held up his hands, cursing vehemently under his breath, but I turned towards Julius with a speculative expression. "I see you finally succeeded in your endeavour to force entry into my private chamber. I did suspect it was only a matter of time."

Asher glared at him. "I was confident I was not misguided in my suspicions."

"Yes, you are nothing if not tenacious, Agent Key."

"What have you done, Julius?" I asked mildly. "Why have you done this?"

Julius sighed deeply, but his gun hand did not falter. "It is not for the reasons you may believe, Astrid, I assure you. I am not a killer by nature."

"Then what is all this?" Asher growled, gesturing wildly about us. "This is a slaughter house!"

"I regret my choices in the matter were rather limited."

"Limited as they may have been," I began, "how can this have possibly been the pre-eminent?"

"It was not my first, but I saw no alternative."

"You murdered all these people and chopped them up into tiny bits," Asher growled.

Julius sighed again, and his expression was grim. "You have no children, Agent Key. You could not begin to understand."

"Then clarify it for me!"

"Explanations will not alter the outcome." For a moment, he looked deeply regretful. "I am very sorry. Despite all of this, I like you very much. It is not my way to harm my friends."

"We are not friends," Asher replied coldly.

Julius smiled wryly. "Then, perhaps, it will hurt me slightly less."

"You intend to kill us?" I demanded, glaring at him.

"It is for the greatest of good, I assure you, Astrid. I would not do it if there were another way to save my Juliana."

"Juliana? What does this have to do with her?" I asked, glancing sidelong at Asher. I lifted a smug eyebrow at him, despite the dire circumstances, and he rolled his eyes.

Julius did not lower his weapon, but he dropped his head, squeezing his eyes shut for a moment. "There is so much you fail to comprehend. All your snooping about, and you have truly learned nothing."

"It is something to do with why she is ill, isn't it?" I asked keenly.

Julius grimaced, and Asher stepped towards him gingerly, as though to seize advantage of his momentary distraction. Julius was not distracted for long, however. His head snapped up, and he levelled his rifle at Asher's chest. Asher held up his hands, but Julius directed his faltering speech towards me. "Astrid..."

"I must know," I told him. "If you are to kill us anyway, I must know why you have done all this. Please."

Asher's glance was incredulous, but I ignored him. Julius' mouth turned up slightly. "If you suspect your stalling will save your life, my old friend, I assure you, there is no help coming, and there is no way out of this room." He shook his head. "I am most aggrieved. I never intended the holiday end in such an abrupt manner."

"Do you think your guests will not notice our absence?" Asher demanded.

Julius lifted an eyebrow at him. "You have been sneaking about, attempting to gain access to places in which you had no business. It would not be completely unreasonable to assume that you, as the others, were taken by exotic beasts or savages."

"There are none, are there? No head hunters, no exotic creatures," Asher said. "What you hunt are people."

"Not for sport!" Julius spat, as though Asher had said something mortally offensive. "Not for sport, I assure you. I am no such man. I am not a cold-blooded killer. I...I do not enjoy it."

"But the servants, the convicts, they all ended up here?" Asher said, gesturing around.

Julius lowered his head. "I had no choice. They were easily explained away, and most of them were not missed."

"But why?" I demanded.

For a long moment, the old professor's face crumpled, and he looked terribly, tragically sad. "I needed them. To save Juliana."

I frowned, glancing sidelong at Asher, but he seemed as perplexed as me. "I regret I cannot fathom of what you are talking, Julius."

"Juliana does not know what ails her. She does not understand what has happened to her."

"But what has happened to her?"

As so many others before him, Julius seemed relieved to unburden himself, as though confession might lessen the horror of his sins and of his intentions. "Her ailment began after we left the island of Papua New Guinea."

Asher frowned, blinking in confusion. "Where you lived with a tribe of savages?"

"Yes, savages indeed they were. They had many rituals, many superstitions..."

"Vampires?" Asher asked keenly.

"No!" Julius growled, scowling. "This has nothing to do with vampires. They are a ridiculous myth. There is something much more real, much more disturbing than that."

"But what is it, Julius?" I asked, breathless in my expectancy.

"They were cannibals."

"Cannibals?"

"They feed upon human flesh."

"I know what cannibals are."

"Juliana's illness...I had seen it before, in the woman and children of the village."

"Not the men?" Asher asked.

"No, not the men. You see, when one of their own tribe is sent to their final burial, the body is feasted upon by the tribe."

"You mean..." I said, horrified. "Juliana consumed the flesh of humans?"

"It is what caused the illness from which she now suffers."

"But you have not fallen ill," Asher said.

"No, it is as I said. The men in the village remained healthy. Perhaps it is the parts of the flesh that were consumed. The women and children were fed... different parts of the body."

Asher's face contorted in revulsion. "Which parts?"

"The parts that remained when the men had finished. The less desirable parts. I was not aware of the ritual, not until it was too late, or I would have stopped it! I would not have allowed my daughter to engage in such a barbaric ritual, certainly not when she might fall ill and die of it."

"How did you learn of her condition?" I asked quietly.

Julius did not lower his weapon, but he seemed almost to have forgotten it in his grief. "When she began to grow pale, one of the village shamans visited her. He had learned some of our language, and he explained their rituals to me. I do not know why he did not stop it. I do not know why he allowed Juliana to fall ill. If he had only warned me of the ritual...but it is not their way. Their rituals are sacred. In order to remain with them in the village, we were expected to observe their customs. Had I known, I would have taken her straight away back home."

"She is unaware of all of it?" Asher asked, and for a moment, he sounded as though he sympathised with the professor.

"If she learned, she would be...well I do not know how she would react."

"But is there nothing you can do to cure her, knowing what you know of the cause?" I asked.

"I know nothing of the true nature of the illness; only its symptoms."

"She will die of it?"

"Yes, she will. Eventually."

"It is a tragic story indeed, but what has it to do with the murders of all these people?" Asher demanded.

There was horror in Julius' eyes as they focussed upon us once more. "Do you not see? I thought..."

The significance of his tale suddenly dawned upon me, and I gasped. The revelation sent a frisson of horror down my spine. "You believed if you continued to feed her human flesh, it might prolong the incubation period of the illness?"

For a moment, Julius seemed impressed with my supposition, and he nodded. "Yes. I had seen the women and children of the villages revitalised after a feast. I thought...and it did help."

"But her condition is worsening, no matter how many convicts and servants you feed her?" Asher said in disgust.

"Yes, it is worsening," he whispered.

The silence in the room upon completion of his speech was laden with despair. Even Asher seemed to have no condemnations to voice, though I suspected the young lady's tragic condition had not been sufficient to sway his opinion of Julius' actions. Though I was astonished and sickened by the revelations, I, too, found it impossible to accept Julius' justifications for his horrifying behaviour.

Julius' expression was suddenly arctic and determined. "I am sorry, Astrid, Agent Key. It is not for pleasure or sport that I do this. You see now it is for the life and health of my only daughter, my beloved Juliana."

"It is a noble motivation. However, it is still murder, Julius!" I told him indignantly. "Why did you not bring her to a specialist? Could they not help her?"

Julius shook his head vigorously. "I did not want her to learn the nature of her illness. I did not want her to know the horror I knew."

"And so you prolonged the horror. You yourself became the horror! What would she have done if she knew what you did in order to save her?"

"I would have insisted you let the illness run its course!"

The colour drained from Julius' face as he turned to Juliana, who stood upon the last stair, her face streaked with tears. "Juliana—"

"I would have insisted you let me die!" she exclaimed. "It would have been preferable to witnessing my father come to this, to learn what has been done to me all these months!"

"Juliana, please understand—"

"Xander!" I growled, glaring at my cousin, who hovered behind the young lady, his features frozen in shock. "I told you to take her out of here!"

"She escaped me," he replied unrepentantly, though his voice was subdued. "She would not hear of being kept away. I am sorry."

Juliana's sobs drowned his speech, and she stepped towards her father. "Papa, you cannot continue this. It is a terrible thing. You cannot be condemned such as this for me. I would rather die than perpetuate such a life."

Julius' expression was stricken, but he remained frozen in place, his rifle pointed towards us as Juliana moved around him to place herself between us. "Juliana, no," Julius said, his voice cracking slightly. "I cannot allow you to die. I only wished to prolong your life until I can find a cure."

"But you have found no cure, have you? All these people that have disappeared...You killed them all?" Despite the tears streaking across her face, the young lady was admirably calm, and she remained as poised as a lady of her station ought to do.

Julius quelled slightly under her reproachful stare. "My dear...I did it out of love."

She lowered her head. "I know you did, Papa. I do not doubt your devotion to me, but you must stop. You must allow Agent Key to bring you to justice. You must answer for this."

Julius scowled. "If I do it, you will not receive the care you require! You will not get well, and you will die like the women in the village! You saw how they suffered, Juliana. I would not wish this for you."

"I would prefer to suffer! You cannot kill them, not here in front of me. You must kill me as well to keep your secrets."

"All of this has been to save you!"

"And it is over now, Papa." She stepped towards him, neglectful of the weapon in his hand. She wrapped her hand around the barrel, pushing it away from us to the floor. Julius did not resist her; the rifle dropped to the floor with a soft, final thump, and tears welled in his eyes. Juliana wrapped her arms around him, murmuring softly to him as he wept upon her shoulder.

Asher moved forwards, but I laid a hand upon his arm, shaking my head. He scowled at me, but he sighed, allowing the young lady a moment with her father. When Juliana stepped away from him, she turned to us, nodding. Julius did not struggle or resist Asher as he strode forwards to bind his hands behind his back. I did not pause to wonder why the man carried shackles in his jacket pockets, but I supposed he had been anticipating this very moment since the inception of our journey. "Professor Coffin, you are under arrest for murder," Asher announced, and I admired his composure.

"I am sorry Juliana," Julius told her in a quiet, choked voice, and it was as though all the spirit and life had faded from him. "I am sorry I did not find a way to save you."

"You'll have plenty of time in the gaol to work out a cure," Asher told him mildly, guiding his prisoner towards the stairs. He turned towards me, and I saw the glint of triumph in his eyes. "I will secure the professor, Astrid, and round up Mr Bray."

I nodded, glancing towards Juliana. "I will tend to matters here." When he had marched Julius up the stairs, I strode forwards, folding the young lady into my arms. She sobbed for a long moment upon my shoulder. I patted her back. "There, there, dear."

Xander, paralysed for the moment, I suspected, by a young lady's tears, wrested Juliana from my embrace. She pressed her face against his chest, weeping with renewed verve into the crisp, clean linen of his shirt. My young cousin looked up at me in terror, and I smirked.

"Xander, take Juliana to her room. Watch over her." He nodded, and I laid my fingertips upon his arm. "Perhaps some laudanum would do the young lady some good."

Juliana lifted her head abruptly. "No. I want no drugs. No more medicine."

"It will help you sleep dear," I told her gently. "You need sleep just now."

"Come, Juliana," Xander bid softly, and she recoiled from him, as though she had just discovered him beside her.

"Can you touch me, Xander, knowing what sort of monster I am?"

His mouth lifted slightly at the corners. "It is my chest upon which you have been sobbing for the last several seconds. I did not recoil from you. You are no monster. You did not know of what happened around you."

"But my father..."

"The sins of the father are not always indicative of the nature of the daughter,"

162

I told her, smiling soothingly. "He believed he was acting to save you."

Juliana shook her head, and her eyes were bleary with tears. "It was not right."

"No, but he acted out of love. You cannot hate him for what he's done."

"I do not hate him. I am horrified."

"Rightfully," I agreed. "Accompany Xander to your room. Get some rest. Allow yourself not to think on it now."

She sighed, but she nodded, allowing Xander to lead her towards the stairs. I did not pause to consider the miseries that lay ahead of the young lady. I took one last look at the horrible room and shuddered. My step was rather swifter than could be considered strictly poised for a lady of my station, and I was deeply relieved the other guests were not available to observe my unbecoming flight. At the top of the stairs, I pulled the door closed behind me with a heavy sigh and turned the lock with a final click.

I had rarely experienced such a terrible and unsettling resolution in all my years as an adventurer, and I had never felt less satisfied with my success.

CHAPTER TEN

Juliana's reflection was drawn and pallid in the looking glass above the polished brass vanity in her chambers. She plaited her long, auburn hair carefully and sighed, meeting my eyes in the mirror as I gazed down at her, laying my hands bracingly upon her shoulders. "I must face my guests," she said in a low, resolute voice.

"You need not tell them just now what has happened, Juliana. It can wait, surely."

She lowered her head, and her shoulders hitched. "The disgrace will become known to them eventually."

"But there is no need to present it to them yourself, dear," I replied gently.

She rose from the scarlet padded seat, turning to face me with determination in her gaze. "I feel as if I am somehow responsible, Astrid."

I smiled wanly. "There is no need for anyone to know of the horrors you have experienced and are still facing. There is no need to cause the guests fear of being trapped on an island with two murderers."

She flinched slightly at the words, but, after a long moment, she nodded slowly. "Yes, Astrid, I see your reasoning. Perhaps full disclosure is unnecessary at this juncture. There is no cause to stir up concern in the guests and ruin their holiday."

"It is not the ruin of their holiday for which I am concerned," I told her sternly. "However, I would not wish to see you fall under the eye of unnecessary suspicion and scrutiny."

Juliana nodded, then she lifted her chin and smoothed her skirts. "Will you join me in the parlour for breakfast, Astrid? I must address the guests before my father's absence becomes suspicious."

I smiled. "Of course."

In the dining room, the guests were gathered around the large breakfast table, nibbling on sausages, kippers and eggs. Their conversation was light, and for a moment, I was shocked at their levity, under the circumstances. They were, however, blissfully unaware of the horrors that had been perpetrated under their very noses. Perpetually in the thick of things and privy to the darkest deviations of my fellow men, I often envied the supremely uninformed their untroubled joy. It was the nature of my chosen profession, however, and did not allow it to trouble me.

Xander rose to join Juliana and guide her to her seat, but she put him off, pausing to stand at the head of the table where her father had lately overseen our repast. I poured myself a cup of tea and joined Asher, who glanced at me in interest, as though I possessed the very secrets of Juliana's speech. I did not, though I was unsurprised when she addressed the party thus.

"I regret to inform you all my father will be unable to join us for the remainder of our holiday pleasures," she told them, and I admired the rigidity of her composure. She was a lady of sophistication and grace beyond her years, and I marvelled at the murderous doctor's ability to raise such a fine, gentle woman.

"Oh, has he been called away?" Sophie asked, pressing her hand to her chest in concern.

Juliana shook her head. "No, he is still very much with us on the grounds. However, he has taken ill suddenly."

"Ill? Has he eaten something bad?" Chanha asked, eyeing her plate in suspicion.

"I cannot say for sure what has befallen him, but he is unwell."

"Will he be all right?" Sophie asked.

"I am sure he will make a full recovery soon. However, for the present, he must remain abed. He wishes you all not to trouble yourself over him. He would not desire you to neglect your own pleasure on his account."

Imaron raised his eyebrows, glancing around at the party. I sighed, anticipating his rabble rousing. "Has your father's illness anything to do with the missing men and the attack of Mrs Darby's man?"

Juliana faltered a moment, glancing towards me as if in supplication. I inclined my head to her. "It is possible he fell victim to the snake which attacked my associate, Reinhart. However, as Reinhart has already experienced a full recovery, though he remains abed in order to regain his strength, we are confident the professor will, too, be quite well with a bit of rest and relaxation."

"A snake?" Imaron asked, his full mouth twisting into a cheeky smirk. "Or a vampire?"

I rolled my eyes impatiently. "We have moved past this ludicrous supposition, Mr Behari. There are no vampires about the island. Or anywhere else, for that matter."

"Well," Chesley said, lifting his chin bravely. "We will simply have to go on without the professor. Do you expect he will be abed all the rest of the week, Miss Juliana?"

She inclined her head. "I suspect he must be."

"We shall endeavour to occupy ourselves then, shall we, my friends?"

"But if we are unable to leave the house, to what pleasures might we get up?" Chanha asked speculatively.

Asher smiled. "You have my assurance, Miss Behari, your leisure need not be interrupted in such a fashion. It is perfectly safe to leave the house now. We investigated the island thoroughly and determined the grounds are quite without peril."

The guests murmured in doubt. "But Agent Key, two men have already fallen victim to exotic dangers, our host included," Sophie exclaimed. "How can we be certain we will not, too, be in danger?"

Xander cleared his throat. "We have determined the attacks occurred whilst our man and the professor were outside the grounds. We have canvassed them thoroughly for exotic animals or savage beasts. There is no danger, provided you remain within the previously outlined confines of the villa grounds. There will be no more ventures into the untamed wilderness of the island. Otherwise, you might enjoy yourselves freely."

"Just the same," Sophie murmured as the others exchanged dubious glances. "Perhaps we might remain inside, just to be cautious."

Chanha tossed her mane of long, dark hair. "Oh, I will not!" she declared, rising to her feet to throw the shades open dramatically, bathing the table in brilliant morning sunshine. She turned to us, her face exultant. "Come, all, let us go to the beach again. It was so delightful last time. I cannot possibly resist wading in the sparkling waters another time. Won't you join me?"

Juliana's face illuminated. "Oh, Miss Behari, what a wonderful idea. I could prepare another picnic for us all. The weather is so fine, and the water will be most inviting. I cannot imagine a more pleasant way to spend the day."

"It is decided then," Imaron announced, rising to his feet.

The others murmured excitedly, warming to the idea, but I felt Asher's hand upon my arm, and I glanced at him. He tilted his head towards the stairs, but I lifted my chin defiantly. "May I speak to you upstairs, Astrid?" he asked, a slight hint of impatience in his voice.

"I will have my breakfast first, Ash."

"Will you be joining us on the shore, Astrid?" Juliana asked, her tone slightly supplicating.

I smiled gently at her. "Perhaps we will, Juliana. Asher and I have some business to which we must attend, but I am certain we will find the time to enjoy the sea."

"Business again?" Chanha asked reproachfully. "Why, Agent Key, Mrs Darby, we might begin to believe there is something afoot of which you are not telling us."

I smiled. "Do not fret, Miss Behari. I assure you, our business has nothing at all to do with you."

She lifted an eyebrow, but Asher interjected smoothly. "Miss Behari, we are merely concerned with the professor's and our associate's health and recovery. We wish only to assure they are resting comfortably before joining you all. There is nothing over which to worry yourself."

Chanha smiled at him. "Of course. I should have realised. As a man of authority and virtue, you must be deeply concerned with the wellbeing of our host. We shall await you both on the shore, then."

I rolled my eyes and pushed aside my plate, rising abruptly to my feet. "Shall we be off then, Agent Key?" I asked coolly.

He smirked and inclined his head. "Of course, Mrs Darby."

I did not speak to him as we strode towards the staircase. Behind us, the party was excitedly discussing their coming adventure upon the shore, but I ignored them, my head held high as I stomped up the stairs beside Asher. Amusement radiated from him, but I was unable to join in his good cheer.

"Come now, Astrid, do not tell me you are still harbouring jealous feelings over Miss Behari."

"Your implication suggests I was ever harbouring such feelings, which I was not. I am merely unable to share the party's good humour."

"How can you be? All is well now."

"Yes." My heart was heavy, however, as we closed ourselves into my chambers. "We have completed our assignment; you have solved your case; we have assurances Julius will confess to the Ministry of Defence when we have returned to England, and you will be returned to your active status. All is, indeed, very well."

Asher crossed his arms over his chest, perching on the edge of my writing desk. "Why, then, do you sound so miserable, Astrid?"

I sighed deeply, sinking onto the edge of the bed. "It is not a pleasant circumstance at all, is it? I had expected a far more satisfying conclusion to our adventure. Why, poor Juliana has experienced not only the loss of her beloved father but a horrifying personal tragedy, not to mention in what she has engaged without her knowledge. It is dreadful indeed. I cannot imagine the suffering she must be experiencing."

Asher sighed, and I looked up at him reproachfully. "Are you satisfied simply to have gotten your man?" I asked. "Do you not want justice, too, for that young girl? She is suffering deeply. What will she do now that she has lost everything?"

He frowned, but his voice was gentle. "What do you wish me to do for her?"

I shook my head. "I do not rightly know what might be done for her. It sounds as though she is deteriorating steadily. Do you not think there is any chance anyone can cure her?" I considered a long moment, and inspiration struck me suddenly. I rose to my feet abruptly.

Asher, too, straightened, and his expression was wary. "About what are you scheming, Astrid?"

I nodded slowly, pressing my hands together in satisfaction. "Oh, yes. Yes, I think perhaps it is brilliant."

"Astrid."

I smiled at him. "You, too, have noticed my young cousin has grown quite attached to the young lady, and she cannot be expected to return to her home without guardianship or company. Her father will, of course, provide for her financially, but she cannot hope to live a happy life all alone. She will need someone to be there for her lest she fall into deep despair. It would be a ghastly shame to lose her to madness or despair before her time."

Asher lifted an eyebrow. "What are you proposing, Astrid?"

I strode smartly across the room, falling into a swift pace. "I am convinced I must offer my home to the girl. Perhaps one of the numerous and esteemed doctors and scientists with whom we are acquainted will find some means of help for her."

He frowned. "Astrid, do you really believe that, if her father, who is one of the most renowned members of the medical community, cannot help her, someone else can?"

I glared at him. "Perhaps. Perhaps there are advances he, in his old age and occupation, has not yet realised. Progress is being made all the time. Rather than prolonging the incubation period of her disease, someone might find what is required to cure her."

"But you must realise, Astrid, even in your optimism, her situation is dire indeed."

I nodded. "Yes, Asher, I do realise that, of course. However, for my dear cousin's sake, I must this once err on the side of hope and extend my charity to the girl."

He sighed, considering me for a long moment, but he nodded finally. "That would be very generous of you, Astrid."

I inclined my head humbly and resumed my seat upon the bed. "I will have Xander speak to her about it in more detail at a later time, when she has had time to come to terms with the horrors of the last week. I have no doubt that the idea has already entered his consideration. Julius may have objections to make, particularly about the propriety of the two young people living under the same roof."

"I hardly think the professor has any influence in the matter at this stage," Asher said dryly. "His judgment is clearly impaired."

"Yes. Indeed, it is. It is a decision entirely for young Juliana to make. And I can ensure that propriety will be of the utmost concern to me."

His expression was dubious, and I lifted my chin defiantly, glaring at him. He smiled. "I am certain you and your cousin will treat the young lady with the utmost care and concern. But I have never known you to be so compassionate, Astrid."

I scowled. "Now, that is a highly derogatory remark, Ash. I am often charitable and generous to those less fortunate than myself. Why, just last year, I contributed most grandly to many organisations dedicated to the betterment of youth and the advancement of science."

He smirked. "Primarily on the suggestion of your cousin and your late husband, I shouldn't wonder."

I grunted in outrage. "I am highly offended by your remarks."

"I beg your pardon. I was merely taking the mickey. I shall endeavour to be kinder towards you in the future."

"That, Agent Key, I find extremely unlikely." I crossed my arms over my chest, lifting my chin sulkily, but the sly expression that came over his features caused me to forget my indignation. "I do not like that look in your eyes."

The innocence upon his face was utterly unconvincing. "I hardly know what you mean, Astrid." I glared at him, and he spread his hands. "Well, the job is done. Coffin is languishing in his incarceration. Bray is likewise secured, and Miss Juliana is safe from further disgrace."

"I can only assume you have a general point?"

"Of course." He rose abruptly, striding towards me with resolution in his expression. "You will now tell me what I did to incite your ire two years past."

I opened my mouth to reply scathingly, then shut it with a scowl. "And we were having such a pleasant holiday," I grumbled.

"Astrid..." His tone was warning.

I glared at him. "You hardly deserve my explanation. You know full well what it was you did; you simply were not aware I had discovered you."

"You will explain now. I have grown weary of your baseless malice."

"Baseless indeed. Do not act as if you have no idea to what I refer."

"I can say quite unequivocally, woman, that I do not."

I eyed him for a long moment, then raised my eyebrows in surprise. "Do you really not?"

"I assure you, I really do not."

I squared my shoulders, bracing my nerves for the confrontation which I had been avoiding for two years. "Do you make claim, Agent Key, that you are not in the acquaintance of a young woman by the name of Clara Worthington?"

He blinked, and his flummoxed expression suggested he had not expected me to ever speak the name. "Clara?"

"Yes, Clara. Miss Worthington was quite certain that you two were in quite close acquaintance, in fact." Colour drained from his face, and I glared at him. "What have you to say on the matter of Miss Worthington, Asher?"

He turned away, striding towards the window. "I am certain you are to tell me what you think you know about her?"

"I would prefer not to speak of it, but since you have demanded my motivation for our past parting, I will present it to you."

He sighed and waved his hand. "Do go on, then. Tell me what it is you think you know."

"Do you deny that you were betrothed to Miss Worthington, but that she is now the unmarried mother of a young son?"

There was no inflection in his voice to suggest his opinion on the matter. "No, I do not deny it."

I paused. I had not expected such a simple confession, and I hardly knew how to react. "Well, then, I have nothing more to add. I believe my ire is both reasonable and well-placed."

He spun from the window and strode abruptly towards me, seizing my shoulders to pull me to my feet. "I have more to add, Astrid," he told me earnestly.

I scowled, pressing my hands to his chest to push him away. He tightened his grip however, and I glared at him. "I am not entirely certain I am interested to hear what you have to add, Ash."

His eyes glittered angrily at me, and I turned my head to avoid his intense gaze. "You have had your chance to present your side of the argument, and now it is mine," he told me sternly.

I sighed. "All right, then." He released me, and I sank back onto the bed, scowling at him. "Go on."

He paced as he spoke, and I found myself unexpectedly curious to hear his explanation. "I met Clara many years ago, when I had first become an agent for the Ministry of Defence. She was very handsome, very keen and bright, and she fancied me very much."

I frowned. "And you clearly returned the sentiment."

"Yes, I did, of course. I courted her for a time, and eventually I proposed."

I glowered at him. "So you were, in fact, quite otherwise engaged when we met."

"I was not." I opened my mouth to speak, but he cut me off. "When we met in Brazil, I had not seen Clara in many months. I did not know she was unhappy, but she left me on the day of our wedding. She did not appear to stand in as my bride."

My mouth dropped in shock. "She left you at the altar?"

"She did. She left only a letter stating she could not go through with it, to be unhappy with someone who was never at home, and she had run off with another man. That was the last I heard of Clara Worthington. Until, I recall now, the time you and I parted so abruptly."

When I raised my eyebrows expectantly, he continued. "I had not seen her in nearly three years, but she appeared in London, returning to her family in disgrace. She was unmarried, and the man with whom she ran off had left her penniless and with child. Fearing reprisal from her parents for her imprudent behaviour, she blamed her circumstances on me, claimed I had taken advantage of her innocence and upon learning of her condition, had abandoned her."

"But you appeared for the wedding," I said. "It was she who had not."

"Yes. This was, of course, an utterly foolish and outlandish accusation, but her parents are poor merchants and lacked the necessary faculties to jump to the appropriate conclusion. After you severed your connection with me, I spent many days in court denying the allegations presented by she and her family. I was, obviously, cleared of the charges of philandering and abuse. She had not anticipated I would have kept the letter that detailed her rejection of me."

I was silent a long moment, my mind reeling with the revelations. I pushed them aside, however, for it would not do to allow Asher Key to disrupt my well-ordered life yet again, despite the misconceptions of our previous parting. I rose, pacing myself for several moments as if to clear my jumbled thoughts.

"But how is it you came to meet with her?" Asher asked, lifting his eyebrows.

"I did not."

He blinked, frowning at me. "But, then, how did you hear of her?"

I sighed deeply, pausing to peer at him. "It was a contact of mine in the courts who told me of the impending litigation."

He scowled, striding towards me to catch my shoulders. "Did you think me so cruel?" I looked away defiantly, and he gave my shoulders a shake. "Did it not deserve an explanation from me? Did you not think I might have something to say in my defence?" I sighed, and his tone was reproachful when he said, "Astrid. There was no one else but you. Had I not made myself clear?"

I glowered at him. "No, Ash, you had not."

"Clearly you knew little of me, if it was so simple for you to believe me capable of such wickedness, Astrid."

I extricated myself from his grip, pressing a hand to my head as I sat back down upon the counterpane. I sighed deeply, unable to master the confused jumble of questions and suppositions.

"Well? Astrid?"

I looked up at him, blinking in confusion. "Well what?"

He sighed in exasperation. "Well, what do you intend to do with this information?"

I shook my head. "I do not know what you mean."

"You know the truth now. You know what truly occurred those two years ago."

"Yes, and now you know why I was so cross with you when next we met. Both stories have finally come to light."

He stared at me blankly for several moments, as though he could not believe the words I had spoken. "Does it change nothing?"

I sighed. "Asher, the past remains the past. We have both moved forwards."

"Astrid, the past isn't the past any longer! We are here now, together."

"Yes. And we were successful in the task for which we came. It is business that drew us together."

He scowled. "You know it isn't nearly as uncomplicated as all that."

I glanced up at him. "Please, Asher, I am feeling rather fatigued. I regret I slept little last evening after the harrowing events of the day. I would wish to take a short kip before joining the others on the shore."

He sighed, but he finally nodded. "All right. Fine." He strode towards the adjoining door, but he paused with his hand upon the knob. "This isn't done, Astrid. We aren't finished."

"We are at present, Ash. Please leave me."

* * *

The balance of the holiday passed without further horror, disappearing servants or grave incident. However, though the other revellers seemed untroubled, unaware of the atrocities committed by their host, I was unable to enjoy their leisure. My waking moments were tense and unsettled. Juliana presented a brave face to her guests, though the strain around her eyes belied her ease, and her complexion remained pale and sickly. Xander was a great comfort to the girl, I knew, but I had glimpsed moments in which the tragedy welled in her eyes, as though it were too much to bear.

On balance, my own tumultuous sentiments were of little consequence, but the revelations Asher had presented had unsettled my otherwise quite clearly defined understanding of my feelings towards him. Finding him not to be the philanderer and cad for which I had taken him these past years, I had begun once again to notice the qualities in him I had always admired, that which had, upon our initial encounters, drawn me to him as a moth to a flame. Being a woman of action and firm resolve, I had sought to dissolve our tension, but my petulant dismissal of him had, perhaps, been just the spur he'd required to finally put to rest our turbulent connection.

Or, perhaps, Chanha Behari had been the impetus, for I discovered him on several occasions in her company. It seemed as though the lovely young woman had quite effortlessly replaced me in his affections for, though he was polite when we spoke, he did not visit me in my chambers or seek me out for private audience. In fact, his treatment of me was professional to the degree of indifference, and it was driving me utterly spare.

The final day of the holiday found the party upon the shore once again, enjoying an early afternoon picnic. Despite her private tragedy, Juliana was as gracious and adept a hostess as her father had been a host, and the spread was extravagant, in celebration or commemoration of the holiday's end. Though, in my opinion, the airship that would return us to Britain could not come soon enough, I lounged upon the blanket with Juliana and Xander, nibbling on a biscuit.

Juliana sighed deeply, staring out at the glittering horizon, though her eyes were distant, and I doubted she was at all experiencing the breathtaking sight. "Mrs Darby, I am delighted by your offer of guardianship," she began, and her voice was troubled. Xander turned his head sharply to listen to her words. "But my father will never allow it."

I smiled gently at her. "My dear, I am afraid he is no longer capable of overseeing your well-being." Her brow furrowed sorrowfully, and her bottom lip trembled slightly. I reached towards her, patting her arm gently. "I am sorry to say so, but we are all aware of the gravity of the situation. However, if it will please you, I will discuss the matter with him. I am confident I will be victorious in convincing him of the felicity of the arrangement."

Juliana perked up slightly. "Do you truly believe you will be successful?"

"Dear Juliana, I am highly adept at persuasion when the need arises. You needn't concern yourself further with your father's reaction. There is no better place for you than in my care. Both my dear cousin and I are determined to witness your full recovery, and we've many associates who might offer a suitable solution to your predicament."

She looked for a moment as if she dared not hold out hope for such a providential resolution, and Xander folded her hand into his own. "Juliana, our associates possess technology and knowledge your father does not. There may yet be progress towards curing your ailment. We will leave no stone unturned in the discovery of it."

She smiled at him, her cheeks colouring slightly. I turned my attention from their tender moment and caught sight of Asher and Chanha emerging from the waves, dripping with sparkling rivulets of seawater. They were laughing companionably, as though sharing an intimate joke, and I screwed up my face in aggravation. "Are you quite well, Astrid?" Juliana asked fretfully. "Perhaps you should spend the day in respite. You have, after all, been extremely taxed."

I glanced at her, but my smile was brittle. "I assure you, my dear, I am quite all right. I am a lady of sturdy constitution; I needn't spend my day languishing. I am invigorated by an active life."

She appeared unconvinced, but I made no further attempt to sway her. Chanha's tinkling laughter drew my attention, and I swivelled my head in her direction, finding her swathed in a thick, fluffy white towel which Asher was rubbing vigorously over her arms. I scowled, huffing softly in irritation. "Disgraceful," I muttered under my breath, but Juliana and Xander were no longer paying me heed; they seemed quite content in their private murmuring. I rose abruptly to my feet, marching towards the frolicking pair near the water.

"Asher," I said sharply.

He paused in the act of towelling the young Indian woman's long, black hair, straightening to face me coolly. "Astrid?"

Chanha smiled brilliantly at me, but I ignored her pointedly. "I must speak to the professor at once."

He blinked. "I beg your pardon?"

Chanha glanced between us, her brow furrowed in pretty confusion. "But is he not terribly ill? I am sure he should not be troubled in his condition."

I glanced at her. "I do not intend to trouble him, Miss Behari. However, there is something of great import which I must discuss with him quite urgently."

Asher frowned, stepped away from Chanha to murmur quietly to me. "What are you about, Astrid?" he demanded irritably.

I lifted my chin proudly. "It is most urgent that I secure his blessing in order to take Juliana as my ward."

"You hardly require his permission, Astrid. He is in no position to dispute the arrangement." He crossed his arms over his bare chest, drawing my eyes to the flat muscles of his torso.

I shook myself; it would hardly do for a woman of class and dignity to be caught ogling a half naked man, much less Asher Key. "It is not his permission we require, Ash. Juliana desires his good will."

He sighed. "He is in custody at present."

"Yes, but he has been cooperative, and he no longer presents a danger."

"It cannot wait until we have arrived in Britain?"

"No," I replied firmly. "Once we have returned home, he will be processed and incarcerated. It will be nearly impossible to secure an audience. I must see him before we depart."

"This is highly unorthodox, Astrid."

I lifted a reproachful eyebrow. "So is man-handling a young lady whilst you are meant to be guarding a dangerous prisoner."

His mouth quivered as though he might smile, but he sighed. "All right. I will allow you to see him." I smirked, and he rolled his eyes. "Come on, then."

He did not speak to me as we ascended the stairs towards Coffin's chambers. I glared silently at his back as I trailed behind him, but I did not attempt to shatter the quiet. When we reached Coffin's door, he drew a key from his trouser pocket and rapped once before turning the lock. Coffin was bent over a writing desk when we entered, and he rose quickly in surprise.

He was haggard, his clothes rumpled as though he had not changed them since Asher had closed him in solitary confinement. His skin was stretched tightly across his bones, and there were dark hollows around his eyes, as though he had not slept, either. "Astrid?" he asked, though his eyes flicked to Asher, who lifted his chin.

"Julius, there is something of great importance I must discuss with you," I informed him, striding towards him. Asher did not bid us farewell as he strode from the room, slamming the door behind him.

"Something of great importance?" He gestured me towards the wing-backed

176

chair beside the desk and lowered himself gracelessly into the seat across from me. "I have already given my confession. Is it not enough? What more do you require?"

He sounded defeated, and the life had drained from his countenance. Despite the horror of his actions, I pitied him. "What I wish to discuss concerns Juliana."

His back stiffened. "Juliana?"

"Julius, you must know she is unable to survive alone without guardianship."

"I have been arranging my financial affairs to provide for her, despite the reparations I will surely be required to pay for my crimes. She will be very secure."

"Yes, I am sure you have provided well for her, but she will need more than money if she's to live comfortably."

He lowered his head, sighing deeply. "I have not ceased troubling over her fate. How will she live without me, especially in her condition?"

"Julius, I wish to offer my home to her."

He lifted his head abruptly, his expression astonished. "I beg your pardon?"

"As you know, I have many associates who may be able to discover a cure to her ailment, and I will provide a comfortable and happy home. She need not be alone."

Julius peered at me, and his features shifted with indecision. "It is highly unseemly for two unrelated young people to live together in such a large home with no proper chaperone," he protested.

"I am highly offended, Julius. Am I not a proper chaperone?"

He lifted a dubious eyebrow. "You are not exactly a qualified au pair, Astrid."

"Juliana is eighteen years old. She hardly requires an au pair," I told him, scowling. "And where else might she go, then?"

He frowned. "I have family who would open their homes to her. My sister is very fond of her, and her family struggles. They would be grateful for a monthly stipend and treat my Juliana very well, I am certain."

"Julius, please be reasonable. Only I am able to offer the medical care she will require. My cousin and I will leave no option unexplored in her recovery. Our associates and friends are skilled in many disciplines and have made breakthroughs you yourself have had occasion to admire. If anyone has the resources to discover a cure, it is me."

"I do not wish to reveal the nature of her illness to the world!"

"Perhaps you do not, but she will not survive it. Not unless it can be studied. She would not wish to die without a fighting chance merely to keep her shame a secret from the world. It is unacceptable, Julius. You cannot ask or expect it of her!"

He sighed, lowering his head. "No, you are right, Astrid, I cannot. Perhaps in my own shame and regret, I impeded her recovery. I was mad with my own guilt and grief. I knew not what to do."

"The course of action you took was likely the least productive, Julius."

"I was acting as I thought best. I see my error now, as I have said. You needn't labour over the point."

"You will receive enough admonishment to satisfy me when we have arrived home. I do not wish to press the issue. My concern is Juliana. I can provide her what she requires."

"I cannot allow such an inappropriate arrangement."

I lifted my eyebrows. "You are not longer in a position to refuse, Julius, and it is as she wishes. The perception of polite society is nothing compared to her life. You must see that."

He glared at me. "If I am no longer in a position to refuse, why have you come to me at all?"

"Juliana requires your blessing. Despite your actions, she understands you acted out of love, and she cares deeply for your good opinion. She wishes for this arrangement, but she will be happier still if you are in agreement of its merit." His jaw set stubbornly, and I rolled my eyes. "If it will appease you, I am not opposed to employ a chaperone to preserve her virtue whilst in my home, though I am offended by the suggestion that I would allow impropriety in my care."

He frowned, but his expression softened slightly. "I would wish to select the chaperone myself for my own peace of mind."

I rolled my eyes. "Do you think me incapable?"

"No, not as such. It is merely that I will be unable to look after my own child. I would be much more at ease if I am acquainted with the one under whose care she is placed."

"I needn't remind you that your judgment has been lately slightly impaired."

"Juliana's interest has been my only concern!"

I sighed, relenting. "All right. You may select her chaperone, but, as it will be my responsibility to maintain her companion under my roof, I reserve the right to refuse anyone whom I cannot abide."

He considered, then inclined his head. "It seems I have no other options. I suspect my dear Juliana's mind is quite made up if she has sent you here to secure my blessing."

"I came of my own volition. However, it was to ease her mind as much as my own." I leaned forward, laying a hand upon his arm. "Julius, I will do all I can to find the cure. I will stop at nothing."

He nodded, then lifted a suspicious eyebrow at me. "But by what impetus are you extending such charity to my daughter? You have only just met her, and though I was closely acquainted with Nathaniel, we are not exactly intimate friends."

I smiled slightly. "I have grown quite fond of the young lady. She is bright and charming."

His expression was dry. "Is it not your young cousin who has grown fond of her?"

"And she of him, I am most confident."

He sighed. "Yes. I, too, am quite sure. There are worse matches for her, I reckon. He is, after all, quite brilliant and they share many interests and passions."

I lifted an eyebrow at him. "She is the daughter of a soon to be notorious mass murder, Julius. Perhaps it is not she who enjoys the luxury of selectiveness."

For a moment, he looked highly offended, then he exhaled heavily in a strangled chuckle. "I had not considered the social ramifications of the scandal." He leaned forwards, dropping his head in his hands. "How can I have done this to my own daughter? I have destroyed her life."

I did not argue with him. "She will face difficulties, but I am determined that her life will not be destroyed. I promise you, Julius, I will do everything in my power to find a cure, and, if I am unsuccessful, I will provide her a contented existence until her expiry."

He rose to his feet, pacing for several moments. I leaned back in my chair, allowing him to process the proposal silently. He paused in front of the bureau, and my head snapped up as I heard a drawer slide out. "There may be something left for me to do to save her this shame."

I frowned, and I threw my hands up as he spun towards me, a small, polished ivory-gripped pistol in his hand. "Cor, Julius. How did you come to be in possession of a gun? Did Asher not search this room before locking you inside? We've already established that you cannot kill us. You'll be unable to conceal the evidence with too having to dispose of your own daughter!"

Julius sighed impatiently, seizing the barrel of the gun and proffering the grip to me. "I have no intention of killing you, Astrid, for heaven's sake. It is you whom I wish to kill me."

I blinked, rising to my feet to face him. "But surely you are not in earnest."

"Of course I am in earnest." He sighed, and his chin dropped to his chest. "Astrid, you are my friend. If you do this, it may all be ended here. No one must ever know what has been done for the sake of Juliana. She may live without the humiliation and scandal upon her family name. I trust you will complete the terrible task mercifully and that you will care for Juliana rightly when I am gone."

I peered at him shrewdly, and for a long moment I considered his proposal. It could all be ended here, as he said, in a single heartbeat. Justice could be exacted for his victims, the young lady would live without the shame of her father's reputation, and no one would ever need know. The guests were already convinced of his illness, and his death could be discreetly explained away, his body put to rest at sea or in the flames of a funeral pyre on the shore.

I sighed. Alas, no, it could not be. Asher required Julius' confession to regain his good standing with the Ministry. It would be difficult to explain a gunshot wound, and Juliana would never forgive me or herself for the loss of her father, for the suffering she would inevitably experience at his death. I shook my head. "If you wish to die, Julius, why do you not take your life into your own hands?"

A single tear streaked from the corner of his eye, and he shook his head slowly. He stepped forwards to offer me the pistol. "I have considered it. I have even held the gun to my head and closed my eyes, thinking of death, but I am too cowardly. Please, Astrid. You must do this."

"No, Julius. I cannot. I am an adventurer, sir, not a killer, and your continuing existence is necessary, for the time. I am sorry."

The door banged abruptly against the wall as it swung inwards, startling us both. We glanced towards Asher who burst into the room, his expression dangerous and terrible. "What the bloody hell is going on in here?" He spotted the pistol in Julius' hand a heartbeat later, and he raised his own gun, which I suspected he had borrowed from Julius' impressive hunting lodge. "Lay down your weapon, Coffin, or I will shoot you."

"Ash, don't!" I ordered sharply, spinning on him. "It is not as it seems."

Asher's eyes were glacial, fixed upon Julius, and he did not glance my way. He levelled his gun at Julius, his muscles taut with concentration. He seemed neither to blink nor to breathe. "He is aiming a gun at you."

"If you'll notice, the gun is actually not aimed at her," Julius said dryly, holding out the pistol towards Asher.

"He is not aiming it at me; he is holding it out to me," I argued, scowling at him with my hands upon my hips. "He has no intention of harming me."

However, as if to belie the statement, Julius raised the gun once more towards Asher, his expression stony. I glanced between the two men uneasily. "I cannot shame my daughter in such a fashion," Julius murmured, and his finger flexed over the trigger.

"Julius..." I said, concern in my tone.

"Drop the gun, or I will kill you," Asher told Julius coldly.

"No, Asher, that is what he wants," I growled.

"And I am happy to accommodate him."

"No! You cannot do such a thing to Juliana."

"Do it, Agent Key, or I will kill Astrid." Julius' hand was steady as he swung the gun back towards me.

I sighed, rolling my eyes. "Asher, he will not."

"I will!" Julius hissed. "I have killed so many. What is one more to save my daughter?"

"Not a friend, Julius," I reminded him sternly. "You have never killed a friend, and who will care for Juliana if I am unable?"

His brow furrowed, and a muscle twitched in his cheek. He turned back towards Asher. "Then I will kill him," Julius said.

Asher glared at him. "Not before I kill you."

Julius smiled humourlessly. "Then we will both die and, I daresay, receive our rightful comeuppance."

"Enough, you two!" I growled. "This is absolutely ridiculous. Both of you, lower your weapons straight away."

"Not until he does," Asher replied, his tone slightly petulant.

"Not until he kills me," Julius added, glaring back at Asher.

I rolled my eyes. "Asher, lower your gun."

He glanced incredulously at me for a split second before swivelling his gaze back to Julius. "What? He will shoot."

"No. He will not. If he does, his crimes will be much the worse for murdering an agent of the Ministry. He will not get away with it. He will be put to death, and his daughter will experience great suffering." I glared pointedly at Julius. "Her father will not live to witness her recovery."

For a breathless moment, I feared he would not relent, for his eyes were steely and his jaw was rigid. Then his breath hitched in a deep, shuddering sigh, and he lowered his arm. The pistol slipped from his fingers and dropped to the thickly carpeted floor with a soft, futile thump. Asher strode forwards and scooped it up, shaking his head angrily at the defeated doctor. "You simply cannot seem to remain out of trouble, can you, Astrid?"

I scoffed. "You might have searched the room better," I scolded.

Julius smiled wanly. "Do not blame Agent Key, Astrid. I am very clever, and I concealed it well."

"Astrid, go," Asher ordered coolly.

I glared at him and spun towards Julius, striding towards him to lay a hand upon his chest. "Julius, Juliana will be well again. I will do all I am able."

Julius sighed, but he nodded, pressing my hand in his. I turned, casting a baleful gaze sidelong at Asher before leaving the room, pulling the door closed behind me. I leaned against the wall in the corridor, awaiting Asher's emergence from the prison. It was merely moments, and when he strode from the room, he looked around as though anticipating my continuing occupation of the corridor.

I met him halfway, returning his furious glare blandly. "What the hell were you doing in there?" he demanded.

I rolled my eyes. "I was endeavouring to secure Juliana's future, as I stated when I requested access to the room."

"You nearly got yourself killed!"

I scoffed. "I hardly think I was in any danger. Julius would not have killed me, despite the circumstances. He would, however, have attempted to kill you. Or provoked you to kill him, preferably. How came he to possess a weapon in the first place? Did you not search the chambers before locking him inside?"

"Of course I did. It was simply quite well hidden."

"I trust you have removed any further means of self harm from his room?"

"Self harm?"

"He requested I kill him."

"He did what?"

I sighed. "He was under the conception his death would save Juliana unnecessary scandal."

"Ridiculous."

"He is a desperate man."

Asher glared, but as our eyes met, he relented slightly. He sighed deeply, studying me with an eerie intensity that both unsettled and excited me. We had not been in such close company since the revelations of our prior parting, despite my futile attempts to secure an audience in spite of Chanha Behari. As though he, too, realised the circumstance, he glanced away, clasping his hands awkwardly behind his back. My stomach flipped slightly, and I opened my mouth to say something to him, to voice the thoughts that had crossed my mind since learning of his fidelity.

"So you are indeed taking Juliana as your ward?" he asked abruptly, and my jaw snapped shut.

My brow furrowed slightly, and I nodded. "Yes. I have secured her father's approval of the arrangement. He sees no alternative solution to her situation, and I was most persuasive in my contention. I expect she will take up residence at Darby Manor immediately upon alighting in Britain."

He nodded, and it seemed as though he had nothing more to say on the subject. I opened my mouth again, but he cut me off, glancing sharply at me. "Astrid, I must insist you do not see him again."

I sighed. "Yes, all right. I am content, but Ash--"

Chanha Behari rounded the corner, and when she caught sight of us, her face illuminated. "Ah, Agent Key, there you are." Her expression was slightly colder when she glanced towards me. "Mrs Darby."

"What is it, Chanha?" Asher asked, and I scowled at him.

"Juliana has announced dinner will be served in an hour. I wondered if you might be so agreeable as to accompany me to the library for the interim."

Asher inclined his head, stepped towards her to offer his arm. He nodded curtly at me. "Shall we see you at dinner, Astrid?"

I waved my hand in irritation. "Of course."

They spun away from me, murmuring in low, confidential tones to each other. My stomach lurched, and I glared after them. My breath hitched slightly as I inhaled resolutely, lifting my chin.

"Ridiculous," I muttered to myself, curling my lip in a sneer. "Precisely when did Asher Key begin to enjoy books?"

* * *

The following day, the airship arrived with the sun, its gleaming body practically glowing in the early morning light. I was grateful for its arrival and eager to return home at once, despite the other guests' apparent reluctance to give up the beauty, warmth and leisure of the island retreat and the villa with its exotic dinners, interesting company and every whimsical pleasure.

I had been unable to catch more than a few hours fitful sleep the previous evening, so anxious was I to return to the relative normalcy of Darby Manor and my less unsettling clients and jobs. I could not bear another night in the warm, sultry salt air, the villa in which memories of horrors and suffering lurked in every corner, and the utterly dull inactivity. Most empathically, I was eager to be away from Agent Asher Key and the disquieting sentiments with which I was very unexpectedly riddled.

The guests boarded the ship blearily, and I watched as Asher conducted Julius and Bray inside ahead of the others. They seemed disinclined to present a danger to any of the guests, and I noticed Bray's eyes, like Julius', were shadowed with lack of sleep. Juliana joined her father, smiling bravely at him and folding her hand into his. The long flight would, I realised, likely be the last time they would be in such comfortable companionship. I was relieved Asher did not protest the arrangement.

His uncharacteristic negligence was, I realised, due likely to Chanha, whom he assisted into the dirigible and escorted to a seat near her brother. Chanha, however, did not abide his departure, and she implored him to join her. I had expected a man concerned with the security of his prisoner to rebuff such a dreadful distraction, but he did not refuse her.

Behind me on the ramp, Reinhart, recovered quite well under the careful eyes of Xander and Juliana, nudged me. "What's the hold up, Astrid?" he grumbled.

Ignoring the question, I lifted my chin, striding forwards to perch stiffly on the bench across from Asher and the Beharis. Reinhart and my young cousin joined me, hefting our luggage under the benches. Though Xander peered dolefully towards Juliana, I smiled at him, drawing him to sit beside me. "You will have all the time in the world with her, cousin," I murmured gently to him. "Allow her these last moments with her father. When we have disembarked, there will be few."

He smiled, but he was silent as the other guests claimed their seats, nattering excitedly. The airship ascended. "I will be relieved to return to my flat," Reinhart remarked in a weary voice. "This holiday did not provide the pleasures and enjoyment you promised, Astrid."

I chuckled. "You will forgive my embellishment. I did not anticipate you would spend the most of the holiday convalescing. You did assist in the solving of a dreadful crime. Does that not appease your disappointment?"

He scoffed. "No. I missed all the excitement."

I chuckled. "Not all of it, and you did manage to stir up quite a bit of it yourself with claims of vampire attacks and ghosts."

"I'm still not entirely convinced we were alone on the island."

I rolled my eyes. "I assure you, Morgan, the villains have been identified and will be brought to task for their crimes."

"Will I see you when we are home once again and you return to your thrilling and dangerous life at the Ministry of Defence, Agent Key?" Chanha asked sweetly.

He smiled, but for a moment, I was certain his cobalt eyes slid to me before he replied, "Should that continue to be your wish when you have returned to the rewarding life of a popular socialite, Miss Behari, I am certain something might be arranged."

"If you ask me, someone should fire upon the place with haste," Morgan added gruffly. "Not even the Isles of Jules can withstand the awesome force of directed energy particles intent upon vaporising its bits."

I laughed. "Do you not think that is a slightly disproportionate response to what has befallen you here?"

"No. I am thoroughly convinced. The place is cursed."

CHAPTER ELEVEN

Though I had not been paying due attention to the speech and presentation and was thus unaware of the nature of the great scientific breakthrough at the University of London's Centre of Scientific Research and Uncanny Inventions, I was enjoying the do in its honour. Being the wife of a celebrated alumnus, I was an honorary invitee, despite my well-known lack of propensity for science and its innovations. Xander and Juliana, however, had exclaimed in delight over the invention, which I had noted seemed to be merely a large, featureless brass cylinder which had emitted sparks and arcs of brilliant blue light when the presenter had triggered it.

Despite my disinterest in the dingus, I smiled as I watched my young cousin and ward discussing the invention in excited tones with our fellow revellers. Juliana was looking in brilliant good health, positively glowing with exhilaration. It appeared, most gratifyingly, as thought the treatments prescribed by my old friend Dr Octavious Yeager were working as well as could be expected to combat the deterioration of her condition.

As the orchestra struck up an exultant melody, I swept a glass of sweet, sparkling white wine from a passing server's tray, watching Xander offer his hand to Juliana for a dance. Bubbles popped in my mouth, and I sighed in contentment. Events had turned most favourably since our departure from the Isle of Jules, and I smirked as I considered Reinhart's proclamation. Perhaps the Isle of Jules truly was cursed.

"Why, Mrs Darby, your mien is rather fetching this evening."

I spun in surprise towards Asher, my glass poised midway to my lips. I lifted a wary eyebrow at him. "Agent Key, you are looking roguish as always." He chuckled, ruffling the back of his overlong hair. "I hear the Ministry had taken you back under wing as their golden boy."

He grinned. "Indeed they have, on account of our shocking breakthrough." He nodded his chin towards the stage. "Speaking of breakthroughs, have you any idea of what Dr Strangeways was talking up there?"

I smirked. "Not in the slightest. You know I haven't the inclination towards science. However, if you are interested, I am certain Xander or Juliana will be delighted to explain the significance of the feat."

He waved his hand impatiently. "I have no such inclination myself. How is your lately ward? Has she joined your motley band of adventurers?"

I laughed. "I think perhaps we shall wait until she has had more time to adjust to her new situation before thrusting her unnecessarily into the path of danger and intrigue. However, I am certain she will prove to be a most talented addition to my entourage."

Asher chuckled. "Has her condition improved, then?"

I smiled. "She is very well these days. She is under the care of Dr Yeager, a brilliant doctor who has made much headway into the area of neurological diseases."

"I am most gratified to hear it. I can only hope she will soon reach a full recovery."

"Yes, I am hopeful as well. She is a fine girl, very bright, and much deserving of a fortuitous future."

"Indeed." I followed his gaze towards my young wards, and smiled as he watched them a long moment, as though experiencing vicariously their youth and good spirits. "And what of the elder Coffin?" I asked, drawing his gaze again. "How is your investigation fairing?"

"Quite well. Julius confessed to a veritable gamut of heinous crimes. You will be pleased to learn his fears were unfounded; his story will not be leaked to the press so that young Juliana might experience a life free of the taint of her father's sins."

"That is very good indeed, though I do not expect Juliana shared his fears; I believe it never occurred to her that her father's shame might become her own."

"May her innocence not be equally unfounded."

"Yes, we can only hope word does not eventually reach the ears of the press. They are rather dogged when they are on a scent."

"They will have a difficult time getting anything out of me.:

I laughed. "I do not envy the correspondent who crosses your path. But what will become of Julius now?"

"Ah, his influence with the top boys has kept him from the gallows. His man, Bray, I'm afraid, is likely to face the full might of the law."

"Will he be given the Boat?" My gaze drifted once more to the young girl.

"No. He will be kept at home so that he might spend his remaining days close to his daughter. That is, should she see her way to forgiving him for what he's put her through."

"Juliana is a most tender-hearted girl. She has already forgiven him, though I expect it will be some time before she comes to terms with what's happened." I turned my attention back to him curiously. "Did you learn to whom the bones in the cave belonged?"

Asher smiled, though the expression was grim. "Ah. Yes. We gleaned much through the professor's confession. When he first learned of Juliana's illness, he brought a young shaman from the tribe in Papua-New Guinea to the Isle of Jules in hopes that he might assist in discovering a cure for the girl's symptoms. He was unsuccessful, of course, and when he learned of the professor and his man's solution, he insisted he be sent home at once."

"I can only assume that his wishes went unheeded?"

"Just so. Being of no more use to Coffin, he suspected his danger and fled the villa."

"Staying a time in the cave."

"Exactly."

"But did he die there?"

"No. He was overtaken by Bray and put to use in the manner of the other victims. Julius, however, being somewhat fond of the young shaman, delivered his remains to the cave, where he believed his soul might experience some sort of peace."

I considered this. "I suppose it is no madder than any of his other plans."

"No. I believe the professor has gone quite round the bend since Juliana fell ill, as his behaviour suggests."

"And the man in the woods?"

"Prosser's of course."

"No vampires or ghosts, then?"

"I'm afraid not. The mystic world still retains its mysterious for a little while yet. The servant escaped the formidable Mr Bray and spent some time hiding in the woods until he was caught up again."

"Imaron's fire must have frightened him away."

"I suspect so. He must have believed our search party was, in fact, a hunting party."

"A hunted man is an animal of pure instinct. A terrible pity. Had he only come forwards, he might have been spared. I doubt Julius would have persisted in his attack once the servant had been returned to his master."

"Perhaps, but his story would have exposed the professor instantly. I suspect he would have discovered another means by which to silence him."

"Indeed, it is likely he would have done. He was lost the moment Julius and Bray looked to him. I suppose there is little use lamenting what might have been."

"Too true, Mrs Darby. We did, after all, get our man, as you say."

"We were quite brilliant."

"Our cleverness has never seen the like." His face lit suddenly with a mischievous smirk, and he offered his hand to me. "Mrs Darby, would you care to dance with me?"

I lifted my eyebrows as he bowed low at the waist. "I beg your pardon, Agent Key?"

"Well, everyone who is anyone is doing it."

I laughed and accepted his hand, allowing him to draw me into a spirited waltz. "I have never known you to be overly concerned with what everyone who is anyone is doing."

"Perhaps I am merely inspired by our young friends."

I gazed up at him warily. "And won't Miss Behari begrudge you a dance with another woman?"

He laughed. "Oh, Astrid, how subtly you express your jealousy."

I opened my mouth in outrage. "Jealousy, indeed. I was simply concerned with the continuing good will in your connection with the young lady."

"Is that so? Well, if it pleases you to know, I have not seen Miss Behari since we alighted in England."

"Indeed?"

"Yes, it seems that, with so many young men of higher station and wealth available to her, I no longer present an attractive prospect."

"That is deplorable!"

He chuckled. "Perhaps not so, for, with no one to irritate with our connection, she, too, presented to me a less agreeable companion."

I scowled, opening my mouth to retort, but he spun me abruptly, distracting me from my reply. We danced for several moments in silence as I considered his proclamation. He was as skilled a dancer as when we had first made each other's acquaintance, and I again had occasion to wonder where someone of his upbringing and profession had learned to waltz. Perhaps the Ministry of Defence required their operatives to be well-versed in various social niceties, so often were they in the position to impersonate a gentleman of higher station.

"Were you even invited to this party?" I demanded abruptly.

Asher laughed. "No."

I lifted my eyebrows. "Then have you come with some purpose?"

"Yes, of course. To speak with you."

"And so you have done, unless there is something more you would wish to discuss with me?"

"There is indeed."

"Ah, let us get to the heart of it, then."

"Indeed, I am most eager." He paused dramatically and smirked. "Mrs Darby, your country requires your particular assistance."

I rolled my eyes. "My country requires my assistance?" I repeated dubiously.

"It is a matter of the utmost urgency, I assure you."

I scoffed. "Though you have regained your good-standing with the Ministry, I shouldn't wonder that I am still on their hostile register."

"Your assistance with the discovery and subsequent capture of a terrible and dangerous criminal has rendered my superiors far more amenable and open to reconciliation."

"Ah."

"And you?"

"Me?" I asked, uncomprehending.

"Are you amenable and open to reconciliation?"

I eyed him speculatively. "What is this mission for which my expertise is so urgently requested?"

He beamed. "Our esteemed sources have uncovered a plot to assassinate a world leader with whom we are very friendly and who has a particular importance to the empire."

I considered. "Ah. I have not prevented an assassination in some time. It would be most stimulating."

"I am certain it will be at that."

"Well, I am otherwise uncommitted this week. I suppose it would not be a terrible strain upon my time."

"Indeed, we will be most efficient and the matter will be solved, I am certain, in only a few days' time."

He lifted his eyebrows expectantly, and I sighed, though my lips curled slightly into a smile. "Yes, all right. I will assist you. If you will simply allow me to bid my obligatory farewells, we'll be off."

Asher smiled. "Ah, there is no need to rush so immediately. Perhaps more dancing and wine is just the appropriate beginning to our renewed partnership."

I peered at him wryly. "I believe it was dancing and wine that began our troubles in the first place, Ash."

He laughed, releasing me abruptly to snatch two glasses of the sweet, bubbly wine from a server's tray. "I assure you, Mrs Darby, I have no idea to what you refer." He handed me a glass, raising it to me as if in a toast. "To conciliation, yes?"

I considered him a long, moment, then smirked, raising my glass to clink against him. "To provisional civility."

He considered then laughed, lifting his shoulders in a shrug. "I suppose, under the circumstances, that is the very best for which I may hope."

THE END

Look for

Astrid Darby and the Circus in the Sky, available now.

and

Astrid Darby and the Captain's Club

Astrid Darby and the King of Zombies

Astrid Darby and the Burning Phoenix

Coming soon from DC Dreams

www.diogenesclubpress.com

ABOUT THE AUTHOR

Eleanor Prophet is an author, columnist, editor, lady of leisure and amateur sleuth. Her most popular works include the Astrid Darby Adventures. When she isn't writing books, short stories, essays and articles of questionable veracity, she is typically enjoying the attentions of Mr Prophet, a dashing international man of mystery and intrigue. Her favourite activities include larking about, rule-breaking, mischief-making and getting to the bottom of things. She often receives fascinating, comical and occasionally disturbing mail to her desk which she publishes on her blog for the public's information, entertainment and frequent outrage.

Read Ellie's Blog at:

www.ellieprophet.wordpress.com